I0789019

TRAFALGAR & BOONE AND THE BOOKS OF BREATHING

BOOK THREE OF TRAFALGAR AND BOONE

Geonn Cannon

Supposed Crimes LLC • Matthews, North Carolina

All Rights Reserved
Copyright © 2017 Author

Published in the United States.

ISBN: 978-1-944591-36-6

www.supposedcrimes.com

This book is typeset in Goudy Old Style.

When last we visited our intrepid heroes...

As of the summer of 1920, LADY DOROTHY BOONE and MISS TRAFALGAR OF ABYSSINIA have been partners for nearly a year. Training in the countryside and taking small commissions to learn how to trust and work together. They have also been using their free time approaching their fellow adventurers to join a society that would lead to a more trusting and supportive community of British adventurers. BEATRICE SEK, in the meantime, began seeking answers about her origins from wherever she can find them. She received her first promising lead from a witch named RENATA "DOV" KOESSEL, who warns Beatrice that she is a powerful and prophesized elemental.

Dorothy's friend CORA HYDE had institutionalized herself after a harrowing expedition, and Dorothy decided to do what she can to finish Cora's work. In the process she discovered a connection to her grandmother's final expedition, a mission Eula Boone was never able to complete, and saw the mystery as a chance to honor her late grandmother.

Standing in their way was EMMELINE POTTER, the VIRAGO, an Irish terrorist who raided ancient sites and sold whatever she could loot in order to fund her country's war. The Virago was also magically inclined and, while matching wits against Beatrice, revealed she too was an elemental. Despite their tenuous bond, Beatrice managed to strike down her foe. Unfortunately, Virago quickly escaped custody and returned to Ireland with a promise to return one day to settle scores with Beatrice, Trafalgar, and Boone.

In response to recent attacks, Dorothy Boone chose to recreate the MNEMOSYNE SOCIETY: a collective of explorers who can learn from and assist one another in their adventures. The young and brash CECIL DUBOURNE; the crafty but shell-shocked CORA HYDE; the posh ABRAHAM STRODE; the elegant brawlers LEONARD and AGNES KEEPING; and the invisible assassin IVY SEVER. It is Dorothy's hope that, together, they can face whatever threats the ancient world throws at them.

PROLOGUE

1915

BATTLE OF SUEZ CANAL

The Suez Canal burned. Fire danced along its churning waters, grasping at the armored hulls of the British battleships and troop carriers. The flames were squat and spread flat like a carpet of light, compressed by a wave of blue-violet energy. It was the color as a summer storm and equally as violent. Fire and magic roared enough to deafen those manning the batteries. In addition to the cacophony of energies mystical and elemental colliding, the wind produced by their meeting shook chains and ropes used to secure the ships. The rattle of machine guns and the bark of rifles added to the din until the magicians feared their incantations wouldn't be heard above it all.

Practitioners stood at various points along the battlements, arms extended with their palms flat to direct the wave of magical energy that held the flames at bay. One magician fell as an Ottoman sniper got off a lucky shot. Another rose to take his place so the wall would continue to hold. Still, their enemy attempted to cross the water and still the fires burned.

Behind the magicians was another flank, a wall of armed mundane soldiers whose job it was to prevent assassinations like the one just committed. Their ages ranged from sixteen (the devoted liars) to the elderly twenty-one. The main difference was how well they hid their terror. The young stared wide-eyed across the battlefield while the elders kept their jaws clenched and their hands steady.

The assault began just after four in the morning, and now dawn was beginning to color the sky. The Ottomans had practitioners of their own, mages who were making rafts and floats invisible to the naked eye. Soldiers were being felled by enemies who couldn't be seen. Bullets were striking thin air over the water and heavy splashes indicated a body falling but no one saw the victim.

It was during the third hour of fighting that three soldiers reached the limits of their false bravado. Two white men and a dark-skinned woman who had been fighting alongside the British. They were not coconspirators, two of them not even aware of the third's name, but cowardice had made them allies. They left the battlements and entered the town of Suez. They left their weapons behind where stronger soldiers might still make use of them and ran through the cramped and dirty streets. They stripped off their identifying uniforms and exchanged them for thick white robes they found hanging from lines outside of dark homes.

The buildings all looked the same in the colorless light of dawn - squat, grey, ugly - but they soon reached the railway where a train waited as if expecting them. They clambered into one of the train cars near the middle and prepared to wait as long as it took to depart. The two men sat shoulder to shoulder against the wall facing the door in case anyone came looking for them. The woman sat closer to the back where she couldn't be seen from outside.

Their shoulders heaved as they tried to catch their breath, mouths hanging open and upper bodies rocking back and forth with the effort. Sweat dripped from their chins and stained their stolen robes. One man noticed his hands were shaking and balled them into fists, squeezing the thumbs inside his fingers as a distraction. The woman muttered something in her native language, the same phrase over and over, with her eyes closed and her face aimed toward the ceiling.

Outside the battle continued to rage. Each agonizing minute was sharpened until they could feel the seconds dragging across their skin. When the train finally began to move, all three stowaways were startled by a man hurling himself at the open door. They all feared they had been caught but this man was not Port Police. He flattened his hands on the floor and scrambled to keep up with the train's increasing speed, but it was clear he would fail.

The men facing the door moved forward. They each took a hand, hauled the man inside, and then retreated back to their wall. The man lay on his stomach for a moment to catch his breath. He wore baggy clothing, the pants slightly darker than the shirt, and he wore a fez which had miraculously remained perched on his head despite his mad dash. There was a bag strapped to his chest, and he took a moment to examine it before moving to lean against the wall.

"*Shukran*," he said when he finally found his breath. They were already in the desert outside of Suez, the mountains moving past the open door at a great clip.

"They only speak English," the woman said, although both men wondered how she could know this about them. "British."

"I see." He was cradling the bag to his torso like a pregnant woman would hold her stomach. "My name is Feisal. Thank you for your assistance."

One of the deserters said, "If we hadn't, you would have ended up smeared on the tracks. Figured we spent the last couple hours trying to end lives. Might as well try to balance the scales and save one." After a moment he added, "I'm Oliver."

The other man said, "Roland."

Feisal gave them a nervous smile. "Well. Now that we have all been introduced to one another..." The woman, whose name was Hasina, arched an eyebrow but said nothing. "Where does this train go?"

"Alexandria," Roland said. "From there we can go wherever we want."

Oliver said, "How far do you think we have to run to get away from this war?"

Roland snorted and shook his head. "What about you? You're no soldier. What are you running from?"

"Oh. Oh..." Feisal looked down at his bag, then twisted to look out the door. He was like a stick man, his bones and muscles clearly visible beneath the surface of his thin brown skin. "I found something. Something very precious. Something magnificent. Already there have been two attempts on my life since the item came into my possession, but I am too clever for them. Much too clever. I traveled all the way to the fighting and then used magic to conceal my movements, see? Yes?"

Oliver said, "Anyone following your trail would lose it in that quagmire back there."

"Mm, yes, yep, like using a smoke pass in a room on fire." He laughed but kept his head twisted so he could keep looking out the door.

"What did you find?" Hasina asked.

The men looked at her. Feisal tightened his grip. "Treasures... ah, items, items from long ago. Buried."

Hasina switched to Egyptian Arabic. "Valuable?"

Feisal answered her in kind. "No. No, only academic interest."

"People would kill for academic research?"

His grin revealed a gold tooth toward the back of his jaw. "You have never been to college."

"And you are terrified of sitting on a train with three people you do not know and admitting that what you have is worth money."

Oliver said, "What the hell are you talking?"

She ignored him and focused on Feisal. "You said treasures."

Feisal shrugged and shook his head. He brought his knees up and squeezed the bag. "I misspoke. Going from language to language, words are slippery."

"Not that slippery."

Roland said, "Oy! You two stop that babbling right now. You're making me anxious."

She continued in Arabic. "If I can ensure your safe passage to Alexandria, will you give me a portion of your reward?"

"I told no lie. There is no monetary reward for what I am carrying."

Roland and Oliver looked at one another, annoyed at being left out of the conversation. Oliver reached under his robe and gripped the handle of his knife, the one weapon he hadn't discarded with the rest of his uniform. Roland had no weapons, but he was confident that he could physically overpower any of the others in the train car with them. He eyed the bag in Feisal's arms. He didn't even know what it was, but the mystery around it was enticing. He didn't care a whit about the other people riding to safety with him. He would have what was in the stick man's pack.

Hasina relaxed against the wall of the car, arms rested casually on bent knees. She could see what lay in store as clearly as if she had Sight; one of the men she deserted with would kill the other. The survivor would attack Feisal, who she suspected of being wilier than he looked. None of the men would consider her threatening. They would save her for last. So when she was finally attacked, she would only have to kill one man. Her alone against three of them would be tricky. But she was confident she could defeat any of them one-on-one.

The train rolled on through the early morning. It was nearly two hundred miles to Alexandria, which meant it would be nightfall before they arrived. The four stowaways had plenty of time to scheme their plan of attack, each one certain they would be the one to emerge with the mysterious pack and whatever treasures it held. When the train finally stopped and the victor carried their prize to a safe location to discover what had been purchased with three lives, they would find a small statue and less than seventeen pounds in the local currency.

It would earn another five pounds at the local antique shop. From there the statue would pass from hand to hand, briefly residing on one dusty shelf before being moved to another, exchanged for money or debt forgiveness or stolen. Six years passed, a war ended, and still the statue moved along the rocks and sand of the Egyptian coast until it finally arrived at a curiosity shop in Port Said.

It stood on a shelf for three full days before a museum docent named Leola Kidane took notice of it. The statue depicted a bare-chested man, holding his arms out, bent at the elbows so the hands were even with his face. It was carved from gray stone, very aged, and she recognized the style as a ka statue. It looked remarkably realistic, though she couldn't imagine what one would be doing in a shop like this at such a ridiculous price. But if it were real, she figured, it surely would have come through the proper channels at the museum.

Still, she couldn't quite bring herself to leave it behind. She tucked it under her arm and continued shopping. It was a lovely little trinket which could be utilized as a gift for the right person. She knew that her very dear friend Trafalgar didn't celebrate birthdays, but Leola did still owe her a debt for getting her the job at the museum.

And if anyone would appreciate having a fake ka statue on her shelf, it was the indomitable Miss Trafalgar of Abyssinia.

CHAPTER ONE

1921

Focus on the positives.

Her grandmother once told her that nothing was ever wholly bad, so matter how dire the situation, one should always find and focus on the positives. With that in mind, she focused on the city of London spread out before her like a jeweled quilt. Fog was rolling off the north bank of the Thames, softening the pale golden lights with an icy blue. She could hear voices echoing up and down the streets and the quiet rumble of motors. The world was serene and beautiful and bathed in moonlight. It was a sight she otherwise wouldn't have seen, and for that she was grateful.

The circumstances, on the other hand, left much to be desired. The wind turned her into a pendulum beneath the wide belly of the airship and, if not for her goggles, would have been pummeling her eyes too much for her to keep them open. She gripped the straps of her harness, the cloth tugging tight across her chest and under her arms, and peered up at the gondola. Her parachute had deployed into the room and was now spread web-like across the window through which she'd fallen. The canvas was sturdy enough to resist being pulled out as well, and she could only hope that strength didn't fail while they were cruising at this height. It might not be the worst thing in the world if she did fall. The parachute might glide her toward the river and slow her descent enough to land gently. Then, of course, she might end up tangled in the cords and canvas. Either way, it wasn't an issue worth worrying over. Not yet.

From above, she heard something hit the wall hard. Trafalgar called out, "Dorothy! Are you all right?"

"Just ducky. Relatively speaking, of course." She heard a blow and a grunt. "Don't worry about me. Protect the boy!"

"I was planning on it!"

Sounds of the fight grew quieter as Trafalgar fought her way off the wall and pushed her attackers back into the center of the room. Glass shattered and something heavy fell. Dorothy despised being so removed from the fight, but she didn't dare trying to climb up. Pulling herself up the cords would only risk having the parachute come free. She wouldn't be doing Trafalgar any favors by ending up in the Thames with two broken legs.

The fight began just as the captain announced London was in sight. Dorothy had been in the lounge with Trafalgar watching the boy they were escorting. His name was Rowan Sullivan, ten years old and mainly interested in bicycles and motorcars based on the one-way conversation he'd been carrying for most of their return trip. He had been kidnapped by enemies of his father, a historian working for Oxford. The kidnappers hoped to force Professor Sullivan into translating a map they hoped would lead to treasures untold.

Dorothy and Trafalgar were enlisted by Desmond Tindall, the man the public believed to be her fiancé. She quickly discovered who was to blame for the crime and traced them to a city in Wales called Swansea. Dorothy disliked Wales with a great passion. "Their language is incomprehensible," she'd complained to Trafalgar on their journey out. "Letters sorted at random with no sense or logic, only forming recognizable words by sheer coincidence. I'd have better luck trying to decode a cat's conversation."

The two of them found the kidnappers' base of operations and got away clean with the boy. Or so it had seemed until they were almost home. Apparently a group of kidnappers had followed them to the hangar and snuck aboard the *Skylarker* before it could take off. They dispatched with the crew and then went after the boy again. Dorothy's defenestration happened embarrassingly early in the fight.

It was sheer, dumb luck she'd been wearing the parachute when they were attacked. Threnody had put the pack together and Dorothy was demonstrating to Rowan how it worked when they were startled by the door crashing open. One of the kidnappers drew a gun, Dorothy tackled him to throw off his aim, and the bullet had gone through the glass. The man had then shoved her against the window hard enough for the glass to shatter and tried to throw her out. She had instead twisted in his arms, grabbed the D-ring in the center of her chest, and deployed the chute. The carefully-folded fist of fabric exploded out into his face with just enough force to knock him back, but Dorothy still tumbled forward into the empty air.

Now they were drifting over neighborhoods, low enough that she could see the detail on each shingle and the brick of chimneys, but still high enough that she would suffer greatly if she dropped.

From above, Trafalgar shouted, "Look out below!"

Dorothy looked up and swung to one side to avoid the unfurling rope ladder that had been dropped from the window next to the one blocked by her parachute. She swung toward it and grabbed one rung, grunted, and twisted her body around to grab the other. Her leather walking shoes were perfect for hanging about in the lounge, not so much for ascending a ladder. The sole slipped along the rung until it was caught in the wedge formed by the heel.

The ladder swung in a wide, nauseating arc as she tried to steady herself against it, well aware that anyone in the gondola could disconnect it at any moment. She knew keeping the parachute on would provide a safety net - so to speak - but the cords might also entangle her as she climbed. She decided on the safest of the dangerous options and undid the clasps, letting the harness slip off one arm and then the other. The pack swung in one direction while she and the ladder went the opposite. Steeling her nerves, she began to climb.

It was more arduous than she expected. By the time she was level with the windows, she had a deep and burning pain across both shoulders. There was a small lip where she could precariously rest her foot as she reached for the glass. Her heart skipped a beat as her fingers curled around the edge. She had to let go of the ladder in order to pull herself inside, but fear kept her hand from releasing.

She could see inside now. One man was on the floor, his head surrounded with the shattered remnants of the water pitcher. Trafalgar was holding her ground against the other two. She parried one, spun to deflect a blow from the other while the first was recovering, and then back to the first. She was keeping them away but she was obviously beginning to flag. Rowan was huddled in one corner, eyes wide and face ashen with terror.

Dorothy threw herself over the sill into the room, turning her tumble into a roll that took her into the fray. She stood up, goggles slightly askew and hair wild from the time she'd spent outside. She grabbed the arm of one man, threw her weight against his shoulder, and spun them both toward the wall. He tripped over his feet and they both toppled. Dorothy was able to brace herself for the fall but he wasn't quite so lucky. He crashed against the side of the table and cursed, bringing up his hands to grab her collar.

"He's weak in the left shoulder!" Trafalgar shouted.

"Good to know!"

Dorothy grabbed his shoulder and dug her thumb in under the bone. Her opponent howled and clubbed the side of her head with his other hand.

"Bloody bastard," she grunted, bells ringing in her skull. She rolled on top of him and sat up, planting the meaty part of her hand on his shoulder and laying her weight on him. He tried to wriggle away but Dorothy reached for the table and grabbed the book she'd been reading. She swung it at his head and made solid contact, but he didn't even come close to losing consciousness.

"Go to sleep!" she said, hitting him again.

"Stop hitting me!"

"You're lucky I'm not hurling you from the window."

Trafalgar said, "Dorothy, to your left!"

Dorothy rolled off her opponent. He sat up just as Trafalgar bum-rushed her henchman toward him. The men collided, one man's head rebounding off the other's jaw.

"The parachute cords!" Dorothy said.

Trafalgar ran to the window and retrieved the chute. She

held the pack, tossed the canvas to Dorothy, and together they bound the men. One man tried to headbutt Trafalgar but she only glared at him.

"Know when you are defeated, my friend."

"Well done, Trafalgar." Dorothy was breathless, her adrenaline wearing off. Her legs felt rubbery beneath her, worsened by the vibrations of the engine under her shoes. She took off the goggles and rubbed her eyes as she collapsed onto the divan. "And thank you for the assistance with the ladder. I was in the middle of debating some very unsavory options."

Trafalgar nodded to her. "And I thank you. I was uncertain how much longer I could have held them at bay on my own. Are you positive you're all right?"

"A bit sore, but otherwise in one piece." Dorothy looked to the corner where Rowan seemed to be recovering from his fright. He smiled nervously at them both. "How about you, young man? Are you injured?"

"No, ma'am!" he said. "That was swell! You clobbered 'em, just like back in Swansea!" He laughed and clapped. "This has been so grand!"

Dorothy shrugged at Trafalgar. "Well. At least we know he's not been traumatized by the ordeal. I'll take care of securing the unconscious fellow. Would you check to make sure Minty and the rest of the crew isn't in need of medical care?"

"Of course."

As she left, Dorothy gestured to Rowan. "Bring me something to tie this unconscious gentleman up with."

Rowan looked around and grabbed a sash from the curtain. He brought it over and watched as Dorothy secured the thug's hands. The boy sat next to the divan, hands folded on his lap. He watched her hands as she tied the knot, then looked up at her face.

"You went out the window."

"I remember. It was quite harrowing."

"And then you beat up that man. A-and the other woman, she beat up all the men."

Dorothy grinned. "She's good at that. You should see my other friend. I call her Trix. She puts both of us to shame."

"Wow. I can't imagine that!"

"Maybe you'll meet her one day. After we get you home

safely to your parents."

Trafalgar came back. "A few crew members were knocked unconscious, but they'll recover. The rest of the crew were barricaded on the bridge. I let them out and apologized to Captain Crook for the window."

"I should probably apologize to her myself. Minty's been fantastic, but I think we've finally worn out her gratitude. We may have to start paying for our trips, if just to cover the damages. Did she mention how soon we'd be landing?"

"We're twelve minutes from the Rookery," Trafalgar said.

Dorothy sighed. "Fantastic. Just enough time for a nice drink."

She walked to the wet bar and opened the cabinet. She scanned the labels, chose a bottle, and poured herself a glass. Trafalgar shook her head when Dorothy gestured with the bottle, so she replaced the stopper and carried her drink back to the divan. She took a seat and sighed heavily as she sank into the cushions, one leg casually draped over the other.

"To Threnody using the strongest of cords when constructing that parachute."

Trafalgar laughed and also took a seat. Rowan, still elated, laughed and clapped his hands. "You two are just jake!"

Dorothy lifted her glass to him and looked out the window, smiling as she swirled the liquor around in her mouth. Now that the danger was past and she didn't have to worry about the attackers, she could truly focus on the splendor of the city passing beneath the ship.

It truly was a beautiful night.

The Rookery was a connected cluster of hangars on the banks of the Thames. Despite the lateness of the hour, there was a fair bit of activity on the ground as the *Skylarker* settled into its berth. Other airships were returning from voyages or preparing for departure. Ground crews scurried across the sprawling port. Araminta's communications officer had called ahead to let Desmond and Rowan's family know the boy was okay.

Minty left the bridge to join Dorothy, Trafalgar, and their young charge on the departure deck. She accepted Dorothy's apology for the broken window but did not accept her offer to pay for its replacement. "You gave me one last day with the woman I loved," Minty said, "and I told you my debt to you would never be repaid. I meant that. Replacing a window is nothing." She held out one leather glove to Dorothy. "I look forward to your next trip with us, wherever it may lead."

Dorothy shook her hand. "Thank you, Minty."

Rowan hadn't stopped babbling to any crewmember who happened to catch his eye. "~and then she went out the window! But her parachute got caught in the window! She was dangling over the city! An' the other lady had to fight all three of the palookas by herself! But hoo, she was..." He bobbed and weaved, punching at the air with both fists.

Trafalgar tried to disguise her smile, but Dorothy could tell she was proud of her part in the story. The boy saw her as a hero, a feeling which in Dorothy's experience rarely got old.

The airship successfully landed, and the group disembarked. Professor Sullivan and his wife were waiting near the dock with Desmond, along with a trio of constables who had been enlisted to take the kidnappers into custody. Rowan brightened when he saw his parents, and the family rushed toward each other under the shadow of the *Skylarker*. Desmond was smiling as he approached, but the expression faded to horror when he saw the swelling on their faces. Dorothy was all but guaranteed to develop a nasty bruise on the curve of her jaw.

"What happened to you two?"

"You sent us after kidnappers, Des," Dorothy chided him. "There was bound to be a scuffle."

Rowan said, "It was more than a scuffle, Ma! There were killers on the airship. But the lady here, she knocked the gun out of his hand. She got knocked out the window! The other lady had to fight everyone else off by herself!"

Desmond had been watching the boy, but he snapped his gaze back to Dorothy. "I'm sorry, did he say 'out the window'? Of the airship?"

"I had a parachute," Dorothy said. "It was far from the most dangerous position I've ever found myself in."

Professor Sullivan stood and cleared his throat, wiping a hand over his face in an attempt to control his emotions. He held out his hand to Desmond.

"Thank you, Desmond, for getting my boy back."

Desmond stared at the outstretched hand. "Weren't you

listening? I didn't do a blasted thing. These two ladies deserve your thanks."

Sullivan shifted his gaze to Dorothy and Trafalgar. He didn't withdraw his hand, but Dorothy noticed a slight curling of his fingers.

"Yes," he finally said, "of course. Thank you, ladies, for everything."

Dorothy smiled tightly, choosing to ignore the slight for the time being. "You are quite welcome. He's a wonderful young man."

"He most definitely is. And we enjoyed meeting him." Trafalgar smiled at Rowan. "Stay out of trouble, young man. We shall be very cross if you get into trouble again."

Sullivan lowered his voice and looked at Desmond again. "Is that a possibility? That these men will try to take Rowan again?"

"Desmond," Dorothy said, "you may tell Professor Sullivan that it's extremely unlikely that these men will have need of his services again, for I took the opportunity to relieve them of the map they wished to have translated."

Sullivan looked confused. "I can hear you, you know."

"Then you can speak to me just as well. Trafalgar and I are the ones who risked our lives to save your son. The very least you can do is acknowledge our presence."

He huffed. "Yes. I... apologize. I merely--"

She waved off his excuses. "The map is in safe hands. If these men resurface, which I doubt they will, I shall be their target. You and your family will no longer be bothered."

"You have my gratitude, Lady Boone, as do you, Miss Trafalgar."

Trafalgar said, "We are happy everything came to a good conclusion for everybody."

Dorothy looked past him, where Mrs. Sullivan was still clinging to her child. "Your family requires your presence, Professor."

"Indeed they do." He touched a finger to the brim of his hat before he turned and went back to them.

Dorothy said goodbye to Minty and thanked her once more for the use of her airship. Desmond straightened his jacket and fell into step beside Dorothy as she and Trafalgar walked away from the dock.

"Now, about this window incident..."

"For God's sake, Des," Dorothy said. "Tell me you're not angry. This job was your idea!"

"Yes, it was," he said. "And in the course of doing a favor for me, you could have both lost your lives. If I had known what you would be facing~"

Dorothy stopped and faced him. "Then I hope you would have come to us regardless. That young man's life was in danger. And if his father had capitulated to their demands and the map turned out to be real, it could have been devastating. Danger is part of our job. It always has been. You saw that for yourself last year when your hand was crushed by Virago's goon. You refused to blame me for that, so do not blame yourself for this ordeal. Am I understood?"

He looked far from satisfied, but he could tell when he'd been defeated. "If you insist."

"I do." They walked from the Rookery to where Desmond had left the car. He held the back door open for them and made sure they were comfortable before he went around to the driver's side. He paused and flexed his hand, now fully-healed, and thought about Dorothy's words before he got behind the wheel. It was one thing to know how perilous their work was. It was quite another to be content staying safely behind while they faced all the danger.

He wasn't sure what could be done about his feelings. He was hardly qualified to stand against any of the foes Dorothy and Trafalgar faced on a regular basis. Regardless, something had to be done if he was ever going to sleep comfortably again.

CHAPTER TWO

There were two places Beatrice Sek should have been that night, and neither of them was the cramped little flat above a decrepit tavern. She could have been watching over Dorothy's townhouse until she returned from Swansea. The trip was expected to be short and uneventful, so she had been allowed to remain behind in London. She could have been tidying up the library or cataloging the veritable museum of artifacts that were stored in the empty house next door.

She could also have been at the Inkwell, the base of operations for the fledgling Mnemosyne Society. The tavern had become neutral ground for the disparate group Dorothy put together, a place where they could meet and compare notes. Beatrice had become the bartender, an easy enough job at a tavern with only eight customers, but she enjoyed it more than she expected to. Agnes Keeping provided the alcohol and Beatrice made sure everyone had a full glass.

Instead, she was lying in a stranger's bed while the flat's owner was in the other room washing up. She didn't know why she'd left home and gone searching for a warm body. She didn't exactly know why she'd chosen the woman she eventually went home with. Her name was Sarah. She was Asian, and she had tattoos on her arms that disappeared under the sleeves of her blouse. Seducing her was just a means to an end, a way to get her shirt off and examine the ink. It was a wasted effort, however; Sarah's tattoos were nothing but colored ink.

She'd been seeking other people like her - "elementals," apparently - since her encounter with the Virago, Emmeline Potter. Each one was tattooed with a symbol of the element their magic controlled. Beatrice had a tree for the earth, Virago had waves for water. There were two more somewhere, elementals of wind and fire, waiting to be found. A mystic called Dov told her that when the four were united, they would summon a fifth: void. She didn't know what that meant, but it certainly didn't sound like something good.

Beatrice turned her face toward the window. Outside, the lights of airships cut through the fog as they circled the Rookery. Dorothy could have been aboard one of them, on her way back from rescuing the son of Desmond's friend. She knew nothing of Beatrice's quest to find the other elementals. She would want to help. And as clever as she was, as ingenuitive as she was, she would make short work of the quest. When the quest ended, she would be forced to decide what to do next.

She didn't want to create "void," no matter what that entailed. Void seemed bad no matter what the details were. But finding the others may provide clues to who she was and where she came from. Maybe her parents were still alive. Maybe she had brothers, sisters. She needed time to decide if getting the answers was worth the consequences.

Sarah came out of the bathroom in a robe, hesitating before she moved closer to the bed. Beatrice sat up and reached for her clothes. When Sarah spoke, there was more than a little relief hidden under her scouse accent.

"I wasn't sure if you'd want to stay the night..."

"I have somewhere to be. But thank you."

"You're welcome." Sarah sat on the edge of the mattress. "I don't usually do anything like this. Bring someone home. Let alone a lady. I've... I've *never* done that before."

Beatrice didn't tell her that fact had been evident in her performance. There was no need to be cruel. She retrieved her clothes from the floor and dressed quickly in the darkness.

"It's probably not going to happen again."

More relief. "Oh. Okay. Do you need me to walk you back

to the pub?"

"No, I remember the way." She paused at the door. "Thank you for tonight. It was... it was good."

Sarah smiled. "I enjoyed it more than I thought I would."

Beatrice said, "That's all that matters. Sleep well, Sarah."

She shut the door quietly and went downstairs, back out into the night. It was just over a kilometer back to Threadneedle but the night wasn't cold enough to discourage her from walking. She quickly regretted her decision as the clouds overhead finally made good on their threat and began to sprinkle the street with a gentle but freezing rain. Beatrice tugged the collar of her jacket up over her head and quickened her pace, jogging under the trees and awnings to try minimizing the exposure. Despite her efforts, she was still soaked by the time she reached the familiar front steps of her home. She stood on the stoop to dig her keys out of her pocket but, before she could find them, Desmond's car pulled up at the curb. She went down to greet them, now ignoring the cold fingers of rain slipping under her collar to run down her back.

Dorothy burst from the backseat with a coat in hand. She draped it over Beatrice's head and ushered her back toward shelter. Beatrice huddled gratefully against Dorothy's warmth and allowed herself to be ushered inside.

"Trix, you foolish woman," Dorothy chided gently. She plucked at the soaked clothes. Trafalgar, who had followed them inside, went upstairs to retrieve towels and a robe. "Who told you to wait outside for us? How did you even know we were coming back now?"

"I didn't know." Her voice was shaking from the cold. Trafalgar returned and draped a towel across her shoulders. "Thank you, Trafalgar."

"Of course," Trafalgar said.

Using the towel as a shroud, Dorothy helped Beatrice take off her wet clothes. "I was coming back from an evening out."

"Aha," Dorothy said with a smile. "And your mind was not on the weather. I see. Was she a beauty?"

Beatrice couldn't help but return the smile. "I've seen prettier."

"Fresh."

Trafalgar cleared her throat. "I'll start a fire."

Dorothy helped Beatrice of her pants, then held out the

robe for her. "You'll have to tell me all about this little minx. What was her name?"

"Sarah." Trafalgar returned and switched on a lamp. In the new light, Beatrice saw the swelling on Dorothy's face. Her eyes flared with anger. "Who hurt you?"

"Nobody I wish to spend any more time discussing this evening." She looped her arm around Beatrice's and guided her into the parlor. Your coconspirator is a much better topic. Dry yourself by the fire. I'll make you something warm to drink and then you can tell me all about your lovely lady." She placed Beatrice in the chair by the fire and turned to Trafalgar. "You deserve a drink as well. After all, you did save me from plummeting out of an airship."

Beatrice said, "I beg your pardon?"

"It's not important, love," Dorothy said. "Trafalgar? Coffee?"

"That would be wonderful. Thank you."

Dorothy said, "Back in a mo'."

Beatrice waited until Dorothy was out of the room before she focused on Trafalgar. "How bad was it?"

"Not as bad as it could have been. We took the kidnappers by surprise in Swansea, so there wasn't more than a scuffle there. But three of them managed to stowaway aboard the *Skylarker* and attacked us during the return trip. Dorothy was dropped out of the window, but she was wearing a parachute that caught against the frame. I pulled her back in and she helped me subdue the men. It was nothing more than a skirmish."

"But it could have been disastrous."

Trafalgar smiled and watched the fire. "Everything we do has the potential to be disastrous. And Dorothy tends to be a magnet for danger more than most. We can't prevent her from ending up in those situations, we can only hope to be there for her when she discovers how deep she's gotten."

"I'm grateful you were there."

"As am I." She glanced toward the door to see if Dorothy was returning. "As for yourself... I can't help but notice you don't seem... what I mean to say is, you don't have the bearing of someone who spent the evening in someone else's bed. The past two years, I've frequently seen you, ah... your..."

Beatrice said, "Afterglow?"

Trafalgar smiled. "Yes. It's absent now. So either you're lying to Dorothy, or there's more to the story that you aren't telling."

Beatrice tugged at the robe and avoided looking at Trafalgar. "I did spend the evening with someone. But it wasn't necessarily for any romantic or libidinous urge. I had ulterior motives for taking this particular woman to bed."

"I see. Reasons you're not willing to confess?"

"Precisely."

"I can respect that. But I would suggest putting on a better show when you talk to Dorothy. If I can tell you're lying, she most assuredly will be able to as well."

"Thank you."

Trafalgar nodded and looked at the clock. "I should not have agreed to the coffee. I'll go tell her that I've changed my mind and I've decided to retire." She stood and inclined her head to Beatrice. "Good night, Miss Sek."

"Good night to you as well."

In the past year, Trafalgar had been using the spare room so frequently that Beatrice and Dorothy both considered her to be cohabitating with them. She still hadn't officially moved in, but it seemed like only a matter of time before the spare room ceased to be available to other guests. Beatrice was pleased to have her in the house. When they met, she considered Trafalgar her enemy because she was Dorothy's enemy. Now that the rivalry was ended and she'd actually gotten to know the other woman a little better, she was honored to consider her a friend.

If something did happen to her, if her search for the other elementals took her away from Dorothy's side, she was grateful there was someone like Trafalgar to take her place.

Close to a week after rescuing Rowan Sullivan from his kidnappers, Dorothy's bruises had faded enough that she no longer bothered concealing them with makeup. Desmond was obviously still feeling guilty for his part in what had happened and seemed to be keeping his distance. Dorothy sent him a message on Tuesday asking him for an evening out, but he'd never bothered to reply. She would have to speak to him before his nonsense carried on too long. She bore him no ill will for putting her on the airship, but she would definitely be irate if he used it as an excuse to ignore her.

She spent the majority of the week in her office, working on a map. She sketched coastlines whenever a mission allowed her the time, and on slow afternoons she transferred those segments onto a single larger piece of parchment. Drawing a map was such a relaxing pastime that she often did it in a sort of trance. She loved the way the paper felt under her hands. She even loved the smudges of ink that were left on her fingers and the side of her hand, though the stains could be a pain to remove.

Working from home also meant there was no need to dress up. She wore loose trousers and a sleeveless white blouse, her hair down and barefoot. It was a uniform she'd kept since she was a child and she saw no reason to wear it again in the privacy of her own home. Comfort above all, and damn anyone who thought differently. She cloistered herself in her den, behind the large oak desk which housed the instruments of her work and hobbies. Calipers, sextants, pencils, and pens were scattered among scattered pages of half-finished maps, while her research books stood like uneven walls on whatever surface was available when she set it down. It was a mess, but it was her mess.

Dorothy loved the smell of the room and the way the air felt in the room. It was comfortable. It was home. The carpet under her desk was smoothed by many afternoons of brushing her bare feet across it, or her toes curling over it.

The sun shifted, altering her light, so she decided it was time for a quick tea break. She left her study in search of something to eat.

Trafalgar appeared on the stairs in response to the door opening. She was dressed casually, in a blouse that was open at the collar under a cloth vest. Her dress swayed against her legs with the movement that had carried her out of the study.

"Dorothy! Do you have a moment? I received an item in the post and would like your opinion on it."

"Of course." She changed direction and followed Trafalgar into the parlor. "I wasn't aware you were even here. When did you arrive?"

"Just after lunch. Beatrice offered to interrupt you, but I was willing to wait."

"That was hours ago! I wish she had told me. I wasn't

doing anything particularly important."

"It was no trouble waiting. You have a magnificent library, and this was a chance to take advantage of it."

Dorothy gestured at the shelves. "Feel free. Books do no one any good gathering dust. Now... what brings you here today?"

Trafalgar picked up a box from the coffee table and presented it to Dorothy. She glanced at the postmark and stamps and smiled. "Cairo? A gift from Leola?"

"Indeed." Trafalgar clasped her hands behind her back. "We've been keeping in touch. Mostly day-to-day things from the museum. She's met someone. A grocer named Khalid."

"Ah, a wonderful profession. The world shall always need grocers."

She had examined the outer package before opening it. Even though she knew Trafalgar had opened it once, she was always careful about opening her mail ever since a package blew up in her face. Once she was confident the package wasn't rigged, she placed it on the table and opened the flaps. Trafalgar watched as Dorothy examined the contents, refraining from explanation so she could draw her own conclusions.

Dorothy lifted the slender statue from the box. It depicted a man standing on a small platform, his left foot extended with the other slightly behind. He wore the striped nemes headdress of an Egyptian pharaoh and stared forward with a small knowing smile. A pair of arms extended from the top of his head, sticking out to either side before bending upward at the elbows.

"A ka statue," she said. "Interesting. Pharaohs believed these held their soul after death. It was often placed in the tombs alongside their mummified remains." Trafalgar remained silent. Dorothy was barely aware she was even speaking aloud, only noting the facts to refresh her own memory. She brushed her thumb over the rough stone. Very strange. A forger would mostly likely have gone to the trouble of sanding it down to make it more tactilely pleasing to rubes who wouldn't know better. "Whoever carved this was very talented... very meticulous. Is this limestone?"

"Alabaster."

Dorothy raised an eyebrow. "Indeed? I didn't get to know

Leola well, but I highly doubt she would have taken something from the museum's collection. Where did she acquire this?"

Trafalgar was leaning against the back of the divan, arms crossed over her chest. "A curiosity shop. It was gathering dust alongside earthenware pottery and dishes meant to entice tourists. She got it for an absolute steal because the owners assumed it was fake. Leola sent it to me as a souvenir, but the more I investigate, the more I believe it may be authentic."

"It's difficult to say without more research."

"You're welcome to borrow it for as long as you need."

Dorothy nodded. "Thank you. I'll keep you apprised of anything I discover." The eyes of the statue were very interesting. They seemed to have depth, somehow, a perception that made her feel as if the statue was returning her gaze. Her intrigue quickly turned to an unsettled feeling, and she suppressed a shudder as she placed it carefully back into the box. "Are you staying for dinner?"

"Beatrice asked me the same thing," Trafalgar said with a smile as she followed Dorothy out of the room. "I have already accepted the hospitality."

"Excellent. You know, you really must get into the habit of calling her Trix."

Trafalgar didn't seem overly keen. "I feel that is more of a nickname between the two of you. I would feel awkward using it."

"I doubt she would mind."

"Then I shall consider it. But only if she asks me."

"That is more than fair."

As Dorothy closed the door, she cast one final glance toward the box holding the ka statue. It seemed extraordinarily unlikely that it was authentic, but there was always the possibility that something slipped through the cracks at one dig or another. Or perhaps it was the product of an undiscovered tomb, an item recovered by a grave robber who had no idea what they possessed.

Whatever the statue's origins, she couldn't deny the fact that she felt an inexplicable unease in its presence. She was grateful to shut it behind the study doors to focus on dinner and conversation with her friends and compatriots. Any mysteries it might conceal could wait until after they'd eaten.

CHAPTER THREE

It rained again over the weekend. Dorothy, suffering from a bout of cabin fever, asked Beatrice if she would mind relocating to the Inkwell for a few hours. At least there she could drink liquor she didn't have to buy for herself. She gathered a translation she had been working on - an academic exercise more than anything else - and, on her way out the door, picked up the box containing Trafalgar's statue. She tucked the box under her arm and allowed Beatrice to carry the umbrella over her head as they crossed to the car.

Beatrice drove her through flooded streets to the quaint gated building where the Mnemosyne Society met. The windows of the ground floor were lit with a soft yellow glow, and Dorothy was relieved to see someone else had gone to the trouble to warm the place so she wouldn't have to shudder while the furnace rattled to life. Her gratitude was short-lived, however, and died quickly as soon as she stepped inside.

Cecil Dubourne, the youngest member to take up their profession, was seated at a table near the front window. Abraham Strode stood over Cecil in the middle of some beratement, his natty jacket pushed back so he could rest both fists on his hips. Cecil's face was skewed by a smug smile, his posture indicating he felt he'd already won the argument. Strode was distracted by the new arrivals, and Cecil merely tipped his head to them in greeting as Dorothy shook the rain from her sleeves.

Leonard Keeping was seated at the bar and sighed with relief when he saw the new arrivals. "Ah, Lady Boone. Thank God. Someone who can talk some sense into these yahoos."

Dorothy sighed wearily. "What is it now?"

Cecil said, "I merely made a comment about Mr. Strode's pocket handkerchief~"

"Using coarse language he should not repeat in front of a lady," Strode interjected.

Cecil rolled his eyes. "And he took offense."

"He has been taking potshots at me all month. He is an insufferable man who doesn't have what it takes to be a part of this club. His father would be ashamed to see what his son has made of his legacy."

The humor evaporated from Cecil's face. "Now, watch your tongue, fellow."

"Oh, you can offer insult but once the tables are turned it's another story."

Leonard sighed and looked helplessly at Dorothy. "Would you please intervene?"

Dorothy began to say something but then thought better of it. "Very well." She stepped forward. "Mr. Dubourne, Mr. Strode, thank you for your time but you will no longer be necessary in the Society. Please take a few minutes to gather any belongings you may have left in the building and then show yourselves out. You may leave your keys on the bar."

Cecil and Strode both stared at her. "I beg your pardon?" Strode gasped, shocked.

"The entire purpose of forming this group was to overcome petty bickering like this. I did not gather you all together and provide this place for us so I could play mother hen to a bunch of grown men who should know how to behave. If you cannot be civil to one another, then we have no use for you. But if you wish to remain, then you will respect one another. And if one of you cannot do that, then the other must learn how to let things go. Am I understood, gentlemen?"

Both men muttered that they understood and returned to their respective tables. Strode pushed in the chair which he'd been using and chose a position with his back to Cecil's table.

Dorothy straightened her jacket. "Splendid." She noticed

Beatrice watching everything with a bemused expression. "And one more thing. Beatrice tends bar because she likes it, not because it's her job. You are not to treat her as if she's hired help. She is here because I would be dead without her assistance. She is an equal member of the Society, a fact which may one day save your lives. If you wish for her to make you a drink, you will ask politely and you will thank her. And you could make a drink for her from time to time as well."

Leonard cleared his throat. Cecil and Strode awkwardly shifted in their seats. All three made muttered agreements.

"Fabulous. Trix, if you wouldn't mind..."

"Tea?"

Dorothy smiled. "And one for yourself. I'll be on the first floor. You are gentlemen. Start acting like it." She paused by the bar long enough for Beatrice to pass her a cup of tea, which she accepted with a dip of her head, and continued upstairs.

The first story was a library which had been filled with books from the libraries of every society member. Dorothy placed her things on one of the long tables in the center of the room. She put down the box with the ka statue and rested her hand on top of it for a moment. It wasn't her intention to dig into its mystery, but there was a chance the Inkwell's library held more useful information than the one she had at home. She could look up a few things while she got settled.

She took off her wet outer jacket and hung it on a rack near the stairs. The space between the shelves was tight and dark, so she took a torch with her so she could read the spines. It was quiet enough that she could hear the rain rattling against the shingles even with another floor above her. The library was a cave, its small windows completely darkened by the storm. The chill was a physical entity clinging to the floor and the corners, pushed from one spot to another by her presence. It seemed like the storm was picking up. She also heard voices from below under the steady drumming of rain, conversational rather than argumentative, so she tuned it out.

The shelves revealed a book on Egyptian iconography and another on Egyptian funereal practices. Her shoes made hollow clicking sounds as she navigated the aisles. It took a bit of digging but she also found a journal that was marked as a reference guide to hieroglyphics. She flipped open the front cover and smiled when she recognized the handwriting.

"Cora. I'll have to remember to thank you the next time we see each other."

Dorothy took the books back to the table. In the time the statue had been in her possession, she'd noticed a string of characters carved on the base. She sat the lantern close enough to see the shapes and opened Cora's journal. Occasionally forgers would include something accurate just to throw off appraisers or collectors of ancient artifacts, but the phrases would be gibberish. On the other end of the spectrum were authentic but mundane carvings. She'd once been positive "TENTAMUN ENJOYS SEXUAL ACTS WITH CAMELS" was a modern prankster, but the item was confirmed to be from the thirteenth dynasty. It would seem even ancient women had their honor impugned on restroom walls.

She placed one finger on each symbol as she deciphered it in the book, slowly transcribing it down. "Here imprisoned... gathered to the bosom of... time?" She tapped her pencil against the book as she double-checked the work.

Beatrice appeared at the head of the stairs. "Dorothy?"

"Mm?"

"More tea?"

Dorothy looked at her cup. She would have assumed it was only tepid, but she was surprised to see it was completely empty. "Yes, Trix. Thank you."

Beatrice retrieved the cup and went back downstairs. She paused a moment to take in her surroundings. Still raining. Maybe a few more voices from the bar below. She hoped if anyone joined her in the library they respected the fact she was hard at work. It was a gathering of minds, not a social club. She picked up the statue and examined the face, then focused again on the faded carvings around his feet. At some point Beatrice returned so quietly that Dorothy was unaware the cup was back until she'd absent-mindedly reached for it. She smiled as she brought it to her lips. Perfect, as always. Dorothy had always been particular about her tea, but Beatrice hadn't learned that method. The truth was that she brewed tea a certain way and Dorothy found she preferred that style to her own. She took another sip and let it roll over her tongue for a moment before returning to work.

"*Here imprisoned, gathered to the bosom of the* not time, but

*ages, lies Amenemhat, High Priest of Amun. Beloved advisor...
trusted...* and so on. *Here released, the beloved Amenemhat, granted
new life and freedom from the warm embrace of Amun.*"

Her voice caught in her throat and she swooned where she
sat. She closed her eyes to fight the sudden lightheadedness.
One hand reached out for her tea, but her fingers trembled
too much to grip the handle. She coughed roughly, tasting
spittle on her lips as she pushed her chair back and rose
unsteadily onto her feet. She felt like she was choking or being
choked from within. She felt as if the room was spinning was
room the if as felt she felt as if the room was~

Strange.

He placed his hand on the table and stared it at. Small.
Feminine. Pale and pink. He straightened his back and looked
down at his body. Female. Trousers, a belt. White. There was
the taste of something on his tongue. An herbal drink. His
stomach was empty. He examined the room again for clues as
to where he was and how long he had been imprisoned. There
were not many. Bound books lined the shelves, dozens of
them.

He heard voices from below and moved to the top of the
staircase. Lights. Men and women speaking a language he
didn't recognize. He looked back at the table, the statue which
had been his home for centuries untold stood near the
lantern. He would return for it before leaving. For the
moment, his most pressing desire was learning about his
circumstances. He began descending the steps and hoped
whoever waited below would pay no attention to a scholar
stepping out for a moment.

He paused at the bottom of the stairs. A woman behind
the bar. A blonde man sitting at a table, with a brown-haired
man in a booth behind him. An older woman leaned upon the
bar, elbows bent and fingers steepled in front of her. With the
exception of the Oriental bartender, everyone in the bar
seemed to be White. After a moment to examine the people
without being noticed, he crossed toward what he hoped was
the exit.

The beautiful woman with brunette hair looked in his
direction and smiled. "Hu-low da'r'thee," the woman said.

He continued walking, eyes on his goal.

"Da'r'thee?"

He was almost to the door now, but someone was approaching from behind. He heard rapid footsteps on the wooden floor. Someone touched his arm and he turned to see the Oriental woman. She returned his gaze with concern. She spoke too quickly for him to decipher. Now everyone in the room was looking at him. The elderly woman at the bar seemed concerned. He met the Oriental woman's gaze in time to see something harden in her eyes.

"U'ah *not* Da'r'thee Bune."

Whatever her words meant, it was clear they knew something was amiss. The woman's grip tightened on his arm. He twisted at the waist and pulled free, his other arm coming up almost without thought to shove the woman away. She stumbled, eyes widening with shock before she recovered and advanced again. Again he moved without conscious thought, shoving his arm out like a piston and hitting her hard in the chest. When she stumbled, he punched with the other arm and caught her on the chin.

"Blu'de 'el!" one of the men said. Both rose from their seat and rushed toward him. He didn't have much faith in his chances against two men while he was in a female vessel, so instead he threw open the door and ran. Cold water doused him from head to foot, startling him into stopping just over the threshold. Was he underwater...? No. It was a storm. He looked up into the skies as he was grabbed from behind. Powerful male arms closed like a vice around his breasts and he was easily lifted off his feet.

The man babbled something in his ear. He twisted and fought, but the blonde man came around and grabbed his feet.

"Hold 'er, Seh-sull!" the man behind him said.

"Um bloody try'n'!" the blonde man said. "She kicks like a damned mule!"

He kicked out with one dainty, feminine boot and caught the blonde man on the chin. He barely even registered the fact he could understand them better. He swung his fist back and hit the man behind him on the hip. It was enough to weaken his hold, so he squirmed free and spun on the ball of his foot. He already knew his host well enough to stop thinking and let the body take over. He looked at the man, declared him an enemy, and let the muscles take over. He lunged, punched, shoved, kicked, and in a matter of seconds, his foe was on the ground.

The bartender was back in it now. She swung at him and he deflected, kneed her in the stomach, and sent her reeling into the wall. She hit at an awkward angle, her shoulder impacting the wall first before her head cracked against the plaster. The impact caused her neck to snap back and she crumpled to the floor without trying to break her fall. He assumed she was dead. Cecil, the blonde man whom he'd kicked, came back inside. The rain had smeared blood across the whole lower section of his face, but he was still spoiling for a fight.

"I don't know what's gotten into you, but I'm going to stop pulling my punches soon."

He grabbed Cecil's fist and twisted until he felt resistance. Then he twisted again until he heard and felt something snap near the elbow. Cecil howled in pain and fell.

With his foes dispatched, he jumped over the fallen man's body and fled into the dark, wet evening. The rain was freezing and his clothes were heavy with it, clinging to his body as he ran blindly. The city! The city was immense and constructed of stone. Peculiar scarab-like constructs roamed the streets, lights burning on their fronts. Each one grumbled from within as if powered by individual motors.

This certainly couldn't be Egypt. No amount of time could account for his home becoming so alien and foreboding. He ran through the alien world, shivering from fear as much as the cold. He only stopped when he reached an immense stretch of grass. More grass than he had ever seen in his entire life, and it sparkled with rainwater as if someone had spilled an entire treasury worth of gems on the ground. He dropped to his knees and pressed his palms against it. He was fairly sure he hadn't been followed but, worse than that, he knew he couldn't find his way back. The statue was lost to him now. No matter. He didn't plan to need it again.

He brought his dripping hands up to his face and pressed them to his cheeks. He was Amenemhat. High Priest of Amun. He had bound his spirit to the ka statue so, upon his death, he could be brought back. He'd sacrificed passage to the afterlife in exchange for the promise of a second birth and now he knew it had worked. He didn't know how long he'd been gone, but it must have been an immense stretch of time. He laughed and turned his face back up to the clouds, letting the rain cascade over his features and into his long hair.

Amenemhat knew he couldn't remain in the body he'd taken. It was female and too weak for a permanent host. But there were bound to be others nearby who would be more appropriate. Without the statue, he wouldn't be able to return the body to its proper owner, but perhaps that was a blessing in disguise. This "Dorothy" was powerful, clever, and capable of fighting men who were twice her size.

She would make a marvelous host for his beloved.

CHAPTER FOUR

"She just went batty and started whipping all of us!" Cecil's voice was nasal and muffled by the rag pressed under his nose. Trafalgar frowned at Cecil's assessment and turned to examine the rest of the room. He was seated on the edge of the booth being tended to by Cora Hyde, who had managed to escape any kind of harm during Dorothy's inexplicable to-do: a chair broken by Strode's fall, the pool of rainwater where the door had stood open while Dorothy brawled with her fellow Society members, the blood spray from young Cecil's broken nose, caused by a boot to the face.

And then there was Beatrice. Beatrice had been knocked unconscious and was lying across one of the long padded benches that ran along the northern wall. Desmond, who had driven Trafalgar to the tavern upon receiving the call from Cora, was monitoring her to ensure she didn't slip away from them before a doctor could arrive.

"It doesn't ring true," Trafalgar finally said.

Cora looked apologetic. "I was here, Trafalgar. I saw it with my own eyes. She didn't say a word. She came downstairs and, when Beatrice tried to stop her from leaving, she attacked everyone without provocation. Cecil and Abe were only trying to subdue her when she assaulted them."

Strode muttered, "Well, not everyone..."

Cora glared at him. "Would you feel better if I had been knocked unconscious as well, Mr. Strode?"

"All for one, as the book says."

Trafalgar held up a hand to stop their arguing. "I believe events transpired exactly as you said, Mr. Dubourne, but I can't make sense of it in my head. Given the right motivation, I can see Dorothy fighting anyone in this room, myself included. The exception being Miss Sek. I cannot fathom a scenario where Dorothy would cause her injury and yet, here she lies, hurt worse than anyone else. You all know how they feel about one another."

Cecil said, "We do?"

Trafalgar flinched. "They are extraordinarily close."

"Like sisters," Cora supplied.

"Yes. And yet you say she hurled Beatrice against the wall with such force that she has yet to regain consciousness? That is not the Dorothy Boone I know."

Beatrice sat up, her movements stiff. Her voice was rough. "Because it was not her."

Desmond put a hand on her shoulder when she tried to sit up. "Stay right where you are. A doctor is on the way to examine you."

"That's not necessary." She pushed his hand away and sat up. "I looked into her eyes. The woman I saw looking back at me was not Dorothy Boone."

Desmond said, "How is that possible?"

Strode said, "It is possible. Possession, of course. It could also have been mind control. What was she working on upstairs?"

"A translation..." Beatrice stood up and stumbled almost immediately. Rather than chiding her to remain seated, Desmond slipped her arm across his shoulders and guided her to the stairs. Trafalgar followed and, after a moment of silent debate, the rest of the society went as well. The chair in which Dorothy had been sitting was knocked over. Desmond righted it and Beatrice gingerly lowered herself into the seat, scanning the items spread out in front of her.

Trafalgar instantly focused on the ka statue. "This is what she was working on?"

"I believe so. She was so transfixed when I brought her tea that she didn't even notice me. Do you know where it came from?"

"Indeed I do. I gave it to her. I received it from Leola, who believed it was a reproduction. It would appear she was incorrect." She picked up the statue and examined the carvings on its base. She had examined them herself, but she'd been unable to translate any of it. She looked at the notebook open on the table. "Had she made progress?"

Beatrice rested her elbow on the table, two fingers resting on her forehead. She rubbed in slow circles as she focused on the page. "Much progress. She'd translated most of the phrase. '*Here imprisoned—*'"

"Ah!" Strode said, interrupting her with a snap of his fingers. "Until we know what happened, perhaps it would be wise not to read anything aloud."

Trafalgar said, "Good thinking." She gestured for the notebook and Beatrice handed it to her. She read the completed translation to herself. "Imprisoned and released... Amenemhat. Oh, good lord. It would appear the statue is authentic after all."

Cecil said, "What is it supposed to do?"

"The Egyptians believed the soul was free to wander the earth after death. The ka statue was designed as a focal point it could return to. A home once its body decayed. I believe this statue was created for a High Priest called Amenemhat and his soul remained tied to it even after all this time." She touched the statue's face. "I believe Dorothy inadvertently freed him, and he took possession of her."

Beatrice said, "So the person who attacked me was Amen... Ah-mun..."

"Amenemhat," Trafalgar said, "wearing Dorothy's body."

Desmond said, "So where is Dorothy? Her... her soul or identity or whatever you wish to call it?"

"It could be where it's always been, just overwritten by the priest. Or... alternatively..." She held up the statue. "She may have swapped places with him."

Beatrice took the journal back. "*Here imprisoned, the—*"

"What are you doing?"

"If Dorothy was imprisoned in the statue, then perhaps repeating the incantation will free her."

Trafalgar said, "If that is true, then she will take your body and leave you trapped."

"I'm willing to take that risk."

Cora said, "If there is any truth to this madness, I'm not sure a potentially concussed brain should be... swapped about."

Trafalgar said, "Not to mention the fact that I'm certain your participation will be necessary if we are to find Dorothy's body. She can't afford to have you sitting on the sidelines when she's in this much peril. I should be the one to do it."

Beatrice said, "Dorothy will need you more than she needs me. This man will most likely try leaving London for familiar territory. Egypt. As a girl, you traveled from Cairo to London with nothing but the coat on your back. If anyone knows what he'll do and where he'll go, it's you."

Before Trafalgar could counter the argument, Desmond said, "It has to be me." The room turned to face him. "Am I wrong? When you go off to reclaim Dorothy's body, I will be left behind. I'm unnecessary to your adventuring and I would be next to useless in a fight. But I can be a vessel for Dorothy's mind, which is one of the most formidable weapons one can wield."

Trafalgar said, "Even if this works, we have no idea if the process will be reversible and we have no idea how much time we'll have to act if it is. You are putting your life at risk."

"I put Dorothy's life at risk when I asked her to find my colleague's son."

"She didn't blame you for that."

"I blamed myself. This is a chance to put things right. For everything she has done for me in the past, I owe her."

He didn't have to explain what he was talking about. If anyone at Oxford knew about his sexuality, they would immediately remove him from his position. He would be arrested, put on trial, imprisoned. Dorothy provided him with an alibi that not only prevented speculation but allowed him to date without arousing suspicion.

"If the worst does occur, my affairs are in order. I'm a professor. The world has thousands of us. But it only has one Dorothy Boone. It needs her in whatever vessel she can get."

Trafalgar looked like she wanted to continue arguing, but she had no recourse. "If you insist. But this means Dorothy will be inhabiting your body. A male body. There may be ~"

He waved his hand. "I trust she will use discretion and

return my body to me unharmed. Now, if you wouldn't mind... the journal?"

Beatrice said, "It may require contact with the statue as well."

Desmond nodded. He held the book in one hand, the statue in the other, and read Dorothy's translation. He cleared his throat and spoke the words aloud. He stumbled a bit over the name but corrected himself the second time he had to say it. When he finished, he stood as still as possible and waited for... something. A sensation or a flash to tell him it had worked. He flexed his fingers on the statue and looked at everyone else in the room, their eyes locked on him to see if it worked.

"I'm still me," he said.

"You said Amenemhat," Cecil said. "He's not imprisoned anymore. Lady Boone is."

Trafalgar said, "Excellent point. Substitute her name."

Desmond cleared his throat. "*Here imprisoned, gathered to the bosom of the ages, lies Lady Dorothy Boone...* ah. Clever adventuress, erudite and stubborn. *Here released, the beloved Lady Dorothy Boone, granted new life and freedom from the wa~*" He choked on his words and coughed, the hand holding the book trembling so violently that it fell to the floor. He stumbled backward and Strode moved to catch him by the elbow so he wouldn't collapse. He thrust out the statue and Beatrice took it before he could drop it as well.

Violent tremors passed through her, and she held so tightly to Beatrice's hand that she feared she might cause injury. She didn't remember Beatrice being in the room when the fit began, and who was holding her up? She felt ill. Seasick. Nauseated. The room swam in her vision and she realized everyone from downstairs had surrounded her. When had Trafalgar arrived? Why did everyone look so concerned? It was just a spell, albeit an unusually strong one. She was horribly parched.

"What on earth..." She stopped herself and cleared her throat. "Good lord. What... wh-what on... what... I'm..."

Trafalgar stepped forward. "Easy, Dorothy. Just relax. You've... you have apparently been through quite the ordeal. Just relax."

"What's wrong with my voice?" She turned her head to see

where Desmond was. Why could she feel him just over her shoulder? Why did she feel an odd pressure in her throat every time she spoke? She looked down at her body and saw a waistcoat, a tie, and slacks over a distinctly male physique. The timbre of her voice suddenly made more sense, but her mind rebelled at the sight. "What happened? What... what is... what's..."

Trafalgar cupped Dorothy's face. There was something on her cheeks - good lord, she had a *beard* - and forced her to remain still.

"We believe your body was abducted by a spirit which resided in the ka statue. Desmond volunteered himself~"

"Des...?"

"~to provide you the opportunity to help us retrieve it. But first you must calm down. Can you do that for us, Dorothy?"

She blinked, holding her eyes shut for a moment. "I don't know. I'm... this... this is all very peculiar. I feel as if I'm s-seeing and feeling everything through a veil. My mind is..." She furrowed her brow. "This is Desmond's voice. Everything I think is coming out in Desmond's voice. I can't..."

Beatrice said, "Perhaps this was a poor plan."

"No. No, I... I-I think it was a fine plan. I just need a few minutes." She shook her head. Beatrice guided her to the chair and helped her sit down. "Oh, Des. You foolhardy... fool... Is he...?"

"In the ka statue," Trafalgar said. "He felt guilty for everything you've done for him in the past."

Dorothy scoffed. "I would say this more than balances the scale." She reached up and touched her beard. "Dear God, how does he stand this thing? Okay. God, this voice. Tell me what happened."

Cora explained the sequence of events, culminating in the fight that ended when Amenemhat fled into the storm wearing Dorothy's body. When Cora got to the part about Beatrice being knocked unconscious, Dorothy reached out to take her hand. She held it between both of hers - well, between both of Desmond's. His hands were so much larger than she was used to, and they made Beatrice's seem miniature by comparison. Her mind threatened to reel again but she forced herself to focus.

"We would have pursued," Cora said, "but Cecil was

injured, and the rest of us were more concerned about Beatrice's well-being."

"You absolutely made the right decision," Dorothy said. "I'm not sure Desmond did, but time will tell." She reached up to her collar and frowned as she loosened the tie and tugged at the top button. "Lord, how does he... ah, much better." She cleared her throat again, even though she knew it would do nothing to help the "problem" her voice had. "What is our first plan of action?"

Abraham said, "Well, her... ah, his? What is the etiquette here?"

"Him," Dorothy said. "Just for the sake of clarity."

Trafalgar said, "Very well. When we were debating which of us would serve as your host, Beatrice came to the conclusion that his first objective will be to flee the city. If he truly is a High Priest from ancient Egypt, London will be utterly alien to him. He'll seek familiar territory before attempting anything else. Does he have access to your mind? Your memories?"

Dorothy said, "How would I know?"

Cora said, "Do you have access to Desmond's?"

"Oh. Right. Um..." She closed her eyes and tried to think of something she didn't already know about the man. She pictured his classroom, which she had seen dozens of times, and his home, which she had also visited. She thought of the Thames, viewing London from an airship, driving in the country... any number of images that could have been culled from her own mind. She remembered a man Desmond brought to a dinner party at the end of Spring. He was young and attractive, just young enough to be one of Desmond's students. She remembered how they had excused themselves at the end of the evening. She remembered his hand sliding into Desmond's trousers and~

"Ah!" She opened her eyes. "Yes. It seems I am capable of accessing Desmond's memory. But it was a targeted search. I had to focus on a specific memory and then follow it to unknown territory. There's a chance Amenemhat won't be able to do that."

Cora said, "Unless he simply thinks 'flee' and your mind fills in the blanks for him. It's a simple enough prompt that could lead him to a boat or an airship."

"Could it lead him to Minty?"

"Possibly," Trafalgar said. "We should contact her, warn her to avoid 'you' at all costs."

Dorothy said, "No. If our priest attempts to engage the *Skylarker*, she should restrain him. If she turns him away, he might find other means of getting where he wants to go. At least then we'll know where he is and where he intends to travel."

Beatrice said, "He may also know where we live. If he can access your armory..."

"Crumbs. You're right. We must get there at once."

Beatrice stood and immediately lost her balance, bumping the table with her hip. Trafalgar steadied her.

"You're not going anywhere like this," she said. "You're staying right here and getting checked out by that doctor, if the bloody bastard ever bothers to show up."

Strode said, "I'm sure it's just the weather delaying him."

Cecil said, "I want someone to look at my nose as well."

Strode snorted. "It gives you character."

"I'll show you character, you ponce..."

"Bloody seriously?" Dorothy bellowed, surprised at the depth of her own voice. "Now? You insist on continuing this petty bickering even in the current circumstances?"

The fire went out of both men, and they looked at their feet rather than meet her eye. She stood up and smoothed down the front of her suit. She had no means by which to describe the feeling of being in another body. Even relaxed, it felt strangely rigid, as if he was tensing for a blow. She wondered if Desmond went through life with this constant edge. She tried to relax and adjusted her tie again. She touched her face, touched the bristles of Desmond's beard, and suppressed the chill that threatened to run down her (his) spine.

"All right. We'll find Trix somewhere to rest and then the rest of us will head out to find this bastard. I'm going to get my damned body back."

CHAPTER FIVE

The doctor examined Beatrice and determined she had a mild concussion. She would be fine with bedrest, which meant she would have to sit out any search for Dorothy's errant body. When Beatrice attempted to protest, she lost her balance and had to be held up by Trafalgar. After that she gave up trying to convince anyone she would be useful in the upcoming fight. She relented to letting Cecil drive her home while Abraham and Cora went to the Rookery to see if their quarry showed up. They also called the Keepings and asked them to look through their library for any reference to Amenemhat. If they knew who he was and what he wanted, there was a greater chance of catching up with him.

Dorothy and Trafalgar rode with Beatrice in the backseat of Cecil's sedan. They had brought the ka statue with them, just in case the opportunity arose to return everyone to their rightful bodies. Beatrice leaned against Dorothy's shoulder, awkwardly touching her hand and arm.

When they got back to Threadneedle Street, Trafalgar asked them to remain in the car while she and Cecil checked to make sure Amenemhat wasn't lurking. Dorothy wanted to help, but she didn't trust her ability to control Desmond's body well enough to engage in a fight. So she remained in the car, holding Beatrice. She looked down and saw Beatrice was staring up at her. She smiled self-consciously.

"I can't imagine this is easy for you. Being cradled by Desmond."

"On the contrary. When I was fighting... what's his name?"

"Amenemhat."

"Him. One look in his eyes and I knew it wasn't you. Looking at you now, it doesn't matter what face you're wearing. I see you."

Dorothy smiled and touched Beatrice's cheek. "I'm glad to hear that, Trix. I'm just sorry you got hurt so badly at my hand. Even if I wasn't the one in control of it."

Beatrice grimaced. "That was my fault. Even though I was aware you weren't in control, I still couldn't bring myself to harm you."

Dorothy smiled. "I hope you don't expect me to consider that a flaw."

"If I hadn't been pulling my punches, I could have restrained him. Prevented all of this. We wouldn't have required Desmond to take such an enormous risk." She sat up and looked at Dorothy. "Any injuries I might have inflicted would heal. It would be better than this."

"We'll find him. We'll undo all of this."

Beatrice said, "And if we don't, you'll simply be Desmond for the rest of your life?"

"Of course not. That wouldn't be fair to him." Beatrice tilted her head, waiting for Dorothy to continue. "If we determine there is no chance of recovering my body, I shall simply recite the spell again and return to the statue. Desmond will have his body back."

"And you will effectively be dead."

"I won't steal someone else's life just to prolong mine."

Beatrice looked away from her. "Take my body."

"Trix..."

"No, Dorothy. I would give my life to save yours in any circumstance, but especially this one."

"I won't."

"You can't stop me. Even if you return your soul to the statue without telling me, I'd merely recite the spell myself. If my purpose in life is to save yours~"

Dorothy put her finger across Beatrice's lips. "Stop. We don't have to worry about that now."

Beatrice turned her head to get it away from Dorothy's extended finger. "Do you know I've never kissed a man?"

"Is that so?"

"I doubt this would count."

She moved her hand to the back of Dorothy's head and leaned in. She pulled back a bit at the first touch of their lips, but committed to the kiss and curled her fingers in the awkwardly short hair at the back of her head. Beatrice put her hand on Dorothy's chest but, feeling it flat and masculine rather than what she expected to find, moved up to her shoulder. She whispered, "I don't like the beard."

"It is a pain, isn't it?"

Beatrice smiled and kissed her again as the back door opened.

Trafalgar leaned in and flinched at what she saw. "Dear god, that looks obscene."

"It doesn't feel much better," Beatrice admitted. "No offense to Desmond."

Trafalgar said, "The house is secure. Cecil is preparing a fire."

They both helped Beatrice out of the car and into the house. Dorothy set up a small nest for her in the den, where Cecil had succeeded in starting a fire.

"I'm not an invalid," Beatrice groused. "I'll be fine in a few hours. There's no need for all this fuss."

"You are worthy of the fuss," Dorothy said. "And while you may resent being left behind, I'm grateful to have you watching the house while I'm gone, as always. I would trust my home in the hands of no one else."

Cecil said, "So, what now?"

"Now we gather a few things before we go in search of our enemy." She stood up and took off Desmond's jacket. "I would prefer to subdue my body thief with non-lethal weapons, but I don't think I have anything that will do the trick in my armory. We'll have to visit Threnody."

Trafalgar said, "Short notice, unannounced? She won't like that."

"Needs must. For now, I must change clothes."

"To what?" Trafalgar said. "You have nothing in Desmond's size. Even if you did, I doubt it would be any more comfortable than what you're already wearing."

She looked down at herself and realized Trafalgar was right. "Damn. You're right. Fine, I'll go as-is. The airship is covered. Where else should we be looking, Trafalgar? Trains?"

Trafalgar shook her head. "He wouldn't take a train. If he's anything like I was in his position, he'd be too frightened of them to even try jumping one. I think our best chance of finding him will be the docks. Odds are good that he'll be much more comfortable on a boat."

"Then that is where we shall go once we're armed. Cecil, go to the docks. See if anyone matching my description is attempting to book passage... well, anywhere, really." She looked at Trafalgar. "I'll need you to lead the way with Threnody. She doesn't know Desmond and I fear she would attack first and accept ridiculously implausible explanations later."

"You are probably right." She looked at Beatrice. "Get your rest, Miss Sek. I shall take care of Dorothy in your stead."

Beatrice said, "Trix. I've had enough of 'Miss Sek' from you. Call me Trix."

Trafalgar tried to disguise her emotion, but she only barely managed to suppress a smile. "As you wish, Trix."

Dorothy smiled as well, leading Trafalgar and Cecil out of her house and back out into the rain.

The clothing he wore was soaked and clung obscenely to his body, this female body which he was surprised to discover had remarkable strength and endurance. His borrowed mind was also starting to provide information about his surroundings. He was in London, it was the year nineteen hundred and twenty-one, whatever that signified, and his vessel was named was Dorothy Boone. She was an adventuress. She knew how to fight. His hands, although small, were strong and bore the callouses of hard work. He withdrew his previous complaints and thanked Amun for his good fortune. He had found a body capable of getting him home but unassuming enough not to draw suspicion.

He would, however, have to do something about his clothes. They clung to his curves in a way that drew the eye of everyone he passed. They gawked openly at him, and it was all he could do not to attack each and every one of them. If they only knew his true identity. If they had but an inkling of the power he could wield in the right form. He suppressed his rage and looked for something to cover himself with.

His mind knew that the motorized carts were called vehicles, and within one he found a hooded cloak. He pulled it across his shoulders and flipped the hood up over his head. Boone's hair had become a mass of tangled tendrils, thick and curled strands of seaweed that hung in his face and obscured his vision. This London was a swamp, a perpetually drowning city that no doubt served as a colony for the wretched and unwanted.

He searched Boone's mind for any potential escape routes. She would have elected for an air-ship, one of those ponderous bags anchored over the river. He watched them from an alleyway, their bellies lit from below by huge shining pits that glowed warmly but without the benefit of any flame he could see. Boone didn't know precisely how far it was to Egypt, but she knew it was far. He wouldn't be able to travel the distance without help.

The word "Minty" appeared in his mind, and it took a moment to connect it with the name Araminta Crook. It was a dark-skinned woman in a brown coat and trousers, her hair braided and covered by a peaked cap with a shining black brim. She commanded one of the airships, so he immediately discounted her as a possibility. There was no chance he would risk his newly-returned life aboard one of those strange conveyances.

That left the sea. He didn't know what sort of advances had been made in maritime travel, but he highly doubted it would be a fast journey. Time was of the essence. His love had waited long enough for rescue and every minute he wasn't with her was an ache in his chest. But how could he escape when he was working at such a disadvantage? Boone had stubborn friends who were apparently willing to fight for her. He had little doubt that they would rally themselves to rescue her. They would likely know the city and block any possible avenues of escape.

"I will not fail you, Henuttaui," he whispered under his breath, speaking in the light tones of his host. He was still unaccustomed to the melody of her accent, the way her throat and tongue moved to form words unfamiliar to him. The entire language was simply there, in his brain. He supposed it made a sort of sense. Boone's ability to speak was so ingrained that it couldn't be forgotten or erased. She knew language like she knew how to breathe or walk. He was grateful for that. He doubted anyone would be able to understand his native language in this bizarre era.

Amenemhat tugged at the hood so it better concealed his face as he pushed away from the wall. He missed the heat of Egypt, the dryness of the air. The rain in London seemed like it would never end, but everyone he saw on the streets seemed resigned to its existence. With the rain came chill, a pervasive cold that seemed to have grown less bearable in the time he'd been conscious. Surely no one chose to live in a place like this. Madness.

He was near enough to the river that he could see large ships being loaded with cargo. He wandered closer and listened to the sound of stevedores as they went about their duties, looking for any vessel marked to show Cairo as its destination. He had no way to book passage - Boone carried no money, which he knew he would need for the promise of a berth - but perhaps he could find a way to sneak aboard.

He was so absorbed in examining the ships that he nearly didn't notice the young man until they were moments away from a collision. Cecil, the man who had been kicked in the face during his escape from the pub, was dressed in a rainslicker and a wide-brimmed cap. His nose was swollen, colored red and black, with tape across the bridge. They both seemed startled to recognize one another and froze for a moment, each debating what to do next.

"Lady B... I mean... you... whoever you~"

Amenemhat grabbed the collar of Cecil's coat with one hand and raised the other in a fist. He yanked the young man forward hard enough that he tripped over his own feet and fell face-first against Amenemhat's knuckles. Gravity had done most of the work for him, and blood once again spurted from his nose as he fell to his knees. Amenemhat allowed Boone's skills to take over. She kneed him in the face and then kicked him onto his back, leaving him sprawling in a medium-deep puddle with both hands clapped over his face.

Amenemhat was startled by the sudden appearance of two brutes at either shoulder. They glared down at Cecil, who was whining about the injuries to his face. One of the stevedores put a hand on his shoulder and looked down at him.

"This your fella, miss?"

"I... I must get away from him. I haven't any money. But I have family in Cairo..."

The hand tightened on his shoulder and he was turned away from Cecil. The man holding Amenemhat's shoulder guided him toward the ship while the other stevedore advanced on Cecil. Boone's friend realized what was about to happen and began scooting backward on his buttocks begging for the goon to listen to reason.

"We'll get you where you need to go," her escort said. "Fellas like that, sometimes they just need to be taught a lesson, you savvy?"

"Yes." Amenemhat looked back and saw the other stevedore hauling Cecil to his feet. The rain muffled the sound of another blow landing, but he saw Cecil's body go limp in his attacker's grip. "Y-yes, I appreciate your assistance in this matter."

The large man nodded, his face grim. "Fella like that hurt my mam. I swore if I ever saw anyone tryin' it, I'd make 'im regret raising his hand. Now... I know I can find you a ship going where you need to go. But I can't promise it'll be comfortable."

Amenemhat didn't have to force a smile, so complete was his relief. "Whatever you find will be more than acceptable. I simply must get out of this city as quickly as possible."

"Let's see what we can do for you."

He looked back once more and saw Cecil being tossed against a brick wall. He brought his hands up to protect his face, but the brute was moving in for another round.

"Good riddance," he muttered, tightening his hood as he followed his savior toward one of the ships that would deliver him to his queen.

CHAPTER SIX

With Beatrice out of commission and Cecil on his way to check the docks, Dorothy and Trafalgar were forced to make their own way to Threnody's. It wouldn't have been a difficult walk in ideal weather, but the rain forced them to hire a taxi. Neither of them felt comfortable discussing their predicament with the driver eavesdropping so they rode in silence. Dorothy reached up and touched her lips, the fingers sliding to one side to again feel the bristles of her beard. She winced and turned to Trafalgar.

"Do you think he would mind terribly if he had to regrow this beard?"

Trafalgar pitched her voice equally low. "Do you trust yourself enough with a razor to place one against his throat?"

"Hm. You have a point." She rubbed her knuckles against her throat. "I've no idea how he stands it. The things I have to suffer for the benefit of having a woman's body, and men do this to themselves."

"Actually, the presence of a beard indicates a lack of effort. There's grooming, of course, but all a man must do to grow a beard is stop shaving."

Dorothy sighed. "Very true."

The cabdriver glanced back as they exited the backseat, no doubt confused by any part of the conversation he may have overheard. Dorothy stood under an overhang as Trafalgar performed the rituals required to gain access to Threnody's workshop, then followed her inside through the concealed basement doors. The interior was as dark and foreboding as always, but with an added depth to the shadows due to the storm. Dorothy remained close behind Trafalgar so as not to startle their host. Threnody could be a bit volatile when it came to strangers.

Trafalgar stopped at the top of the stairs. "Threnody? It's Trafalgar. Under normal circumstances I would never come to you unannounced, but we are dealing with a matter of great urgency."

"This is beyond the pale!"

Threnody's voice came from their right. They both turned to see a dark shape step into the kitchen. It was more the sense of movement than anything visual; black flapping against black.

"You dare to bring a stranger here?"

"No, I assure you. The truth is far more complex than that. No matter how it looks, this is Lady Dorothy Boone."

Threnody still didn't show herself. "I have seen Lady Boone's male disguise. She is talented but she is not that convincing."

Dorothy said, "Please, Threnody. It really is me. My consciousness was swapped with someone else's by an artifact. My companion Desmond Tindall offered his body to me so I could participate in recovering my own. I can itemize every weapon I've purchased from you in the past if that would make you believe me."

"Anyone can read an invoice. Perhaps if you were to pay off the balance of Lady Boone's seven thousand pound debt..."

Dorothy couldn't stop herself from laughing. "Seven thousand pounds? I owe you two hundred. And if you expect me to believe you would extend that much credit to anyone, perhaps your mind has been swapped as well."

Threnody moved out of the shadows to face them. Even in the low light, they could tell she was wearing the mask of a plague doctor, her standard disguise to cover the failed experimentation that had been done to her face.

"All right. Perhaps you are truly Dorothy Boone. What do you require from me?"

"We were hoping you might have some non-lethal weapons we could use," Dorothy said. "The less self-inflicted damage I have to recover from when I get my body back, the better."

Threnody said, "There is no such thing as a non-lethal weapon. Anything can be lethal if wielded correctly. Or incorrectly as the case may be."

She thought for a moment and then stepped between them to go upstairs. She gestured for them to follow her, and Dorothy noticed the Crafter smelled like clove cigarettes and oiled leather. She had never noticed the scent and wondered if it was stronger today or if Desmond just had a stronger sense of smell than she did. She ignored the mystery and followed Threnody upstairs to her shop.

"I have a few prototypes that may fit your needs."

She sorted through the debris on her work table until she found an oblong wooden box with a lid that flipped open on the short right side. Dorothy instantly recognized it as an ammunition box from the Great War, though it was not information she recalled learning. Obviously more of Desmond's mind slipping through. It was disconcerting and something she hoped she could somehow learn to prevent. She had a feeling that getting her body back would require her full attention. She could ill afford to be distracted or confused at the wrong moment.

Threnody removed a weapon from the box. It had the butt of a pistol, but its barrel had been shaped into a wide, open circle which had been filled with opaque glass. She aimed it at the wall and squeezed the trigger. The glass came to life with a series of quick, fluttering flashes of bright white light. Dorothy flinched and turned away, and Trafalgar held up one hand to block the light.

"More of an annoyance than anything else," Trafalgar said.

"You wouldn't say that if I'd aimed it at your face. Hit someone in the eyes with this and it affects their nervous system. I heard stories of people in the trenches of the Great War being blinded or temporarily paralyzed while watching muzzle flashes or sparks of magic while at night. Quick bursts of light in an otherwise dark environment can disable your opponent without lasting harm."

Trafalgar took the weapon and examined it. "Splendid.

This will do nicely. You really are ingenious, Threnody."

Threnody ignored the compliment and moved to another shelf. "Simple and effective, the ravdi." She held out her hand to reveal a short stick that spanned the width of her palm with a few inches left over. It resembled Trafalgar's emei piercers, but with blunt ends instead of sharp. She closed her fingers around the hilt and demonstrated a few blows. "A strike will cause pain on bony areas such as the knuckles or sternum. Fleshy areas like the arm, flanks, throat, or eyes will obviously be vulnerable as well."

"A stick?" Dorothy said. "I expected more from you."

Threnody glared at her. "Grab my arm, 'Lady Boone.'"

Dorothy stepped forward and grabbed Threnody's arm. Threnody tossed the ravdi to her other hand then brought it down on the web between Dorothy's thumb and forefinger. Her hand convulsed and Threnody twisted, escaping from Dorothy's grip entirely. She swung the ravdi at Dorothy's hip, hitting with far more force than it seemed possible. When Dorothy doubled over from that, Threnody casually adjusted her grip on the weapon and thumped the curve of Dorothy's neck and shoulder with barely any force behind the blow at all. The pain still made her cry out and she fell to her knees.

"I stand corrected," Dorothy said, still down, her hand massaging her shoulder. "Hopefully Desmond will be understanding about any bruises he has when I return this body to him."

"Hmph." Threnody handed the ravdi to Dorothy and looked around her workroom again. She searched a different shelf and returned with another wooden box. "These pellets will burst upon impact. They're filled with sulfur. Be careful with this one, because it would be very easy for anyone deploying it to be as affected as their enemies."

"I'll keep that in mind." Trafalgar looked at Dorothy. "Are you all right?"

Dorothy was still massaging her shoulder. "I'll be fine. These will be more than effective for our needs, thank you."

Threnody said, "One more item." She opened a drawer and withdrew a small ovoid object made of metal. She pinched one end and the sides bloomed open like a black flower. The center shot forward and withdrew almost too quickly to see. "Squeeze to open, then slap it onto your opponent's skin.

Arm, hand, neck. Clothing might work, but skin is better. The needle with deliver a small dose of sedative. Your body will have some marks where the legs dig in, but those will heal as quickly as any scrape or bruise."

Dorothy took the object and carefully examined it. "Quite ingenious. Can we add these items to my debt?"

Threnody shook her head. "As I said, these are prototypes. I have no idea how effective they'll be in the field. Consider this a test run. Let me know how they work, any flaws I need to work out, and I'll consider it a fair exchange."

"Seems fair enough," Dorothy said.

"I'll remind you that you said that if these fail when you need them most. Good luck."

Dorothy packed the weapons into her pockets, letting Trafalgar take the sulfur pellets. When they turned to leave, Threnody said Trafalgar's name in a way that indicated she should hold back.

"I'll see if I can hail a cab," Dorothy said, leaving them alone.

Threnody stepped closer and lowered her voice. "It's true? Dorothy Boone's soul is in that man's body?"

"Soul, consciousness, essence. I doubt there is any true scientific word for it. But yes, those who last saw Dorothy's body insisted it was under someone else's control. And having spent quite a lot of time with Professor Tindall, I can swear to you that the man who just left is not him. So whatever the truth may be, it is undeniable that some sort of exchange occurred."

Threnody turned away, the dark oval goggles that covered her eyes reflecting nothing. She had been born as Ida Kearney, the daughter of an inventor. She was assaulted by a man who rewarded her struggling by bashing her face in with a bit of masonry. She repaired the damage to bone and muscle using metal and leather straps. As she aged, she updated her parts as needed but she still considered her appearance ghoulish.

"Would it be possible?"

She didn't have to finish the question. "Not without great sacrifice by the host. From what I understand, you would have to displace someone from their body in order to take it."

Threnody nodded. "I understand. I had to ask."

"Of course." Trafalgar put a hand on her friend's shoulder

and squeezed. "Have I ever told you that I find your scars beautiful?"

"If you're asking if you've ever lied to me, then no."

Trafalgar said, "It's no lie. It's not softening the truth, either. When I saw your wounds for the first time, I was stunned. It's evidence of the brutality you've survived and the brilliance with which you saved your own life. I am amazed by your face, Threnody. I am humbled by it. I have never seen anyone wear their strengths so brazenly."

Threnody had turned her back on Trafalgar. When she spoke, her voice was soft. "You should go. Time is fleeting for your friend."

"Can we meet afterward?"

"Oh... right, your sling. I'm afraid it won't be ready for a few more weeks."

Trafalgar said, "Not for that. As friends."

Threnody turned to face her again. "If you wish."

"Excellent. I shall look forward to it." She patted the pocket which held the pellets. "I thank you in advance for the help you've once again given to us."

"Of course. You're my best customers. If anything happened to you, I would lose two-thirds of my business."

Trafalgar smiled and left the workroom.

Downstairs, she found Dorothy waiting on the front stoop. Desmond's hair had flattened to his forehead, his clothing sopping wet and wrinkled at the collar. She'd never seen him look so disheveled and, once she thought about it, she had also never seen Dorothy looking less put-together. She was standing with her back to the wall, head turned to watch the street, arms crossed over her chest. Though the body was undeniably male, there was something feminine in the way his legs were arranged and the slope of his shoulders. If she squinted her eyes, she could have sworn it was actually Dorothy in one of her guises.

Dorothy noticed Trafalgar's approach and stood up straighter. "No cabs yet. We should have asked our driver to wait."

"May I make an observation?" Dorothy nodded. "You stand like a woman."

"I should hope so."

Trafalgar said, "You miss my point. You stand, walk, and

comport yourself as a woman. Desmond's body isn't built for that. You're making it behave unusually. That may be the source of your discomfort. If you were to simply stop focusing on it and let the body relax into a more natural pose, you would feel more at ease."

Dorothy furrowed her brow and pushed away from the wall. Her posture remained fine, but her hips and shoulders relaxed slightly. She hmmed and moved her arms as if testing the fit of a jacket.

"You may be onto something there. Now if only you could find us a cab."

"Perhaps..." Trafalgar looked down the street and saw a cab approaching. She stepped onto the sidewalk into the rain and lifted her arm. The cab immediately slowed and pulled up next to the curb. She turned and smiled at Dorothy, who glared at her from beneath Desmond's knit brows. She shrugged and opened the back door of the cab. "Never underestimate the compassion of a cabbie who sees a damsel in distress."

"You? A damsel?"

Trafalgar said, "It comes in useful from time to time. And besides, you're not looking particularly damselesque today. Not that you ever do, really..."

Dorothy heaved a sigh and settled in the backseat. She gave the address of Leonard and Agnes Keeping to the driver and slumped against the back seat.

"I never thought I'd see the day when I missed a man treating me like a dainty flower."

Trafalgar patted her on the knee. "You'll be sick to death of it again in good time, Dorothy. I have faith."

The cabdriver looked over his shoulder at them, confused but unwilling to give up the fare. Dorothy smiled at his confusion as he pulled away from the curb.

Amenemhat was escorted through the alien ship by her savior, who revealed his name was Paul. He kept one hand possessively on his shoulder, letting it slip lower as he guided him through doorways and narrow passages. Amenemhat did not appreciate the constant pressure of the man's hand, but he didn't want to risk his deliverance by saying anything. It had taken hardly any time whatsoever to find a ship bound for

Cairo. He was pleasantly surprised by the estimate of how long the trip would take. One week wasn't anywhere near as fast as he would hope, but also it was not as bad as he feared.

Paul spoke quietly with a few members of the crew until he was passed along to the captain. Amenemhat used the name "Dorothy" when asked for his identity but refused to tell them what he was fleeing. The men seemed to have come up with a scenario in their heads, for they looked at her with an odd combination of pity and scorn. To them, he was a woman who had angered her man or perhaps refused to perform wifely duties. They thought whatever had turned him into a runaway was his own fault. Let them think what they liked, so long as they took him home.

He was given a small, cramped cell with walls of curved metal. There was a small bed, a circular window, and a narrow desk attached to the wall by two chains. Clanks and thunks traveled through the belly of the ship and seemed to echo in the tiny chamber. He didn't know how anyone could be expected to sleep in such a place, but he wasn't going to complain. Paul also found a pair of men's clothes, black trousers and a white shirt, so Amenemhat could change out of his soaked outfit.

"Let's get you out of those wet clothes," was how he phrased it, eyes skimming hungrily over his borrowed body.

"I can manage," Amenemhat said.

"I insist, pretty little Dorothy."

Paul reached for her. Amenemhat drove the flat of his hand into Paul's throat and felt the fragile construct of his windpipe crunch under the force of the blow. Paul's eyes went wide, his tongue extending as he gasped for air. Amenemhat pulled Paul deeper into the room, grabbed the back of his head, and quickly introduced his face to the metal wall four or five times before letting the man fall like a bag of wet bread. He exhaled sharply and adjusted his blouse, which had gone askew in the brief interlude. He composed himself and dragged the heavy dead weight from the center of the floor to the space beneath his bed. Hopefully he would find a more permanent solution before smell became an issue.

He removed his wet clothes and paused to look down at his body. Deceptively muscled, though petite. The woman Boone had fight training and, judging from some of the scars he could see, she'd been in her fair bit of actual fights. He again thanked Amun for providing him with such a worthy host. It was a good omen that he was on the right path and that his objective was blessed by god.

Someone knocked on the door. He turned, looked at the blood on the floor, and stepped forward to block the door from opening.

"Who is it, please?"

"Bennie. Cap'n wants to know if Paulie is gonna sail with us, 'cause if not, he's gotta go ashore now 'fore we shove off."

Amenemhat said, "He... he's going to spend the trip here. With me. Taking his... rightful reward for rescuing me on the docks."

The man on the other side of the door chortled. "Well, I think the rest of the crew deserves a bit of that reward as well, don't you?"

Amenemhat closed his eyes and stifled a groan. Would he have to kill every man aboard this vessel to remain unmolested?

"Paul is quite greedy, you know..."

"Heh. Don't I know. I'll tell the cap. Don't be too rough with 'er, Paulie!"

Amenemhat listened to the sound of receding footsteps and let out the breath she'd been holding. She walked back to the porthole and stared out. Rain streaked the glass but he could still clearly see the city shrouded in fog, its golden lights glowing like starlight. Amun had brought him this far, and he had faith his god would continue blessing his quest.

"Soon, Henuttaui. I am coming to wake you. Soon."

He smiled and went to the bed. He was exhausted and needed sleep, and the trip would afford him much time to plan and learn about this strange new world in which he'd found himself.

By the time he arrived in Egypt, he would have everything he required to wake his beloved.

CHAPTER SEVEN

Upon their arrival at the Keeping house, Agnes immediately ushered Trafalgar and Dorothy upstairs to offer them a change of clothes. Dorothy was forced to take something from Leonard's wardrobe. She paused before removing his trousers, standing in front of the wardrobe completely nude and very aware of that fact. She glanced down and immediately averted her gaze. Well. There *that* was. She cleared her throat and tried to avoid thinking about her new and unusual anatomy, but when she stepped forward she felt it move against her thigh.

"Good lord, that's distracting..."

Apparently Leonard's preferred style of undergarment was a pair of pale pink linen shorts. She stepped into them and was forced to adjust things. She grimaced and tried to finish the task as quickly as possible, but it seemed to be more difficult than she expected. There was no arrangement that felt comfortable to her. She tugged at the linen, shifted her hips one way and then the other, and nearly gave up on the idea of underwear altogether when she somehow found a position that worked.

She quickly donned the trousers and a tan shirt. The material felt strange against the bare skin of her chest and she left the bedroom feeling as if she were only half-dressed. It was no wonder men were able to prepare for an evening out so much faster than a female counterpart; they had a fraction of the tasks to perform before showing themselves to the world.

Leonard and Agnes were in the study, standing over a table where they had spread out an impressive collection of books, journals, and reference guides. Dorothy had no idea how long the two had been married, but they operated as a single entity. They were in their sixties, contemporaries of her grandmother and still very active in their field. Leonard's white hair had grown long enough to tend toward curly, while Agnes wore her black-and-silver hair tied back in a long plait. Agnes looked up as she approached.

"Desmond, there you are. I..." She shook her head. "I apologize, Dorothy."

"It's all right. I'm feeling a bit confused myself." She stood across the table from them. "What have you learned?"

Leonard said, "Nothing specific on Amenemhat, of course. I didn't expect to have anything immediately on-hand which referenced him by name. I focused instead on the ka statue and the inscriptions Trafalgar described. I thought perhaps it might be a spell from the Book of the Dead so I did a bit of digging."

Trafalgar entered the room in one of Agnes' dresses and stood beside Dorothy, nodding for Leonard to continue his speech.

"The Book of the Dead is, of course, a funerary text meant to prepare souls for their journey to the afterlife. From what I can gather it's your basic 'ashes to ashes' litany. Nothing special or significant about it. But it also doesn't contain the characters you described from the statue. So I dug a little deeper and discovered the Books of Breathing."

Dorothy prompted, "And that would be?"

Agnes said, "They are also funerary texts, but with a different purpose. The Book of the Dead was a guide to send a person's soul to the afterlife. The Books of Breathing contained spells to ensure the person's soul continued to exist in that afterlife. I believe it was a way for them to retain consciousness and awareness even after losing their earthly vessel. It stands to reason this Amenemhat fellow used a spell from the Books of Breathing to release his soul without taking the next step and moving on to the next life."

"When we know more about who he is," Leonard said, "We'll have a better idea of what he wants and how to stop him."

"Stop him?" Dorothy said. "The damage is already done."

Agnes said, "To you, yes. But there is still immeasurable damage that could be done. He has the ability to leap from one body to the next. Imagine what havoc could be wrought with such an ability. If it ever got into the hands of a despot or a criminal, they would be unstoppable. I can't even fathom if Genghis Khan or Napoleon Bonaparte had the ability to switch bodies."

The front bell chimed and Leonard excused himself to answer it. Dorothy picked up one of the books and flipped the pages.

"You bring up a valid point, Agnes. I don't suppose there are any copies of this Book of Breathing lying around, or any reference to how we might reverse the process from afar."

Trafalgar said, "The process may be irreversible." Dorothy's eyes snapped toward her. "Not that I'm saying this is a permanent situation. If push comes to shove, we can merely... shuffle everyone back to the correct bodies. If you are barred from returning to the statue or back into your own body, I will step in as a... as a, uh... waystation. You into my body, my essence into Desmond's, then Desmond and I shall..." She furrowed her brow. "I will require pen and paper."

Leonard came back from the door. "Pen and paper will have to wait, Miss Trafalgar. Agnes, please get the first aid kit!"

The women turned and saw Leonard half-dragging Cecil into the room. He had been beaten until his face was a bloody ruin. Most of the bloodstains on his clothes seemed to be seeping through the cloth from within rather than dripping from his damaged face. One eye was already swollen shut. "Good lord!" Dorothy gasped, moving to help transfer him to the divan. Trafalgar laid down a blanket so he wouldn't bleed into the cushions.

"The poor man collapsed on the stoop after ringing the bell," Leonard said. Agnes returned with the medical supplies. "Thank you, darling. Cecil? Can you hear me?"

"My ears are the one thing they didn't break." His voice was slurred and lisping. Leonard began tending to the worst of the wounds. "Bloody bastards attacked me on the docks.

Dorothy... er, the fellow in Dorothy's body... tol' them I was comin' after her. They decided to be chivalrous. Didn't give me a chance to explain."

Dorothy said, "So you saw him? Amenemhat?"

Cecil nodded carefully. "While I was getting the stuffing beat out of me, I heard where he's heading. One of the dockworkers put him on a boat to Cairo."

"As expected," Trafalgar said. "It's unfortunate that Mr. Dubourne had to suffer so grievously to learn something so trivial as Amenemhat's travel plans."

Dorothy said, "It's not trivial at all. We know where he is going. And he's traveling there as a stowaway, which means he will have to travel at their pace. He'll be at sea for at least a week."

Agnes said, "There can't be many vessels departing for Egypt what with all the revolutions and anti-British demonstrations going on. Finding out exactly which vessel he's on should be child's play, and then we simply track his journey."

"Brilliant." Leonard stood and gestured for Agnes to take over for him with Cecil's wounds. "I'll contact my associate Stavrou at the docks. If he doesn't have the information we require, he can find it for us within the hour." He hurried from the room to make the call.

Trafalgar looked at Dorothy. "I leave it up to you. We can pursue and hope to catch up with them at some port between here and their destination, or we can get ahead of him. Go to Cairo and await his arrival in the hopes of laying a trap."

Agnes sat next to the divan, taking over where Leonard had left off. "Why do you have to choose? Wasn't the Mnemosyne Society founded on the spirit of cooperation? The two of you can go to Cairo and lay a trap while Leonard and I pursue to ensure he doesn't slip away at any point of the journey. Or vice versa. We'll go to Cairo and you pursue in case there's an opportunity to regain your body before he arrives."

Dorothy said, "You're absolutely correct, Agnes. The question now becomes where will we do the most good."

Trafalgar said, "Or where we can cause the most harm. If we pursue Amenemhat in the hopes of retrieving your body, we'll have to take the ka statue with us. The risk of losing or damaging it will be far greater if we're in transit. Going to Cairo and waiting will not only provide security, we can also use the time to learn about our adversary."

"I hate to take advantage of Minty so soon after our last journey, but an airship is the only way we could reach Cairo before he does."

Agnes paused in the process of bandaging a wound on Cecil's face. "Well... not the only way."

Leonard returned in time to hear the end of the conversation. "Agnes! They already have a means of traveling to Egypt."

"Yes, but~"

"But nothing. We cannot betray a confidence."

"Yes. But," Agnes continued, glaring at her husband, "if they can shave even a few hours off their journey, it could mean the difference between success and failure. We must tell them."

Dorothy said, "What on earth are you talking about?"

Agnes wiped smears of blood off her hands as she stood up. "We have access to a plane." Leonard groaned and pinched the bridge of his nose, but Agnes ignored him. "It would be your best option."

Trafalgar said, "A plane capable of traveling from London to Egypt in the time required?"

Leonard sighed, "Yes. It would have to make a fuel stop somewhere on the Continent, but it could get you where you need to go by tomorrow."

Dorothy raised an eyebrow. "Why haven't we heard of this before?"

Leonard fixed his wife with a withering look that may have worked on a lesser woman. "The aircraft is a prototype. Its inventor is a friend of ours and asked that we keep its existence confidential. But I suppose given the circumstances..."

"The circumstances being our colleague's life being at enormous risk," Agnes interjected.

"...we could convince her to help you out. The plane only sits three, so you won't be able to bring Beatrice with you."

Dorothy said, "I would probably want her to sit out anyway, given her injury."

"She won't like that," Trafalgar said.

"So I won't tell her before we leave. I'll ask forgiveness

later."

Trafalgar raised an eyebrow but didn't comment.

Agnes headed for the door. "I'll call her and see if the plane is even available and if it can fly in this weather. Won't take a minute."

"Meanwhile," Leonard said, "my friend at the docks found the information we required. The only ship departing for the Mediterranean scheduled for a stop in Cairo is the *Bessemer*. Once you're underway, I'll make arrangements to begin our pursuit." He looked at Cecil, who had passed out. "I assume someone will have to remain behind to care for poor Mr. Dubourne."

Dorothy said, "Yes, I can't help but feel utterly responsible for the drubbing he took. I shall have to find a way to make it up to him."

Leonard made a sound of agreement, then looked toward the window. "The storm looks to be lessening, but let me get you a rainslicker before you go out in this mess again."

Dorothy nodded her thanks. "I'll get the clothes back to you as soon as I can."

"At your leisure. I'll have Desmond's clothes washed and dried, and they will be ready for him to retrieve once this whole situation is settled."

He left the room and Dorothy reached down to tug on her trousers.

Trafalgar cleared her throat. "A bit obscene, don't you think?"

"Crumbs," Dorothy said. "I'm sorry. There seems to be a science to dealing with... this... that I have yet to grasp. Perhaps I haven't given men enough credit for keeping it under control. Or perhaps Desmond is remarkably endowed. I'm not exactly an expert in that area..."

"I doubt he would appreciate this discussion."

"You're absolutely correct."

"Although..." Trafalgar furrowed her brow. "We're contemplating a week in Egypt waiting for Amenemhat to arrive so we can capture him and reclaim your body. I find it difficult to believe you won't need to bathe or... evacuate... in that time."

Dorothy said, "I've been trying not to think about that, but you're absolutely right. We'll cross that bridge when we have to."

Agnes appeared shortly after their conversation ended. "You're in luck. Isidora has agreed to the journey. You have time to go home and pack for the trip, but remember to pack light. The plane has a very strict weight limit."

"I should go to Desmond's... do you have clothes at Threadneedle?"

Trafalgar said, "Yes, but I believe it would be easier to pack something at my actual home."

Agnes said, "I'll drive you. Come, ladies. Our lead grows shorter by the minute."

Beatrice couldn't stand lying on the couch for more than a few minutes, so she set out to make the most of her time as an invalid. She was still lightheaded but she could maneuver through the house well enough. She knew the best spots to pause and rest, and she knew everything she could use for support or lean against as she checked the locks and windows. She also decided she could work on the inventory, a job which would require her to remain seated for long stretches. It would also allow her to serve a purpose, be useful to Dorothy in a time of great need.

The townhouse next door had been transformed into a vault for items Dorothy brought home from her travels. Fragments of ancient maps, stone statues like the ones that had caused the current mess, golden idols, gold coins which had been collected in cloth bags, and many other things which seemed valuable but were otherwise unremarkable. Dorothy removed them to dissuade thieves from ransacking the sacred sites and then made it her duty to research each item's history to discover which culture it belonged to. Then, if possible, she returned it to the proper owners.

Beatrice remembered six months ago when she and Dorothy had taken a quick jaunt to Mexico so they could return a chalice to the tribe who had lost it when they migrated north from South America. The ceremony in their honor had been a joyous affair in which she and Dorothy were both seduced by a young woman named Narida, who insisted on thanking them both in a very athletic and acrobatic manner.

She smiled just thinking about it. The tent had been

sweltering and all three women were dripping sweat. Narida was seated in Dorothy's lap, allowing Dorothy's fingers to do all sorts of vulgar things between her legs, and she had leaned forward to put her head in Beatrice's lap. Dorothy had looked up and met Beatrice's eyes across the span of Narida's back and she'd smiled, face ruddy and shining, hair dark and hanging tangled in front of her face.

Beatrice shuddered at the memory. Dorothy had taught her so many things about pleasure and sex. She meant what she'd said. If they couldn't retrieve her body from Amenemhat, if it was somehow fatally damaged or straight-out killed, then Beatrice had no qualms about offering hers in exchange. Besides, the idea of having Dorothy Boone inside of her body...

"Stop it," she whispered to herself, urging calmness before she got herself worked up. She needed tea. She pushed back from the table and went back downstairs. At the bottom of the stairs she turned and started down the short hall to the kitchen. She was almost to the door when she recognized the sound of water running. At first she thought it was the rain, but it was definitely coming from inside the house. She stopped and turned to see if she could determine the origin, but a powerful force of energy hit her in the chest before she could fully turn.

She hit the side of the stairs hard enough to knock the wind out of her. She brought up both hands and summoned as much energy as she could in the space of a second. Fire in the form of blue energy twisted around her fingers but she never had a chance to release it. Something twisted the flames and pushed them back around her hands and tightened until both hands were squeezed into fists. The energy guided her hands down and pinned them to the plaster behind her.

"Come out and face me!" she bellowed.

A woman stepped through the study doorway into the hall. The ground floor was too dark to see her features, but there was no mistaking the lilt when she spoke. "I merely wanted to ensure you wouldn't do anything rash when you realized I was here."

Beatrice bared her teeth. "I thought I made it perfectly clear what would happen if I ever saw you again."

Emmeline Potter, the Irish terrorist known as Virago,

grinned, the meager light catching her teeth as she moved closer to where Beatrice was pinned.

"Now, Miss Sek... I know Dorothy Boone was spotted boarding a ship bound for Cairo earlier this afternoon. I've no idea why you didn't go with her, but I'm not one to question opportunity. It's time you and I had a chat."

"I have nothing to say to you, beast."

"On the contrary, I believe I have information you've been quite desperate to uncover. I know you've spent the time since our last meeting in search of the other two elementals. The last two members of our odd little family."

Beatrice said, "And how would you know that?"

"I've been keeping tabs on you, of course. I'm sure you would have done the same for me, had you been able to find me." She chuckled and reached out to adjust Beatrice's collar. Beatrice twisted away, but Virago grabbed her chin and forced her to hold still. "I know where another elemental is. I'm willing to take you to her. But only if you ask."

Beatrice said, "I'll find her myself."

Virago laughed. "Oh, I highly doubt that. The offer is on the table, Miss Sek. It's up to you whether you take it or not." She turned and walked toward the door. She lifted her right hand, and both doors swung open. "A water elemental in a storm like this... I have the keys to the entire world in the palm of my hand. It's really quite magnificent. I hope to see you soon, Bao Tai Sek."

Beatrice closed her eyes and hung her head, ashamed of what she was about to do. But Virago was on the front steps and, when she left, there was no way of knowing when their paths would cross again. Beatrice and Dorothy had both been trying to find her since their last encounter, and neither had any luck. Now she'd discovered that even their most sacred place, the townhouse, was vulnerable. At the very least Beatrice could spend the time with her trying to find vulnerabilities in the damn woman's powers. She raised her head and looked at the woman who was now completely shrouded in rain.

"Virago. Wait."

The terrorist stopped and turned. Even in the darkness it was easy to see the poison in her smile. Beatrice pushed down the bile that threatened to rise.

"Show me."

CHAPTER EIGHT

Dorothy had the benefit of dressing in men's clothing for years, so she had some experience in knowing what to pack. There was a moment in Desmond's bedroom where she was worried about intruding on his privacy, but it couldn't have been worse than actually borrowing his body. She packed lightweight shirts and trousers, then went into the bathroom and took whatever looked essential. Desmond liked to keep his facial hair neatly groomed and, sure enough, she found a grooming kit. A razor, brush, scissors, cream, aftershave, mirror...

"Beards as a sign of laziness indeed," she muttered as she added it to her things.

Before she went back downstairs to where Agnes and Trafalgar were waiting, she took the opportunity for an experiment. She was in a relatively familiar space, without the pressure of time, and she did suppose there was a pressing need that required tending. She unbuttoned the fly of her trousers and the underwear. Out of habit, she started to lower herself to the commode, but realized it wouldn't be necessary. She cleared her throat, closed her eyes, and relaxed. She had grown up with brothers so she knew that aim was a necessity, and she did the best she could with a minimum of actual contact.

Afterward she declared the mission a success. There was a bit of confusion about returning everything to its proper confinement but she thought she was getting better at it.

"Sorry, Des," she muttered. "But on the brighter side, we'll be closer than any true husband and wife could ever be. If nothing else this will make me a much more convincing decoy for you."

She took her bag downstairs and Agnes drove them across the river to Trafalgar's home. It was full dark by the time they arrived and, though the rain had stopped, the heavy cloud cover meant there was no light from the stars or moon.

Trafalgar turned on lamps as she moved through her space, a private sanctuary which she had been spending less and less time in. She said it was just more convenient to stay with Dorothy and Beatrice, but the truth of the matter was that the building hadn't felt like a home since Adeline's death and Leola's subsequent departure. Now it was little more than a waiting room where she kept her tools and personal items. She didn't have an armory or vault like Dorothy, and she certainly didn't have anything like her library.

She stood for a moment in the parlor. There were memories in this place, good memories, but perhaps it was time to let them go. She would always cherish her friends and the time they'd spent living under this roof, but there was no reason to keep it now that they were gone. Adeline was gone. Leola was in Egypt building her new life. Trafalgar knew the time had come for her to move on as well. She packed a bag and went back out to the car.

"It's a grand house," Dorothy said. "I can see why you would be reluctant to leave it."

"It's very large," Trafalgar said, "and quite empty. Although I fear adding another body to the Threadneedle house might make it overcrowded."

Dorothy shrugged. "Nothing wrong with a little crowding."

Agnes drove them to Wanstead Flats, an area Dorothy had always considered anomalous within the confines of London. It was an unsullied stretch of grassland, pastures, and lakes that had remained free of homes or businesses. Agnes found a place to park and apologetically informed Trafalgar and Dorothy they would have to walk the remaining distance.

"Mazzi is overly cautious, but not without reason. She doesn't want just anybody discovering the existence of her plane."

"How has she managed to keep it unknown?" Trafalgar asked. "People must have seen it in flight."

"Of course. And they have seen her transferring it from hangar to hangar. It looks ordinary enough, as planes go. People saw enough of them during the War. It's only if they become interested in the specific technology she's using, or if they notice the range and speed of the ship, that it becomes problematic. She's very careful when flying over London but, for the most part, it's impossible to tell just how special it is just by looking." She smiled at Trafalgar and Dorothy. "I believe that's something all three of us have experience with."

They walked through knee-high brush, startling some grazing cattle, to a semi-circle of trees which surrounded a corrugated metal hangar. Lights shone from within and made the archway opening look like the mouth of a mythical cave. The plane stood within, shrouded in shadows. Dorothy didn't know the color: it may have been yellow or simply appeared such due to the golden light washing over it from the lanterns. The winds spread ten meters in either direction, taller than any of them, and a good fifteen meters from nose to tail. A woman was crouched on top of the plane, her knees pointed out to either side like she was a cat getting ready to pounce. She wore tight tan pants, a brown leather jacket, and a flight cap. She was basically every newsreel image of a fighting ace Dorothy had ever seen.

Agnes whistled to the pilot. "Mazzi! Come down and meet your passengers."

The woman unfolded and climbed down from the wing. Her face was square, her nose thin and pointed, and a crown of dark brown curls peeked out from underneath her cap. Her eyes were green underneath slender eyebrows that were arched in surprise.

"The adventurers!" She spoke heavily-accented English, the vowels betraying the fact that her first language was Italian. "Isidora Mazzi. You can call me Mazzi."

"It's a pleasure to meet you," Trafalgar said. "I am Trafalgar, and this is my associate, D—"

"Desmond Tindall," Dorothy interrupted. She had decided it was far easier to simply play the role than explain the situation to everyone who crossed their path.

Trafalgar looked askance at her but seemed to pick up on her intention. "Yes. Professor Tindall and I are immensely grateful for the use of your ship. Agnes wouldn't have betrayed your confidence unless it was a matter of grave importance."

Mazzi said, "I know Agnes well enough to believe she wouldn't have spent the currency of my trust without thinking it was a worthy expense. And I've heard stories about you, Miss Trafalgar. Not so much you, Professor. No offense."

"None taken," Dorothy said. "I tend to operate in more of a support capacity."

"Perhaps when we arrive at your destination, I can meet your other associate. Lady Boone? I have to admit, I've always admired her."

Dorothy couldn't resist a smile. "Truly?"

"Oh, yes, very much so. She is an inspiration."

Agnes grinned at Dorothy. "Well, I'll leave you ladies to it. Good luck!"

Mazzi smiled, confused. "'Ladies'?"

Dorothy said, "Ah, I-I am in the minority, it would seem. As I often am."

"You seem like my kind of gentleman, Professor Tindall. Come, I will help you stow your baggage and then you can help me with the pre-flight. We won't be able to talk much once we're up, so I'll go over a few hand signals just so you're not completely in the dark about what I'm doing."

Trafalgar said, "I'm sure we can trust you to keep us safe."

Mazzi laughed. "Spoken like someone who has never flown with Izzy Mazzi before! We'll go over the hand signals. Just in case."

Dorothy looked back at Trafalgar, trying to hide how excited she was at the prospect of a daredevil flight over Europe. Judging by the eyeroll she received in return, she was less than successful.

Amenemhat risked leaving his quarters after they had been at sea for several hours. He had spent the time lying on the cot trying to organize the thoughts and memories of his host. She was extremely well-educated as well as being handy in a brawl. She remembered wars and a great deal of history, including portions from his part of the world. The pyramids still stood!

His people were not only remembered, they were revered! Several of them were even remembered by name, although it seemed Henuttaui was not one of those immortalized in history books. He would change that. Soon the world would know her name.

But first he would have to survive the journey home. He had waited until the sounds of the ship grew quiet before he went outside. It was night, and it seemed as if most of the crew had retired for the evening. A few of the men peered at him as their paths crossed and he was once again reminded that he was in a woman's body. Boone remembered that women on a ship was considered superstitious by many sailors but he didn't care to reassure their misconceptions. Let them fear his presence.

He found the larder and prepared a small meal for himself. He was half-starved. He took his food out onto the main deck and sat cross-legged near the railing. They had sailed past the edges of the storm and the moon shone down on the water. He could see the shoreline of the unknown country they were sailing past. He chewed the meat carefully, grimacing at the taste but knowing it was better than nothing. Who knew what kind of delicacies these people ate? He was lucky to find palatable meat and bread.

Amenemhat thought of Henuttaui, the most beautiful woman in any kingdom, mother of the king and holder of the title God's Wife of Amun. He was a High Priest and therefore should never even have met her eye but she was too utterly appealing for him to ignore. He often lingered when he knew she would be passing by just so he could get a glimpse of her. Eventually she took notice and graced him with brief smiles when he caught her eye.

She was the also one who did the unthinkable and came to him, who met him in prayer and knelt beside him on the mat. They didn't exchange a word during that first communion. He was too terrified to say the wrong thing and she did nothing to ease his tension. When the prayer was finished, she stood and left, still without a word. He'd watched her go, confused but emboldened by her taking the first step.

The first time they touched, his finger to the smooth back of her hand, he'd had an embarrassing physical reaction that was impossible to hide. She had noticed it, which only increased his humiliation. But she said nothing and turned her back so he could save face. Soon he was accustomed to the touch of her hand, the feel of her skin on his. Soon he had tasted her breath and felt her mouth on parts of his body that had never been touched by another.

He opened his eyes and realized he had become distracted by the memory. He looked around and saw that he was still alone on the deck. The food spread out on a napkin in front of him now seemed horrid and unappetizing. He gathered it up so he could eat later without risking another trip out of his quarters. It would be a long journey home and anything he could do to minimize contact with these barbarians was worth the effort.

Back in the safe confines of his room, he placed the food in the satchel he'd found in the closet, then looked at the floor next to the bed. The hand of his savior and would be rapist, Paul, had fallen out. There was also a small rivulet of blood seeping along the edge of the wall. The corpse would have to be dealt with soon. He sighed and decided there would likely be no better time, so he pulled the man out and swaddled him in a sheet.

On his way back below deck, he encountered a pair of sailors. "Show me Paul's quarters."

The men smiled at each other and one moved closer to her. "We could show you to mine. I bet they're a lot more comfortable."

Amenemhat closed his eyes and sighed. He punched the man who had spoken in the throat, stomped on his ankle, and shoved his face into the hard metal wall of the corridor. He then grabbed his quarry under the chin, the other hand on his forehead, and twisted quickly until he heard a snap. His friend stared, too stunned to react, and Amenemhat grabbed the collar of his shirt to slam him against the opposite wall.

"Must I make an example of you as well?"

"No! No. No, Paul's quarters... they're... th-they're at the end of this corridor. 3B-1O2."

Amenemhat released him. "Dispose of this man's body. Tell no one what happened or you will be the next one sent overboard. Am I understood?"

"Yes. Y-yes, ma'am."

Amenemhat turned and walked away. Paul would have

clothing he could wear and, though it would likely not fit well, it would be better than wearing the same thing for the entire trip to Egypt. He looked down at Dorothy Boone's hands. They had now felled two men, neither of whom Amenemhat thought she could stand a chance against. Henuttaui would be very, very pleased with the woman he was bringing to her. He wished he'd grabbed the statue before leaving, but it wasn't entirely necessary for what he needed to do. Henuttaui's statue would be more than enough to perform the ceremony.

As for Dorothy Boone's consciousness, he hoped it was very comfortable staying right where it was. Her body now belonged to his beloved.

Mazzi called her plane Valkyrie. It was indeed gold in color, as Dorothy confirmed when she climbed into the middle seat and fastened the harness. It took off at half past nine o'clock, frightening the cattle the group had encountered on their way to the hangar. Mazzi was in the forward seat with Trafalgar at the rear, their positions carefully chosen to better distribute their weight.

"I want to warn you I'll be going slow over the city," Mazzi shouted over the chop of the propellers, "but once we're over the Channel I can make up some time. That's both to reassure you and a warning. It gets a little windy up there."

"I'm sure we'll be fine," Dorothy assured her.

Mazzi said, "Remember you said that in six hours when we arrive at Rome."

Dorothy said, "Wait, I'm sorry, did you say six hours...?"

Mazzi was already facing forward and either didn't hear her or decided not to answer. That estimate would have them traveling at speeds of 250 kilometers per hour. It hardly seemed possible, but as soon as they were airborne, Dorothy believed their pilot may have been overestimating the flight time. Their heads and shoulders were exposed to the air and were soon battered by frigid and relentless winds. They both wore leather caps and goggles which matched Mazzi's, but Dorothy was unprepared for how uncomfortable it would be. For the first time she was grateful for Desmond's beard. She twisted as much as her seat allowed and saw that Trafalgar had wrapped a scarf around the lower half of her face, her features clearly visible through the taut fabric. Dorothy held up her thumb, but Trafalgar shook her head and responded by turning her thumb down.

Dorothy faced forward again and pushed up her sleeve to look at her watch. The next twenty-four hours would be non-stop travel, save for a brief stopover in Albania so their pilot could sleep. They would arrive in Rome in the dead of night for refueling, then jump over to Tirana for their layover. Dorothy thought Rome, being the midpoint of their journey and Mazzi's home country, would be a better choice.

"I'm not entirely welcome in Rome," she said. "Long story. I should be fine so long as I don't leave the airfield. I do hope your passports are in order."

As do I, Dorothy thought. She had Desmond's passport in her jacket pocket, but she had no idea if there would be any issues with it. Hopefully they wouldn't have any problems at their stopovers.

Their speed did increase over the Channel, as evidence by a stronger burst of wind against their faces. Dorothy was beginning to question the wisdom of an experimental craft. But they had to reach Cairo before Amenemhat did.

She looked out over the flat expanse of black sea. Somewhere out there was the *Bessemer*, and aboard it was the man who had stolen her body. Part of her wished it was plausible for Mazzi to turn and sweep across the water until they spotted the ship. Dorothy highly doubted the Valkyrie, as impressive as it might have been, could land on a cargo ship. In any event, they would likely run out of fuel before they even caught sight of their prey.

In a little over one day's time, they would land in the desert. Then they could begin planning.

Chapter Nine

The players were all on the board.

At sea, Amenemhat aboard the *Bessemer*. Pursuing him aboard another ship were the Keepings. Cora Hyde and Abraham Strode were back home in London pouring through any references to ancient Egypt for references to their quarry. Dorothy wished she could assist in that endeavor, but she was board an experimental aircraft called the Valkyrie with its inventor and pilot and Trafalgar. The seat was comfortable but exposed to the air and too cramped for her to do anything but sit and contemplate her current situation.

She was trapped in Desmond Tindall's body.

The worst part was that she was becoming more comfortable in his skin. She actually did manage to fall asleep on the plane, her exhaustion eventually overpowering the shriek of wind. She felt a burst of confusion upon waking but, once she remembered the events of the past few hours, she calmed down. She had taken Trafalgar's advice to let the body relax, to let the muscles settle in a way they were familiar with, and it had done wonders. But now she was concerned about becoming too comfortable. She wanted her body back. She didn't want a period of adjustment, she wasn't *herself* back.

When they landed in Tirana, she sent a telegram home to inform Beatrice of their progress. She also received a telegram from Cora explaining they'd made very little progress uncovering Amenemhat's history. Dorothy wished them luck and offered her own library, although she highly doubted she would have anything relevant.

Mazzi treated them all to lunch from a bistro in the airport and they found rooms to rent where they could sleep for a few hours. When they woke, Dorothy found a telegraph from Cora.

"Went to your house, but Beatrice wasn't present. Will try again later." She furrowed her brow. "That's odd. Where would she have gone?"

Trafalgar said, "Perhaps she joined the Keepings on their pursuit of the *Bessemer*. She can recuperate on the ship as well as she can at home."

"I'm not entirely convinced that's true, but I suppose it does sound like something she would do." She sighed and looked at her watch. They were supposed to meet up with Mazzi in fifteen minutes. "We should get back to the plane. I'm not looking forward to twelve more hours of being whipped in the face."

"Consider yourself lucky. I'm not sure you're aware of this, but those compartments were not made with a woman of my height in mind."

Dorothy winced. "I didn't consider that. Are you all right?"

"I'll be fine. I once traveled eighteen hours folded into a crate." Dorothy raised an eyebrow and Trafalgar smirked. "You're not the only one who had adventures before we partnered up."

Mazzi was waiting for them at the airstrip. She smiled and clapped her hands as they joined her next to the plane. "*Buongiorno*, 'ladies'." She winked at Dorothy, who smiled indulgently. "Are we all rested up for the remainder of our flight?"

"I suppose we shall manage," Dorothy said.

"I have excellent news for you. I have recalculated our flight plan. My sweet Valkyrie has been performing beyond expectations, so we can skip the stop in Izmir and go directly to Cyprus. I can get you there in five hours, and then to Cairo in another two."

Dorothy was stunned. Subtracting the time they'd taken to

sleep, their trip from London had only taken fifteen hours instead of the thirty she would have estimated. She looked at the plane with newfound respect. "This is a mighty little plane you've built here. I'll have to see about enlisting your services for future expeditions."

Trafalgar said, "For Lady Boone and myself, you mean."

"Ah, yes... of course that's what I meant. But when did you have the time to recalculate anything? This layover was meant for rest."

Mazzi looked suspicious, but good-natured about her confusion. "Who can sleep in the middle of a grand experiment? I've always wondered how it would manage a long hop like this. I just could never justify a journey for its own sake. I owe you one, Professor Tindall, and you Miss Trafalgar." She patted the side of the plane proudly. "Okay. hop on board. Sooner begun, sooner done."

"Indeed," Dorothy said.

They resumed their positions and once again they were off, this time crossing Greece. They passed over the Aegean Sea, and Dorothy peered over the edge to see if she could spot the area where she nearly died the year before. She caught movement in the corner of her eye and saw Trafalgar seemed to be doing the same thing. They shared a smile before Dorothy faced forward again. She didn't want to jinx anything but, knowing they only had a few more hours in the air, she was actually starting to enjoy the way the wind whipped against her face.

She also had grown fond of the back of Mazzi's neck, as odd that statement seemed. The curl of her leather jacket, the way her hair danced in the constant stream of air pushing over her shoulders. She admired the set of the woman's shoulders as she commanded the plane through invisible eddies and currents, pulling up or dipping down based on indicators only she could see. She was fortunate she didn't have to stare into the woman's emerald eyes for the entire journey, or hear that magnificent accent. The two combined were highly dangerous—

"Crumbs," Dorothy muttered, gazing down at what was happening in her lap. It was barely noticeable through her trousers and the tail of her jacket, but her body was definitely giving away the prurience of her thoughts. She flushed behind her beard and moved her hands to cover the embarrassing rise she had caused. She would have to be more careful about her thoughts. She focused on the scenery and, soon enough, her anatomy was no longer causing her distress.

She idly wondered how the other members of their little society were faring on their missions. She wondered what Amenemhat was doing on his longer journey. What was he plotting? How was he filling the time between London and Cairo? What devious surprises did he have up his sleeve for them? And, most worrisome, did they truly have a chance of retaking her body without causing some grievous injury from which she would never recover?

Beatrice blinked awake, uncertain when she'd fallen asleep. She had no memory of drifting off or even getting into a car. The fact that she was almost always a driver caused her to panic. She sat straight up in her seat and grabbed for the steering wheel, her hands landing flat on the dashboard of the passenger side. Her heart slowed when she realized she was a passenger. She looked to her right and saw Virago behind the wheel, revealing their conversation the night before hadn't been a dream or hallucination. She wore a driving cap, a pair of goggles, and a bright red scarf that looked like blood against her pale throat. She glanced casually over at Beatrice, smiled coldly, and faced forward again.

Beatrice scanned the countryside around them. She saw low stone walls dividing the road from a long flat field. The world seemed to tilt slightly at the horizon, as if they were coming down off a mountain, but looking back she only saw gentle mounds of hills. It seemed like she could see for a hundred miles in every direction, the view broken only by the occasional stone building. Up ahead the road was flanked on either side by tall, ivy-wrapped trees reaching up to the grey sky with skeletal branches.

"Where are we?"

"Ireland." Virago's brogue was thicker, as if emboldened by being in her homeland. "We're not far from Kildare."

Beatrice sat up straighter. "Ireland? That's not possible. What day is it?" She didn't remember a boat, and she definitely didn't remember traveling over four hundred miles.

"It's three days since you were last conscious. I didn't want to take the risk you would change your mind before we passed the point of no return."

"You knocked me out?"

"I let you sleep. A little longer than usual, but don't you feel rested?"

There was little Beatrice could do in their current positions. Even if she could angle herself properly to attack Virago, she was driving. She couldn't risk running off the road, and she wasn't entirely sure she would be able to make her way back home without help.

"If you do that again, your life will take a painful turn."

Virago laughed softly. "I do like your fire. Which will be very useful when we get to where we are going."

Beatrice remained silent for the remainder of the ride, which ended on the grassless forecourt of a crumbling church. Virago removed her driving gear as Beatrice examined the grounds. The church was surrounded by a wooden fence that didn't look as if it could deter anyone from knocking it over. Beatrice had been chilly since she woke up but, as she and Virago approached the side of the church, the temperature seemed to rise by several degrees.

"This church was founded by the Brigidine sisterhood long enough ago that we don't need to concern ourselves with the actual date. Brigid lit the eternal flame herself, and it burned here until the sixteenth century, when monasteries were being suppressed. Everyone believed the flame was extinguished, but that was a falsehood meant to protect the flame. A spark remained, and it was transferred into one of the sisters."

Beatrice said, "The flame elemental. That was how she was born?"

They had reached a heavy wooden door with an imposing iron lock securing it. Some magic was incapable of manipulating iron, but all magic could defeat wood. Virago didn't even bother with the lock and simply shoved the door out of their way. The chains meant to keep them out slithered to the ground like the shedding skin of a snake. Virago led Beatrice inside.

"In quieter times, she keeps the fire stoked here, where no one can disturb it. The actual flame is just a symbol. The true power is the elemental." She turned and smiled at Beatrice. "As well you know."

Beatrice sighed. They were in a sanctuary, the pews long removed but with enough trappings that she knew where she was. A lectern on the stage was carved with the image of a flame. Pale blue light came in through the windows, reflecting brightly off the cobwebs collecting in every corner. Virago led the way down what had once been the center aisle, respecting the original architecture. Beatrice followed behind her.

"Leave."

They turned toward the voice, which had come from a balcony overlooking the sanctuary. A woman was staring down at them, her green robe trimmed with gold at the cuffs and the edge of the hood which was lifted to conceal her features. The one word had been spoken softly but with enough power that Beatrice didn't doubt there was a threat behind it.

Virago held her hands out to either side. "We come here as friends."

"And yet you enter uninvited."

"She has a bad habit of doing that," Beatrice muttered.

The robed woman cocked her head. "British? By way of France? Interesting."

"You expected Mandarin?"

"I never expect anything from strangers. It saves disappointment in the long run."

Virago stepped around Beatrice. "My name is Emmeline Potter. This is Bao Tai Sek. You may call us Virago and Beatrice, if you like. And what may we call you?"

The woman said, "Sharing my name would imply you will be here long enough to continue this conversation. I assure you, that will not be the case."

"I hoped this would not be difficult." She looked at Beatrice. "Show her."

"Show her... what?"

Virago said, "There isn't enough water around here to be impressive. But you can control stone, dirt, ivy. Think of something."

Beatrice furrowed her brow and looked around the sanctuary. One of the inner walls had collapsed, leaving behind a pile of rough and broken stones. She extended one hand, gathered energy in the cupped palm, and twisted her wrist to reach across the floor. The energy enveloped the stone and she used her other hand to manipulate the pile into a straight line. She turned sideways and pushed up, lining the stones into a row of steps which led up to the balcony.

Virago chuckled and casually walked up the stones. "My friend--"

Beatrice snapped, "No."

"--my *associate* Miss Sek is an earth elemental. I am a water elemental." She had reached the balcony and reached out, pushing up the hooded woman's sleeves. From below, Beatrice could see her forearms were covered with intricate flame tattoos, the ink spreading around her wrists as if her hands were the source of the fire. Virago smiled. "And you, my dear, are a fire elemental."

The woman pulled her hands away. "I'm nothing of the sort."

"There's no point in denying it. We've come this far. Miss Sek and I found each other through happenstance, and once we were acquainted, I became aware of your existence. In the space of one year, three of the four elementals have found each other. Surely you understand the significance of that."

"Even if I were to accept your delusions and join your cause," the woman said, "to what end? For what purpose have you come here to enlist me?"

Virago said, "Prophecy tells of four elementals who will unite one day to bring about a fifth."

"Aether. That which makes up the stars and the void between them."

"Exactly. The prophecy merely says void, but I'm confident they are one and the same. Once we find the representative of Wind, we will be ready."

Beatrice said, "I still believe 'void' is not something we want to bring about."

"We shall agree to disagree," Virago said, "at least until all four of us have been reunited. Then we can discuss it as a group. Are you with us?"

The woman hesitated. She looked down to where Beatrice was still holding up the hovering set of stones. Beads of sweat had appeared on her forehead, but she appeared capable of continuing for as long as she needed to. Finally the woman looked back at Virago.

"If it truly is fate that brought you here, then I suppose I have little choice in the matter. Where shall we begin?"

Virago smiled.

Chapter Ten

Trafalgar admittedly didn't know much about the demonstrations underway in Egypt. Everything she knew was what she gleaned from Leola's correspondence. She knew that nationalists were involved in a revolution against England's occupation. Leola wrote that she was treated well by the locals, since she wasn't British by birth. Dorothy seemed confident that they wouldn't have any trouble, but Trafalgar didn't share her optimism. Even if Dorothy was able to talk her way through any confrontations, their foe was wearing the body of a British woman with little to no knowledge of what he was entering into.

She looked over the side of the plane as Mazzi began losing altitude and tried not to panic; there didn't seem to be anything resembling an airstrip in the vicinity. There was a possibility that they'd pushed the experimental aircraft too far and it was beginning to fail them, but then she saw a plume of sand rising up on the road that ran parallel to their descent. They were low enough that Trafalgar recognized Leola in the passenger seat. Leola raised an arm in greeting and Trafalgar waved back, so eager to see her friend she actually looked down to see if jumping out and running to her was plausible.

It was not. Just the idea made her a bit nauseated.

They were on the ground just a few minutes later, and

Leola's jeep caught up with them as Dorothy and Mazzi were unloading the cargo. Leola ran to Trafalgar and greeted her with a rib-compressing hug, laughing in her ear as they swayed together. The driver of the jeep approached slower, a small-framed Egyptian man with his black hair left long on top but short on the sides. He wore a sky blue shirt with thick brown suspenders, tight slacks, and shiny black boots which were scuffed and stained by sand around the soles.

"You look amazing, my friend," Leola said against the side of Trafalgar's head. "I have missed you so much."

"I've missed you as well. The house is quiet without you underfoot. And the washing never gets finished on time."

Leola laughed and stepped back to brush her hands over Trafalgar's shoulders. "Is that why you are not wearing your jacket? I hardly recognized you without it!"

"Even I am not foolish enough to wear such a jacket in the desert." Trafalgar laughed and playfully clapped Leola on the cheek. The driver was lingering a few steps away, hands in pockets, observing the reunion with a nervous smile. "Is this Khalid, your grocer?"

Leola laughed. "No, Khalid is at work. This is Denny Razek. He is a friend of the museum. When I received your telegram about the purpose of your visit, I asked for his assistance. He agrees with your associates, the Keepings, that your adversary is seeking the Books of Breathing."

Denny stepped forward. "Yes, it seems clear you were correct to assume that is his purpose for coming here. If he no longer has the ka statue, he will require the books to take a permanent body and presumably regain his power. May I ask whose body it is that he stole?"

Trafalgar looked at Dorothy, who was watching Mazzi from the corner of her eye. It was too late to bring the pilot into the story, and it wasn't something to drop lightly into a simple introduction.

"We'd prefer not to say at this time," Dorothy said, "but we'll enlighten you as soon as it becomes prudent."

Denny had caught the glance at the pilot and nodded his understanding.

Trafalgar said, "Would you happen to know where we can find these Books of Breathing?"

"I'm afraid not," Denny said. "But I know where we can

begin looking."

"That is half the battle." She extended her hand. "Miss Trafalgar."

Denny smiled wider and took her hand. "I'm aware, yes. Leola frequently regales everyone at the museum with stories of your exploits."

Leola nudged him hard, looking bashful. "Denny."

"Apologies," Denny said, but he did not look particularly apologetic.

Trafalgar chuckled and turned to gesture at the other two members of her party. "May I then introduce you to Isidora Mazzi, our pilot, and Lady... Lady Boone's fiancé, Desmond Tindall."

Dorothy extended her hand to Denny, but there was an odd expression on her face. Perhaps it was merely seeing one of her expressions being made with Desmond's features. It was like she was wearing a very close-fitting mask. The effect was disconcerting to say the least, and it could have accounted for the way she seemed to be eyeing Leola's friend.

Mazzi also shook their hands, but said, "I'm afraid I'm not staying. Unless Miss Trafalgar and Professor Tindall need me for the return trip...?"

Dorothy said, "I don't think speed will be a necessity when we return to England. At least I should hope it won't be."

Mazzi clapped her hands together. "*Rocambolesco*. Then I shall take my leave." She reached into her flight jacket and held out a card to Trafalgar. "You're good eggs. Any time you need to be somewhere in a hurry, all you have to do is find me."

Dorothy said, "Thank you, Mazzi. I don't know what we would've done without you."

"You're most welcome. And thank you for the opportunity to stretch my baby's wings." She turned and looked at the plane, hands on her hips. "I didn't want to tell you this when we were still flying, but I had a few pilot friends waiting in Cyprus and Athens, just in case I needed their help."

"Always nice to have a backup," Trafalgar said, "but I'm glad we didn't need it."

Leola said, "Denny, help me load their things into the jeep. The museum keeps rooms for visiting dignitaries. I've arranged for you to borrow a couple for the duration of your stay. You can rest and freshen up, and then we can get started."

"You've gone above and beyond for unexpected guests," Trafalgar said.

Leola's features darkened. "Yes, well, if it weren't for me, you wouldn't be here. I sent you the ka statue in the first place."

Dorothy said, "And a good thing you did. If this happened while the ka statue was still in Egypt, Amenemhat may have been able to fulfill his mission before he was discovered. Who knows what he might have done? You sent him to us and, in doing so, slowed him down long enough for us to get ahead of him. Even if that wasn't your intention, you may have turned the tide of our encounter with him."

Leola nodded her gratitude to Dorothy. "One can only hope. Come. You must be exhausted."

"Indeed." Dorothy said, "Lead the way."

The Valkyrie caught up with the jeep when they were halfway to Cairo. Dorothy and Trafalgar both turned to watch as it sped up on them, the powerful engine sweeping sand off the road. They waved as Mazzi passed overhead, and she stuck one arm out to the side in farewell as she continued on. The plane banked hard to the west and was soon just a glint of sun on metal in the far distance.

"It's a hell of a plane!" Denny said without looking away from the road.

"Once you get past the discomfort of being exposed to the elements," Dorothy said, "it is quite a thrilling ride."

Trafalgar added, "Given you have the leg room."

"Yes, given that," Dorothy admitted. She reached up, expecting she would need to tame her hair, but was again reminded of one more benefit she gained from being in a man's body. If she felt she could get away with a shorter cut in her female form, she would do it in a heartbeat. Unfortunately the fact she preferred trousers to dresses was already too scandalous for some. If she actually styled herself as a man, the rumors would make it impossible for her to serve as Desmond's beard.

They passed a group of veiled women on the edge of Cairo, protestors in favor of making Egypt independent. It was the only sign of the revolution they saw between the so-called airstrip and the small red-brick building where they would be staying. Dorothy hauled both her and Trafalgar's bags from the backseat and shook Trafalgar off when she reached for her own.

"I can handle it. Another thing I'll miss about having this physique. Men can be quite handy pack mules."

"Just be careful you don't strain poor Desmond past his abilities. And try not to be too comfortable in his body."

Dorothy said, "Trust me, any conveniences I'm enjoying will be far outweighed by the comfort of being myself again." She looked to make sure Leola and Denny weren't within eavesdropping distance. Denny was speaking Arabic with the proprietor of the hotel. "Although I do fear there might be concern about bleed-through. Desmond's thoughts, memories, mannerisms... if I remain in this body long enough, my consciousness may fade. There have been moments in which I'm completely at peace with the situation. If that should happen, I'm counting on you to do the right thing and put things right. For Desmond's sake."

"I'm honored you would trust me with something of that magnitude."

"Really? Even now, after all we've been through? My lord, Trafalgar, at this point, your main purpose in this partnership is saving my life when I've gotten in over my head."

Trafalgar chuckled. "I'm still waiting for you to repay those favors."

"In due time."

They were taken upstairs to their rooms. Trafalgar and Leola were obviously eager to catch up, so Dorothy asked Denny to join her in her room.

Denny threw open the curtains to reveal the view. "It's not much, I'm afraid, but it's quite beautiful at sunset."

"I can imagine." Dorothy watched Denny move and, with a glance at the door to make sure they were still alone, lowered her voice. "May I ask you a question? You can refuse to answer but, if you do answer, I promise it will be kept in the strictest of confidences."

Denny looked nervous. "Okay."

"Why do you present yourself as male?"

Denny stared at her for a long moment, then laughed

nervously. "I-I'm not... I'm not sure what you mean."

Dorothy said, "I only ask because I'm uncertain if it's out of necessity, a woman working in a man's world and all that, or if it's because you're correcting how you were born."

"I'm not... presenting..."

"I shouldn't have asked. I apologize."

"I'm male."

Dorothy looked at him for a long moment, reading the meaning behind those two words. She nodded. "Very well. I hope I didn't cause you any embarrassment. I merely thought if it was a ruse, I would reassure you it isn't necessary around Trafalgar or myself. But now that I know the truth, I won't bring it up again."

Denny cleared his throat, refusing to meet her eye. "How did you know?"

"I'm a woman. I have intuition about this sort of thing." Denny's eyes snapped back to her and Dorothy rolled her eyes. "Oh, crumbs. I forgot myself. Ah, I... I am, in fact, Lady Dorothy Boone. I'm the one whose body was stolen by Amenemhat using the ka statue."

"I see. Amazing. How did it..." He closed his eyes and shook his head. "Sorry, no. There will be plenty of time for that later. You need to sleep after your long journey. You can wash up through here... you share the washroom with Miss Trafalgar. Do you want something to eat?"

"Perhaps after I've slept. But I would like to send a telegram. Would that be possible?"

"Of course."

Dorothy had written out a message to Beatrice at their last fuel stop. She handed it over along with the address. She was truly starting to worry about the silence coming from London. If Beatrice hadn't responded by that evening, she would call up the final member of the Mnemosyne Society, Ivy Sever, and ask her to check the house. Beatrice's injury hadn't seemed so dire when they left. In fact she seemed a few hours away from a complete recovery. If there had been complications, if the injury had been worse than it seemed... if Beatrice had been alone...

"Professor? Er, Lady Boone...? What should I call you?"

She snapped back to reality and realized she'd been holding out the address for nearly thirty seconds. She swallowed the lump in her throat and placed the paper in Denny's outstretched hand.

"I'm sorry. I was... my thoughts ran away with me. In private, you may call me Dorothy. In public, Professor would be preferable. Easier than explaining to everyone what has occurred."

"Of course. I'll see that this gets sent right away."

"Thank you for all your help, Denny."

Denny smiled and touched his eyebrow in a quick salute. "After all the stories I've heard about you, Lady Boone, it's an honor to play any small role in one of your adventures. Rest well."

Once he was gone, Dorothy closed the curtains Denny had just opened and undressed down to her underwear. She held her arms out in front of herself, admiring the musculature and the way they moved when she flexed her fingers. She rolled her shoulders and stood on her toes. If they failed, or if they had to cause physical harm to stop whatever he planned, perhaps remaining in Desmond's body wouldn't be the absolute worst thing in the world. She went to the mirror and examined his face. His eyes were quite beautiful.

"The beard would have to go," she muttered, watching Desmond's lips form her words. It was startling how normal it looked.

She shuddered violently and pushed away from the mirror.

"No. God, no, this body is not mine. Desmond will be returned to his proper body when this is all said and done, no matter what that means for me."

She went to the bed, pushed back the blankets, and stretched out on top of the mattress. She laced her fingers behind her head and closed her eyes. In a week's time, she would either be back in her proper body or she would be residing in the ka statue again. There was no third option.

Chapter Eleven

Dorothy dreamed.

In the dream, they were still in Egypt but she was in her proper body. When Mazzi asked if they needed her to stick around, Dorothy requested she stay so they could get to know one another better. The dream was disjointed, like discovering lost memories instead of reliving each moment. In the dream she brought Mazzi back to her borrowed room. She watched herself undo the buttons of the leather flight jacket, exposing the wrinkled white T-shirt underneath. She could almost hear the pilot's voice cooing Italian terms of endearment in her ear as they moved toward the bed.

"I didn't think you would mind, Professor," she whispered, her hand sliding up Dorothy's stomach.

Dorothy said, "Professor...?"

"Would you prefer 'Desmond'?"

Dorothy opened her eyes and realized that Mazzi actually was in bed with her, that the pilot was nearly topless save for a thin slip, and her fingertips had just moved underneath the elastic of the boxer shorts. Desmond's body was doing horrible and awful things in response to her presence. She recoiled away from Mazzi's wandering hand, grabbing the pillow and pressing it over her groin as she slid off the mattress onto the floor. Mazzi sat up, amusement turning to confusion as she watched Dorothy retreat to the wall.

"What on earth are you doing?"

Mazzi said, "I thought... the way you spoke to me, the way you looked at me. I thought you were merely shy or worried about propriety." She folded her legs under her and sat up. "There's no need to worry about that with me. I want you as well. I thought surprising you this way would be proof enough to put your mind to ease."

"I don't... I'm..." Desmond's sexuality was not her secret to spill, even if it might solve her current predicament. "I'm engaged to Lady Boone."

"I've heard enough stories about Lady Dorothy Boone that I'm not worried about insulting her."

Dorothy briefly forgot herself. "Stories? What stories?"

Mazzi sighed. "Oh, Desmond, please. I don't judge her. I've had dalliances in the past myself. Women are just so..." She smiled and ran a hand up her own thigh, momentarily lost in her thoughts. "I know that many would shun her for what she is, and you should be commended for helping divert the suspicion of gossips. But surely you have urges of your own temptations." She moved on her knees to the edge of the bed. "Let me take care of them."

"Well." She swallowed the lump in her throat and tried to adjust the pillow without letting it make contact with her overstimulated flesh. "I... do think you're an immensely attractive woman. And under other circumstances..." She sighed wistfully. "Oh, god, if these circumstances were at all different... but they're not. The situation is far more complex than you could possibly imagine."

"Do you not like aggressive women?"

Dorothy's laugh dissolved into a groan. "Oh, I adore aggressive women."

Mazzi climbed off the bed and approached her. "So..."

"So there are extenuating circumstances. Consent, for one."

"Consent? Desmond, you can do whatever you wish to me. I've been thinking about it since Rome, in fact."

Dorothy cringed away from her. "Yes, you've made your willingness exceptionally clear. But you're not working with a complete set of facts. And without going into details, I'm... there isn't..." She closed her eyes. "Desmond cannot consent to his body being used in this manner."

That brought Mazzi up short. "What in blazes are you talking about?"

Dorothy sighed. "I'm not Desmond Tindall. I'm merely borrowing his body until I can retrieve my own. I am actually Dorothy Boone."

Mazzi's eyes widened. She backed up a step.

"So you see, you would not have been consenting to be intimate with me, and Desmond could not consent to being used for the act. So, yes, while there is an undeniable, ah, physical response, it does not mean I have permission to carry on."

"This is amazing. You actually traded bodies?"

Dorothy said, "It was more of a shuffling, but basically. Yes."

Mazzi scanned the floor and retrieved her discarded jacket. "I'm going to choose to believe you, because there are about a thousand other lies that would be far simpler. You could have told me you found me unattractive..."

"That would have been the least believable thing I could have said, Miss Mazzi."

She smiled and held the jacket in front of her. "I apologize for intruding on your space. In every meaning of the word."

"Apology accepted. And as I said, under ordinary circumstances, this would have been an incredibly welcome surprise."

"I suppose I understand. Would a kiss be entirely out of the question?"

Dorothy smiled. "I think I can explain away a kiss."

Mazzi stepped forward and placed her hand on Dorothy's cheek. Her fingers teased the beard as she pressed her lips to Dorothy's. The kiss was brief but long enough for Dorothy to regret her current circumstances. She smiled and brushed her free hand down Mazzi's arm. Mazzi ran her tongue over her bottom lip and then looked into Dorothy's eyes.

"When things have, ahm, settled down, back to normal? Maybe you can call me? And not about using the plane?"

Dorothy smiled. "That could be arranged."

Mazzi nodded and moved to the door. She stopped before she left and said, "And thank Professor Tindall for the kiss when you speak to him again."

"I'll thank him for the both of us."

Mazzi blew her a kiss and then left the room.

Dorothy blew out a sigh of relief and frustration, then sat on the bed. She kept the pillow on her lap to prevent herself from having to see the lingering evidence of Mazzi's visit. She grimaced.

"And what am I supposed to do with you?" she whispered. She grew up with brothers, so of course she knew of one approach that could be taken. But would it go away on its own if she just ignored it? She sighed and pinched the bridge of her nose.

She didn't care what else Amenemhat had planned. She was going to make him pay for putting her in such an awkward position.

Amenemhat ignored the knocking for as long as he could, but eventually he knew he would have to deal with whoever was outside Paul's quarters. It wasn't ideal. He would have nowhere to retreat, but the door created a bottleneck. He could defeat an angry mob if they came at him one at a time. He'd considered escaping when the ship had stopped in a port for nearly a day, but in the end he decided to remain where he was. The crew had come to the conclusion he was nobody to be trifled with once their compatriots began disappearing, and they seemed to be giving him plenty of space. But now someone had spent the last eight minutes standing at his door, refusing to be placated, and it was time to address the issue.

He picked up a stone paperweight and placed it in his back pocket. Paul also had a firearm, and Amenemhat checked to make sure it was loaded. He wasn't confident in the usage of such a weapon but it seemed simple enough. He felt Dorothy's ability and the fact he would be using it in close quarters would cover for any incompetence.

He opened the door and stared out at the deckhands and other crewmembers who crowded the corridor. He stood so they could see the gun held by his side, but none of them made a move forward. On the contrary, the ones on the front line cringed back as soon as the door swung open. One of them even showed the palms of his hands, as submissive a gesture as Amenemhat could imagine.

"What?" he said.

"We don't want to disturb you," the lead man said. "But we thought a conversation was in order."

"Speak."

He cleared his throat and looked at his friends for support. "We've realized you've killed a couple of us. Men who, ah, took liberties or spoke out of turn. Last night a few men decided to ambush you as soon as you showed your face, but they... well, the ones who came back, they convinced us that this would be a better choice."

Amenemhat barely remembered the group. He hadn't been sleeping well; every time he closed his eyes, his memory was flooded with scenes from Boone's life. He would wake certain that she'd somehow regained control of her body. He thought taking a walk on deck might ease his mind, but the crew had been waiting. One of them had grabbed him from behind, but he went limp and slid out of his grasp. From the ground, he had kicked out two kneecaps and grabbed a handful of bollocks to disable three men in one move. He hadn't given it much thought because the others had fled immediately. He thought the matter was settled.

"We figure all of us could eventually take you down..."

He tensed, and the crewman held up his hands to stop an attack.

"But! But... but we didn't know who would, uh, who would be willing to be one of those you take down, savvy? So if there's a way we can get you off the ship without no one getting hurt, then that's the best plan of attack. We want you gone, get it? Safer for everyone if we just forget you exist, lady. So if you tell us where you're going, we'll make sure you get there as soon as humanly possible. No stops, no delays, just a straight shot to wherever."

He scanned the men looking for signs of duplicity, but they all looked legitimately frightened.

"Cairo."

"Right. Cairo. That's where we were heading anyway. We just weren't sure if you planned to jump ship early, or..." He smiled nervously. "But uh. I'll tell the captain. We'll set a course and we can have you there in just two more days. Will that work?"

"Yes."

"Good. Just... just don't kill any more of us, okay? We'll

stay out of your way, you stay out of ours, and when we hit sand, we never have to see each other again."

Amenemhat stepped back and shut the door in their face. A moment later he heard the shuffle of boots on the deck, whispered voices receding as the men fled. He smiled and returned his weapons to the desk. That had gone tremendously well, he had to admit. He would arrive in Egypt in half the time originally estimated. His foes would have a smaller window in which to foil him, and he wouldn't have to spend a minute longer on this infernal metal prison than necessary.

He took a seat on the bed and looked out the porthole.

It was just a few days now. A matter of hours.

He would be ready.

A small diner stood next to the hotel, and Trafalgar took advantage of it when she woke from her nap. She told the owner she was a tourist and thanked him when he made her a small sample dish of his best sellers. She took it back to the hotel and sat in the lobby, taking a position where she could see the stairs. She tried to remember the name of each dish as she tasted it: the kebab was delicious, as were the fava beans, falafel, and hawawshi. She wasn't entirely sold on the shawarma, but she could see the appeal of it. She made a mental note to return to the diner before they left Cairo so she could get the full experience.

When Dorothy came downstairs, Trafalgar lifted her hand to wave her over. The sight of her was a revelation. The day they left London, she thought she had seen Desmond at his worse. Now there was a new contender for that prize. The short sandy brown hair was uncombed, and lines criss-crossed the face under the beard as if she had been fast asleep only moments ago. She wore a wrinkled white shirt untucked over tan slacks, and her suspenders also hung limp from her hips.

Dorothy stopped by the front desk and spoke with the clerk. Whatever answer she received shifted her features into a look of concern as she joined Trafalgar at the table.

"You look positively dreadful."

"I feel worse," Dorothy said, her tone carefully hidden under the roughness of Desmond's voice. She gestured at the glass of milk and Trafalgar gestured for her to take it. Dorothy took a long swallow and sighed. "The telegram I sent to Beatrice wasn't delivered. No one answered at the house."

Trafalgar tried not to look overly concerned, but that was quite alarming. The only reason she could think of for Beatrice's absence was if she somehow convinced the Keepings to take her along when they left. But surely Agnes and Leonard would have found some way to let them know she was safe and with them. Beatrice had to know Dorothy would check up on her. Simply vanishing would be unintentionally cruel, and Trafalgar had never known the majordomo to be anything close to cruel when it came to Dorothy's feelings.

Dorothy said, "How did you sleep?"

"Wonderfully, I'm afraid. The bed felt luxurious after the plane. Speaking of which, did you know Mazzi is still in Cairo? Apparently she only went as far as the Nile before turning back."

Dorothy avoided her gaze. "Yes, she stopped by my room..."

Trafalgar sat up straighter. Dorothy's disheveled state suddenly made more sense. "Oh, Dorothy. Please tell me you didn't~"

"Of course not! I would never."

Trafalgar arched an eyebrow.

"I would never take advantage of her or of Desmond in that matter."

"That, I believe," Trafalgar said. "So you turned her away."

Dorothy nodded. "It wasn't easy. She was persistent. She thought she would... wake me with a pleasant surprise, so I woke with her in the midst of... things."

Trafalgar said, "Oh."

"Yes."

"I see."

"Right."

"That must not have been~"

"It was not."

"Is it still...?"

"No."

"Did you~"

"Can we stop discussing it? For the record, no. Things have settled down now. But it took this body far too long to realize nothing was going to happen. I barely got any sleep."

She sighed and sipped Trafalgar's milk again, this time not bothering to ask permission. Trafalgar chose not to complain and looked for a waiter to request a second glass. "I had to reveal everything to Mazzi. It was the only way I could dismiss her without feeling like a cad."

"A cad?"

Dorothy met Trafalgar's eye. "Hm?"

"You were worried about being seen as a cad? That's a very... masculine term."

Dorothy rolled her eyes. "I just spent the last twenty minutes with an erection. Forgive me if I feel a bit manlier than usual this morning."

"Quite. But you did ask me to monitor your situation. If there's a possibility you're becoming too comfortable in Desmond's body~"

Dorothy laughed loud enough to draw attention from the staff. Trafalgar used hand signals to request a second drink.

"Trust me, my dear Trafalgar, I am in no kind of comfort this morning. I am more determined to get back where I belong now than ever."

"If you're absolutely sure."

Dorothy grunted. "Finish your breakfast. I want to get to the museum as quickly as possible."

"As you wish, sir."

Trafalgar smirked at Dorothy's angry look and focused on finishing her food.

CHAPTER TWELVE

According to the front desk, a car had been left for them at the hotel. Trafalgar knew the way to the museum, and felt confident enough in her driving abilities to take the wheel. Denny and Leola were waiting for them in Denny's office, dressed much the same as they'd been the day before. Leola had chosen a blue dress with golden accents, something much softer than Dorothy ever remembered seeing her wear in London. Perhaps her relationship with Khalid and a quiet, settled life was something that agreed with certain people. Denny wore a suit with a plaid bowtie, and he smiled when he saw Dorothy. She nodded a greeting to him and tried to smooth out the wrinkles of her clothes as she took a seat.

"I apologize for my appearance..."

Leola said, "No apologies necessary. The circumstances are quite unusual."

Dorothy nodded. "So we've all been apprised on the situation?"

"You are Lady Dorothy Boone," Leola said, "despite outward appearances to the contrary. You believe the man who stole your body is an ancient High Priest named Amenemhat, and he is coming here to Cairo for reasons unknown. But it is fairly reasonable to assume he's coming after the Books of Breathing, which will allow him to transfer his spirit to another body. You wish to regain your body while preventing the knowledge of his magic from falling into the wrong hands. Is that the long and short of it?"

"The broad strokes, yes." Dorothy looked at Trafalgar. "This one is sharp. Why did you let her get away?"

"You try making her stay when she wants to leave."

Leola grinned. "Too right. Now... shall we begin?"

Dorothy gestured at the table. "This is your home, so I shall defer to your leadership."

"Very well. Mr. Razek, why don't you tell us what you've found in regard to our foe?"

Denny stepped forward. "What do you know about *damnatio memoriae?*"

Dorothy looked at Trafalgar, who shrugged and said, "Not a thing. It's a Latin phrase for condemnation of memory. What does it have to do with Egypt?"

"Names had great power in Egypt. To carve your name in stone was to confirm your existence. Conversely, erasing someone's name was believed to erase them from history. Horemheb famously destroyed all shrines or monuments of Akhenaten and used the debris to build his own shrines. It was only fairly recently that the names he eradicated were rediscovered."

Trafalgar said, "Look on my works, ye Mighty, and despair."

Denny looked enraptured. "Nothing beside remains. Shelley. I adore that poem. I suppose most archaeologists have a soft spot for it, of course, but the first time I read it, I got chills. It's so sublime." He looked down at his notes and cleared his throat. "But, ahum, getting back to the matter at hand. After a fair amount of investigating, I discerned that Amenemhat was a victim of such an erasure. After he died, an enemy went to the effort of destroying any written reference to him."

Dorothy said, "What did he do to deserve such a fate?"

"He fell in love with the wrong woman. History is more familiar than some people like to think. The names may change, but humanity has always had the same flaws. Amenemhat lived in Thebes during the Twenty-first Dynasty. He was a High Priest of Amun. They were extremely powerful individuals. Some believe they even held sway over the pharaohs. Despite his power, there was one person who was absolutely off-limits. The God's Wife of Amun. She was the mother of the king, a cult princess, basically the closest thing to a goddess on Earth. Amenemhat fell in love with a God's Wife called Henuttaui. In fact, I believe the feeling was mutual, otherwise the punishment may not have been quite so severe. When the relationship was discovered, they were sentenced to death.

"Amenemhat, in addition to being a High Priest, had more than a passing interest in the occult. He accepted their fate, but he found a way to ensure their spirits lived on. He bound his spirit to the ka statue so that when he was executed, his soul would enter into it rather than passing into the afterlife. He did the same with Henuttaui's spirit. He hoped one of his followers would wait until things settled down and then come to revive them both in new bodies. Unfortunately, his rivals acted first. Every mention of Amenemhat was erased, including the hiding place of the ka statues containing Henuttaui and himself."

Dorothy was staring at Denny. To say she was impressed would be a vast understatement. "A fair amount of investigating, you say? How long did Trafalgar and I sleep?"

Denny shrugged awkwardly. "Once I get my grip on something, I find it difficult to let go."

"So it would seem," Dorothy said.

Trafalgar said, "We obviously know what became of Amenemhat's ka statue. But you said Henuttaui had one as well."

"If he survived this long, then perhaps she did as well," Leola said. "Perhaps in addition to finding the Books, he is coming back to awaken her. I've been in contact with the shop where I originally found the ka statue and the owner has been trying to determine its provenance. I'll get in touch with him later today to see what progress has been made."

"Excellent," Dorothy said.

Denny winced. "Well, not exactly. I'm not confident that will lead anywhere of value. The ka statue was listed as a fake, so it had to have come from someone who had no idea of its origins. It could have been passed down within a family through several generations or it may have been unearthed during the military action of the Great War. Finding its origin through the pawn shop is next to impossible. But I thought we should cover our options."

Trafalgar said, "Do you have any idea where we should look? Luxor? The Valley of the Kings?"

"No. Ordinarily that would be a fine place to start, but the people we're looking for were executed and disgraced. They wouldn't have merited an honorable burial, but they would have had the means to ensure they weren't just buried in the desert and lost to time. I believe Amenemhat and Henuttaui were buried in mastaba. They were underground burial chambers with an above-ground offering temple."

Dorothy waited a moment to see if Denny was going to pull the rug out from underneath them once more. When he seemed to be finished, she said, "So if we find these mastaba, then there's a chance we will find Henuttaui and Amenemhat's final resting places. Will that include the Books of Breathing?"

"I don't know. But Henuttaui's tomb will hopefully still have her ka statue."

Trafalgar said, "And if it does, perhaps we can use it as a bargaining chip. A way of forcing Amenemhat to return your body without resorting to violence."

"A hostage exchange?" Dorothy said.

"I don't like it either," Trafalgar said, "but it would seem to be the least objectionable scenario. If it helps, the hostage we're holding would be completely insensate and unaware of what was happening, so it wouldn't truly be a kidnapping scenario."

"Saved by semantics," Dorothy said. "I suppose I can live with that. Before we do anything, we have to find the tombs and pray they're still intact. The grave robber who stole Amenemhat's ka statue may have also taken the Books of Breathing."

Denny said, "Yes. I... I didn't want to bring up that possibility, but there is a good chance that's true."

Dorothy sighed and looked at the table in front of them. "We'll cross that bridge when we come to it. Do we have any semblance of a plan?"

"Yes!" Denny said. "I don't mean to imply it's hopeless. Mastabas are quite large, and there are records of who is buried where and when the tombs were constructed. We can eliminate some of these so-called cities of the dead as too recent or too old, and that leaves us with only a handful which could possibly have been used for his burial. Out of those... well, many have been desecrated over the ages, and even more were looted during the War, but I believe I've narrowed our options quite considerably."

Trafalgar said, "Narrowed to...?"

"Three tombs. Well, five."

Dorothy raised an eyebrow. "Well done, Denny. You're quite handy to have around."

He averted his eyes, suddenly awkward. "I may be a bit verbose, but I'm enthusiastic. Give me a jigsaw puzzle and I'll have you a picture you can frame in ten minutes. Fifteen if there's a lot of sky."

Dorothy laughed. "And probably talking the entire time. Never let anyone tell you to shut up."

Denny picked up his notebook and tore out a few pages. "I took the liberty of writing down where the tombs can be found. We can split up and take a quick look at each one. As I said, I'm not sure what you should expect to find in them. The ka statue would have been interred behind a false wall. If you find one that's broken and empty, then the odds are good that it's Amenemhat's. Or that... you know... someone else... robbed a different tomb. We'll meet up back here in three hours to share what we've found. If anyone has any promising leads, we can all go and fully investigate. Miss Trafalgar, you can go with Leola so the two of you can get reacquainted. Lady Boone, if it would be all right with you, I'd be honored to be your driver."

Dorothy said, "I'm sure I'll hear a great deal about the history of this great city while we're driving. I can't wait."

"Then let us be off," Trafalgar said. "Amenemhat draws ever closer and time is at a premium."

"Agreed. See you all back here in three hours' time."

Denny moved to walk beside Dorothy as they left the office. "Were you aware that the Arabic name for Cairo is al-Qahirah, which means the vanquisher or the victorious."

Dorothy put an arm across his shoulders. "Really? I wasn't aware of that."

"On our way to our first tomb, I can show you the church in which it's believed that the Holy Family - Mary, Joseph, and the Christ child - sheltered after fleeing Egypt..."

"Fascinating!"

Dorothy looked back to see both Trafalgar and Leola striving not to laugh at her. She winked and focused on Denny's story as they left the museum.

The flame elemental introduced herself as Lasair. Beatrice followed them back to the car, where Lasair chose the dickey seat above the boot despite being exposed to the elements. Beatrice climbed into the passenger seat and stared at the remains of the church as Virago drove them back onto the main road. There was no rain, but the sky threatened a downpour any moment. She thought about the woman in the backseat, the fact that the quest she'd been on for the past year was now half finished, and she furrowed her brow.

"It's convenient, don't you think?" Beatrice said. "Four powerful elementals, and we're all located in Great Britain? Clustered together in a space smaller than some American states?"

Virago laughed. "Nothing convenient about it at all. I was born here, and you were born... well, you don't know, do you? Somewhere in Asia seems the most likely choice there. And you, Lasair?" She looked over her shoulder. Lasair had lowered her hood to reveal she was bald save for a small layer of pale red peach fuzz. "Where were you born?"

Lasair looked as if she wasn't going to answer but, finally, she said, "South Africa."

"So there you have it," Virago said. "The four corners of the Earth. North, east, south, and now we know where to find our fourth."

Beatrice said, "So someone born on the American continents? That narrows it down."

"Well, of course it does. It eliminates almost eighty-five percent of the population. And then narrowing it down further, whoever it is will be drawn to this region just as you and Lasair were as children. The thing that makes us what we are, the power within us, it desperately wants to be complete. We merely have to find someone who is magically adept, who was born in the Americas, and who now lives in Great Britain."

"If you put it like that," Beatrice muttered.

Virago said, "The three of us working together should make short work of the search."

"And what then?" Lasair said.

"A fantastic question." Beatrice looked at Virago. "You're the one spurring us on, the one abducting me and using me to convince Lasair to join our cause. What is the endgame?"

Lasair said, "Void. Whatever that entails."

Beatrice said, "And you're not the least bit curious what that could mean? It doesn't sound particularly pleasant to me."

"It means power. For us. The four who bring it forth will be rewarded."

"My god, you have no idea," Beatrice muttered. "You're simply working on faith."

"I have no doubt that this is what we were meant for. This is why we were created, why we're here on this planet. Our purpose."

"Created?" Beatrice said. "Not born?"

"Do you remember your parents?"

Beatrice said, "That's~"

"The road!" Lasair shouted, the first time they'd heard her raise her voice.

Virago faced forward in time to see the dirt path they were on rising up like a carpet with something moving underneath it. She moved her foot to the brake but there was no time for the vehicle to respond. They drove onto the sloped ground and were immediately tossed to one side, both occupants of the vehicle bracing as Lasair was thrown from her perch. Beatrice gathered her energy as Virago let go of the steering wheel to thrust both hands at the ground they were fast approaching.

The car hit with such force, deafening her with the crunch of metal, that Beatrice assumed the ground must have shattered all around them as well. It began tumbling, throwing her against Virago and tangling their limbs until she finally fell through either the open driver's door or the broken windscreen. She believed she blacked out when she hit the ground. There was an alarming stretch of darkness during the descent, and then she was rolling. Something was broken inside of her, there was no question about that, and she suspected something else had broken through the skin.

When she finally came to a stop, she was facing the

creaking remains of the car. It was upended, wheels still spinning, the air around it shimmering with fumes from spilled petrol. Virago was lying between Beatrice and the wreckage, her legs twisted in a nauseating jumble. Her neck was also twisted at an impossible angle, her eyes staring blindly into nothing. She couldn't see Lasair, but she assumed the worst.

Someone approached. She saw only their legs and the dark slacks that seemed to flap slightly with each step. The newcomer stood over Virago for a long moment, then continued on to stand over Beatrice. She tried to look up at him, but her neck didn't work. Neither did her arms, her legs, or anything below her shoulders.

"Still alive?" a soft voice asked. There was almost concern in the tone, like a nurse who had come to check on a patient.

"Finish the job," Beatrice said.

The person crouched and put a hand on Beatrice's face. They sighed heavily. "Ah, if it were only that easy, love."

Beatrice felt something burning in her head, then a sudden and excruciating pain which flooded her entire body before giving way to blessed and complete numbness.

CHAPTER THIRTEEN

The mastabas were located in Giza, a relatively quick southward jaunt along the Nile. They took two vehicles, splitting up once they reached what Dorothy hoped was referred to as "the ancient part of town." Two pyramids loomed above the smaller mastabas, squat little stone structures with inwardly sloping walls that looked like the foundation of pyramids that were never finished. Each one stood about the height of a home, completely unassuming compared to the grandeur just a few hundred yards away.

Denny drove them past the Sphinx, which Dorothy had to admit was a crushing disappointment. She'd never made it to Giza on any of her travels, and photographs always made the enigmatic sculpture look so impressive. In reality it was just another part of the landscape not far removed from the city center. People were going about their day without giving the wonders a second glance. She supposed living in the shadow of history tended to make one immune to it.

"It's fine," Denny said with a knowing smile. "Everyone assumes it will be more, ah, monumental."

"They are quite impressive. Just..."

"They don't jump out as they should. I felt the same way when my father brought me here the first time."

They were forced to walk from some distance to the

mastaba indicated in Denny's investigations. The entrance was a slender gap between two monolithic stone walls, the bricks of which were carved with intricate carvings. Dorothy paused to examine the artwork and regretted that she didn't have more time to fully explore the tomb. Even if it had been looted, there was plenty of amazing things left to discover. She traced her finger over the delicate cuts in the stone, moving closer so she could examine the ink that had been used in each groove.

She looked at Denny with regret. "This is where you tell me that these will still be here when Amenemhat has been dealt with and we should focus on the task at hand."

"Most definitely," Denny said. "If you require a guide for your return trip, I hope you will keep me in mind."

Dorothy nodded and patted the stone, a tacit promise that she'd return one day, and dropped her hand. She turned sideways to enter the courtyard of the tomb. She was holding a torch which Denny had provided and swept it from one side of the passage to the other. It bent and turned on itself so she couldn't see the end from where she stood.

Denny moved behind her. "Just around that first turn," he said. "The main entrance will be to your right. Then the corridor turns to the left, again to the right, and that is where you should find the false door protecting the ka statue."

"How easy is it to get turned around in here?" she asked.

"Nearly impossible," he said. "It's not a labyrinth. There aren't branching corridors that lead off in every direction."

Dorothy said, "I've been in a labyrinth. I'm relieved to hear this won't be a repeat of that experience."

"That's one of the stories Leola told us. Did you actually see the minotaur?"

"See, yes," Dorothy said, "Although smelling him is the feat I'm proudest of surviving. Wet fur and aged leather."

Denny said, "Yuck."

Dorothy chuckled. "Oh, he was a sweetheart in the end. Spared our lives, killed the man trying to kill us. What more can you ask from a beast, hmm?"

"You have a point." Denny ignited a torch and placed it in the corner where it would illuminate their way. Dorothy could now see that the courtyard was a single passageway with only one entrance. There was no chance they would get lost because there was only one way to go. Denny cleared his throat. "I want to thank you. For letting me prattle on. I've been told that my biggest problem is that I never know when to stop talking, and I continue on long after the listener has become bored or forgotten whatever topic it was that started me off."

"Bored?" Dorothy said. "Nonsense. One never knows what information will become vital one day, or where that information will come from. It's education, and the key to a full life is to never stop learning. You've taught me much in the short time we've known one another, Denny. For that, I'm grateful."

Denny ducked his head and smiled bashfully. "Thank you. That means the world coming from you. A-and now that we're here in this most private of spaces, thank you for keeping my secret."

Dorothy was examining the ceiling with her torch. "Secret? Oh. Yes. Think nothing of it."

"You don't think it's deviant?"

"I sleep with women, my good man. I shall never be called a hypocrite."

They moved deeper into the tomb and Denny laid a second lantern. "The false door is at the end of this corridor. It's the main offering chamber where tributes could be left for the deceased. Family and loved ones would bring in food and treasures and leave it here. The ka statue was protected by the wall, but there are holes the spirit could use to come and go."

Dorothy said, "I've discovered it's far more complicated than that." She aimed her torch at the dead end ahead of her. "The wall appears intact, so this can't be Amenemhat's tomb. Look for signs that it might be Henuttaui's."

Denny took off his pack and sat it on the ground. He removed a squat box made of black metal and began fiddling with dials on the back. Dorothy moved closer and looked at the small screen set into the side of the object.

"What on earth is that?"

"You know sonar, yes?" Dorothy nodded. "This operates on the same principle. Sound waves travel forward, then they bounce back, and I use the data to construct an image of what's on the other side of the wall."

Dorothy crouched next to the machine. "I want one."

Denny chuckled. "Getting the technology into a portable package was a pain. But once I've figured out how to make more, you'll be first on the list." He flipped a switch and the box began to hum. Dorothy expected a visual representation of the sound, but all she got was the shaking loose of dust and stone particles from the walls and ceiling. She thought she could also feel a tremor in the ground that passed before she could confirm it was due to the machine. The screen lit up and Dorothy peered down at a blur of shapes in a generally square area.

"I assume you can make sense out of this."

"To a degree. I can't tell you anything about the fine details, but there is a ka statue in the wall. And the shaft to the burial chamber is just through there. I have rappelling gear if you wish to descend and check it out."

Dorothy said, "We'll save that for after we find hard evidence." She moved closer to the wall and examined one of the frescos. Whatever it had depicted was lost, scraped away by chisels and time. "I wonder who this person was, if not Henuttaui. What did they do to justify erasure?"

"Humanity can always find reasons to erase those they disagree with."

"Hm," Dorothy said. "Too right."

She had turned in time to see Denny avert his gaze, indicating he'd been staring at her. He knew he'd been caught, so he said, "May we speak frankly?"

"Always."

"The, the ka statue. The incantation, the spells. It really... i-it swapped your bodies? It happened instantly?"

Dorothy knew what he was hoping for. "Yes. But Denny, please don't think it's a... a solution to your gender issue. To begin with, you would need someone to swap bodies with. Even if you found someone similar to you - a woman born into a man's body - I don't believe that this exchange was intended to be permanent. From the moment I awoke in Desmond's body, I've been able to access his memories, his mannerisms... I truly believe that if we don't correct things in an expedience manner, soon I will be unrecognizable as Dorothy Boone."

Denny said, "That's fascinating. Terrifying, but fascinating. A slow fade back to the status quo. Do you believe the same thing is occurring on the ship with Amenemhat?"

"I do. As my consciousness fades in this body, I have to hope it grows stronger in my own."

"But then would it be the same version of you who existed before the exchange?" Denny asked. "Or would it merely be a shadow?"

"I prefer not to find out." She walked to Denny and put a hand on his shoulder. "I'm sorry. If I thought there was a chance--"

Denny shook his head. "No, I understand. It wasn't a flawless idea. I would not want to abandon who I am just for the sake of having the proper packaging. I want to be me, not someone else. That's the whole point of Denny Razek as oppose to Dendera Razek."

Dorothy said, "Good for you." She squeezed his shoulder before sliding her hand down to his upper arm. Denny looked down at her arm and, when he looked up again, Dorothy leaned in and pressed her lips to his. He made a muffled sound of surprise but, while he did tense, he didn't pull away. Dorothy slipped her free hand, the one holding her torch, around his waist and pulled him close. Denny stepped into her embrace and began returning the kiss, his hands meeting in the small of Dorothy's back. She felt her body responding and knew Denny could feel it as well.

"What's this?" Denny asked when the kiss ended, neither of them moving to part.

"Remember I said that I'd been assuming some of Desmond's skills, memories, and mannerisms? I believe that if Desmond had truly been here, he would have wanted to do that. And I'm just impulsive enough to follow through on the urge. I hope I haven't offended you."

Denny shook his head. "No, on the contrary. It was very welcome. I'm not sure if I'm actually kissing him or if I'm... I'm kissing Dorothy Boone."

She moved her hands to the lapels of his jacket. "Yes, that is quite the conundrum. But if this were an ordinary excavation, if you were here with Desmond Tindall. Alone and unobserved in an ancient tomb--"

"This is actually the courtyard, the above-ground public offering space. The tomb itself is well below us, past the bedrock, in--"

"Denny," Dorothy said softly.

He looked her in the eye.

"What would you be doing if I was Desmond?"

Denny hesitated, then moved his hands around her waist. He lifted the tail of her jacket and rested his hand on the buckle of her belt.

"I've always... I-I mean, it's been a bit of a fantasy of mine f-for a long time..."

Dorothy nodded. She could feel it in her bones that this was something Desmond would agree to, could almost hear his voice in her head as she looked into Denny's eyes. She backed up until her shoulders touched the wall.

"I would like very much to help you bring that fantasy to life, Denny."

He swallowed and whispered, "Wow. Okay..." He passed his tongue over his bottom lip and looked down. His hands shook as he unfastened Dorothy's trousers just enough to reach inside. Dorothy grunted and closed her eyes when his fingers found her. There was a momentary struggle with the clothes but then Dorothy felt the warm desert air on her bare skin. The palm of Denny's hand felt smooth and cool against her. She felt gooseflesh rising on her arms. She flattened one hand against the wall behind her and, with the other, urged Denny onto his knees. He knelt on his jacket as a mat.

Dorothy focused on a random corner of the tomb. "Des, I do hope somehow you're able to retain this memory fo-ohh..." She closed her eyes, put her hand in Denny's hair, and stopped trying to think for a little while. It felt magnificent, familiar but not. Denny seemed very talented at what he was doing, or maybe Dorothy was benefiting from a lack of experience. Whatever the truth, she could barely focus her thoughts on anything other than what was happening below her waist.

Soon, too soon in her opinion, there was an ending. She gasped and her voice caught in her throat, a rough guttural moan which she swallowed down as she roughly curled her fingers in Denny's short hair. He kept his mouth on her until she was spent and she slumped against the wall, struggling to catch her breath and trembling from the strength of her orgasm. She looked down as Denny produced a handkerchief and proceeded to tidy up. The sure strokes of the cotton made her twitch again, and she put a hand over her mouth as she laughed.

"Thank you for that, Lady Boone."

"I say this having never meant it more... but the pleasure was all mine. Is there a way I could possibly... ah..."

Denny shook his head. "What just happened was physical. Anything you do would be mental. It would be you. And I'm not your type."

"No. I... I appreciate what you did for me." She smoothed her hands over her clothes to make sure she was presentable. Her hands were still shaking slightly. "We should finish looking for evidence as to whose tomb this is. We still have the other tomb to investigate before we reunite with Trafalgar and Leola back in Cairo."

"Yes. Precisely. Business." He smiled at her before he turned to examine the other wall. Dorothy straightened her hair and tugged at her belt. Denny said, "You're wrong, by the way."

"About what?"

"The pleasure being all yours. There was more than enough to go around."

Dorothy chuckled. "I'm thrilled to hear that, Mr. Razek."

Trafalgar moved to the edge of the burial shaft and shone her torch down. She could see tool marks in the stone where centuries ago, slaves and workmen had cut through the bedrock. She didn't relish the idea of descending, but the first tomb had been a bust and there was evidence that this was the one they were looking for. The first clue was that the false wall in the chamber was shattered and the ka statue was missing. Leola identified several carvings which gave honor and glory to Amun, which added to the chances they had found what should have been Amenemhat's final resting place. Unfortunately there was no sign of the Books of Breathing in the above-ground structure, so one of them would have to climb down into the burial chamber.

Leola came up behind her and peered down into the dark. "Shall we make a wager? Winner gets to go?"

Trafalgar grinned. "It is good to know your grocer hasn't tamed you."

Leola walked widdershins around the edge of the hole, thumbs hooked in the loops of her trousers. "He's quite awful to me, if you must know."

"Khalid? How do you mean?"

"Every morning he receives shipments of the finest fruits, brought in from the docks after traveling here from all over the world. I once conversationally mentioned that I loved pears. So now, every morning, he sets aside the finest pears for me."

Trafalgar said, "A true beast."

"I have asked him to stop. But he has already stopped making me paper flowers when the shop is idle. I fear asking him for anything else."

"Well, a man can only be changed so far. Perhaps you will find a way to live with this enormous character flaw."

"I can only hope."

Trafalgar chuckled. "So you are happy?"

"Deliriously so." She looked up. "And you?"

"I am content. Lady Boone has proven to be a fitting partner. Though occasionally frustrating."

Leola said, "The best partners always have a bit of frustration in them. That means they've challenged you. It's a good thing."

Trafalgar said, "I shall endeavor to remember that the next time she is irritating me."

"Hm. Yes..." There was something odd about the tone of Leola's voice, but she changed the subject before Trafalgar could inquire. "Let us decide who shall descend. Paper Scissors Stone?" She held her fist in the palm of her hand, but Trafalgar waved her off.

"I have had my fill of being lowered into dark, ominous places, while you have been starved for adventure. I would be happy to let you go while I remain here."

Trafalgar had never seen anyone look so excited at the prospect of being lowered slowly into a dark tomb. They opened Leola's pack and Trafalgar helped her get into the harness, double-checking each catch and strap before declaring the rig to be safe. She noticed Leola's hands were shaking and looked up into her eyes.

"Are you sure you're all right?"

"I'm fine," Leola assured her. "I love my life. My new job. Khalid. I love it all. But I have really and truly missed this."

Trafalgar patted her on the arm and anchored herself as Leola stepped into the burial shaft. She took a few deep breaths, nodded that she was ready, and began to descend. Trafalgar was wearing gloves to protect her hands as she fed the rope a little at a time, feet planted shoulder-width apart as she guided Leola's careful climb down. Leola was quickly out of sight, but the torch strapped to the shoulder of her harness filled the pit with a soft golden glow.

She was almost halfway down when Trafalgar heard something from the courtyard. Their lanterns were still casting light on the walls, and there was a flicker of shadow as someone passed through the beam. Trafalgar tensed and looked toward the pit.

"Leola... I believe we're about to have company."

"I'm closer to the bottom than the top," Leola said, her voice echoing off the walls of the narrow shaft. "Keep lowering me."

"Be careful." Trafalgar fed her more rope, eyes on the entrance to their chamber. She was completely defenseless and, even if it was a representative from the Department of Antiquities, she would have a difficult time explaining why she seemed to be looting a tomb. If it was an actual tomb robber, she had the weapons from Threnody in her pocket, but they might as well have been left in her room since her hands were occupied with holding Leola's rope.

Another shadow fell across the wall and the newcomer stepped into view. Lady Dorothy Boone, clad in dirty and ill-fitting men's clothing, stepped into the burial chamber and leveled a shotgun at Trafalgar's head. Her hair was raked through, tied off and clipped in multiple places with no skill or aesthetic beauty. He had made a beautiful woman look as if she'd just crawled out of her own tomb.

"Pardon the intrusion," Amenemhat said, his voice a gross imitation of Dorothy's, "but I'm afraid you're plundering my tomb. I suppose there's no harm done as it's about to become your tomb as well."

Trafalgar said the only thing that came to mind. "Oh, crumbs."

Chapter Fourteen

It had been days since Trafalgar had seen her friend in the flesh, and those hours had not been kind to her. Hair unwashed, and face scrubbed free of any trace of makeup so that her freckles seemed to stand out more than usual. Her eyes were wild and rimmed with red as if she hadn't been sleeping. Despite her rough appearance, it was clear that she still had strength in the way the barrel of her gun didn't waver from its target.

"It would be very unwise to pull that trigger," Trafalgar said.

"You have no idea what I'm capable of."

Trafalgar said, "Oh, I have a very good idea, Amenemhat. I've fought Dorothy Boone a few times and I know exactly what she can do."

Confusion passed over the familiar features. The barrel of the weapon wavered slightly. "You know who I am? How is that possible?"

"You believe it's a mere coincidence to find me here, in your tomb?" Her arms were feeling the strain. Every bump and jerk of Leola's weight on the rope transferred up into her shoulders, but she didn't allow her voice to waver. "We came to stop you and retrieve my friend's body."

Amenemhat raised the gun again. "Apologies. I have plans

for this body."

"Do not pull that trigger. If you do, I'll release this rope and the woman I'm lowering into your burial chamber will fall and most likely be grievously injured."

"You presume I care."

The light coming in from the courtyard briefly faded and then returned; someone else had entered the courtyard and was moving furtively forward. Trafalgar raised her voice to cover any sounds that might give away the new arrival.

"You should care. Unless you plan to descend yourself, in which case... who precisely would be here to bring you back up? I presume you're here for the Books of Breathing so you can transfer your essence to a more appropriate host. And these 'plans' you mentioned for Dorothy Boone's body. You intend to use her as a host for Henuttaui."

Amenemhat bared his teeth. "Who are you?"

"I am Miss Trafalgar of Abyssinia, and that is my friend's body that you are wearing."

Dorothy-in-Desmond's-body stepped into the chamber and rushed Amenemhat, tackling him from one side and knocking his aim off. She grabbed the barrel of his gun with one hand as she slapped the other against the back of his neck, slipping her hand under the curtain of hair so she could affix Threnody's sedative spider directly to the skin as directed. Amenemhat cried out when he felt the injection, turning his attention from Trafalgar to the more direct threat.

Dorothy managed to wrench the gun from his grasp as carefully as possible, careful not to break his finger on the trigger guard. Those were her fingers and she intended to use them again very soon. Amenemhat was less concerned about inflicting harm, and proved it by punching her in the face and the side of her head, making her ears ring. His movements were sloppy, his eyelids drooping as the sedative began to work, but he showed no signs of actually passing out.

"How long before the sedative takes effect?" she asked, closing her hands around his throat in the hopes she could choke him to unconsciousness.

"Threnody didn't specify," Trafalgar said.

"That is... information... we should have insisted upon!"

Amenemhat threw his weight against her and the two tangoed forward again, nearing the shaft. Dorothy swept her leg against Amenemhat's, knocking him off balance and sending them both to the ground. Amenemhat, pinned to the ground, grabbed Dorothy's face with his right hand and squeezed.

"All that time I spent on that ship," he said, "was spent preparing for the moment I would be reunited with my love. I need the Books to make our change permanent, but I don't need it to undo what has already been done."

He began chanting, his voice rough, and Dorothy moved to clap her hand over his mouth before he could finish what he was saying. She felt Desmond's thick fingers clap over the lower half of her face and knew it was too late. Her brain reeled from what had just happened, like a rubber band had just snapped around it, and she felt the claws of the sedative taking hold. She muttered against Desmond's hand, looked up into the face which had greeted her that morning in the mirror, and tried to use hand signals to warn Trafalgar before she completely lost consciousness.

"What was that he was saying?" Trafalgar asked.

Amenemhat made sure she was unconscious before he removed his hand. He was trembling. "I don't... ah, I don't know. I couldn't make it out."

"I'm lucky you were here."

Denny had appeared in the entrance to the chamber. "My assistant tracked me down as we were leaving the first tomb. The *Bessemer* docked early this morning, and the Keepings' ship was delayed so they couldn't pursue him once it arrived. Lady Boone thought it would be prudent to warn you that Amenemhat was somewhere in the city."

Trafalgar said, "And a good thing you did. I suppose we can count this as repayment for the time I saved your life in Peru."

Amenemhat chuckled. "Yes, I suppose we should."

The smile faded from Trafalgar's face. "Denny, subdue him."

"What?"

"That is no longer Dorothy Boone. Amenemhat swapped bodies again."

Amenemhat turned and threw himself against Denny, knocking the small, confused man down. He heard Trafalgar curse but didn't look back, running so quickly that he bumped into the stone walls on his way out of the inner chamber. Once again, Boone's friends were forcing him to leave empty-handed, abandoning the tools he required to save his love. But now he was in a new body, a fresh one, and he could think properly without Boone slipping through the cracks. It had been happening more and more frequently during the final days on the boat as they cruised through the Mediterranean.

Outside the mastaba he found two vehicles. He chose one and got behind the wheel, grateful that his new host seemed to know how to operate it. He twisted the key, shoved his foot down on the small pedal, and reversed quickly away from the tomb. He was sweating and breathing heavily, and this new body - Desmond - felt so completely different from Boone's that he was constantly suppressing twitches and nervous tics.

His plan remained unchanged. He would find the spells necessary to resurrect his love and he would find a way to place them in permanent bodies so they could live out their days.

But first he would kill Dorothy Boone and Trafalgar of Abyssinia to ensure they would never again meddle in his affairs.

Denny knelt next to Dorothy, holding her head in his lap. She still hadn't regained consciousness but her vital signs were all strong. "How did you know it wasn't her?"

Leola had reached the bottom of the shaft, so Trafalgar was resting her arms. "I heard Amenemhat saying something just before he passed out. I mentioned Peru, a place Dorothy and I have never been together, as a test. If I was wrong, Dorothy would simply have been confused. I felt it did no harm to confirm."

"A good thing you did." He looked down as Dorothy began to stir. "Lady Boone? Are you okay? Are you... yourself?"

Her eyelids fluttered. "I'm..." She started to sit up, but Trafalgar and Denny held her down. Her eyes were open then. She held her hands in front of her face and released a trembling breath as she examined the rest of her body. "I'm back. I'm me, I'm back. Oh, thank heavens."

Trafalgar said, "Nice to see you again, Lady Boone."

"Wonderful to be seen." She touched her face, walking her fingers over to her lips to feel them smile. "Seen, to be seen, wonderful to be seen. Hah. I've missed the sound of my own voice."

"It gets old fairly quickly," Trafalgar said.

"Cheeky." She grunted, cleared her throat, and looked around the tomb. "Desmond... he went into Desmond's body, didn't he?"

Trafalgar said, "I'm afraid so. I couldn't pursue, and Denny..."

"Denny's not a fighter." Dorothy smiled up at him. "Hello, Mr. Razek. It's a pleasure to actually make your acquaintance."

She could have sworn he blushed. "And you as well, Lady Boone."

"Let me sit up." Trafalgar and Denny both helped her into a seated position. She closed her eyes as her head was spinning. "Tell me what's happening."

"Well, Amenemhat confirmed that this is his tomb. Leola is already in the lower chamber trying to find the Books of Breathing. Since he showed up, we're fairly certain it's here. I suppose we're lucky he chose to retreat rather than fight for it."

Dorothy said, "Right. And the first tomb you checked?"

"Leola confirmed it was someone else's. So unless you had any luck with the one you checked..." Dorothy shook her head. "The fourth one belongs to Henuttaui. It's reasonable to assume Amenemhat is headed there as we speak. The one thing we have going for us is that he won't be able to steal anyone's body without the Books."

Dorothy said, "If there's an inscription on the base of the statue, he could trick someone into reading it aloud. Inadvertently swapping their bodies."

"Yes, but I believe the Books have more powerful spells. Permanent swaps, forced exchanges, that sort of thing. That is why it's imperative we don't let him acquire it."

"How long has Leola been down below?"

"Only a few minutes. She'll whistle when she's back in the harness and ready to be brought up. I would have helped you with the fight–"

Dorothy said, "I understand why you couldn't. Besides, if he had gone into your body and sent your consciousness into mine, I fear we never would have untangled the mess. We'll give Leola time to explore, which will give me an opportunity to regain my bearings. We should also warn Mazzi that the person in Desmond's body is no longer a friend."

"I can do that," Denny said.

"Thank you, Denny."

He nodded and hurried from the chamber. Trafalgar took a seat on the ground next to Dorothy, bending her knees and resting her arms across them.

"You're truly well?"

"I believe so. A bit of a headache, and I'm a bit woozy, but that may be due to the sedative in Threnody's little gizmo." She touched her hair and winced. "I suppose it was a bit too much to hope that the ancient priest to take care of my hair."

Trafalgar said, "You've definitely looked better."

Dorothy poked her tongue out and began working to get her hair into some semblance of normal. Amenemhat was somewhere in Giza, most likely on his way to his lost love's tomb, but she couldn't help feeling optimistic. They had his ka statue and soon they would have the Books of Breathing, the two items he required to continue his body-jumping shenanigans. It was hard not to be hopeful of victory.

Beatrice knew she had died. She remembered the pain and, more importantly, the sudden numbness that came after. Not just a lack of pain but a lack of any feeling whatsoever. It was a nothingness deeper than black. Even when she regained consciousness, proof that she was alive, she still knew exactly what had happened. She kept her eyes closed as she took stock of her situation. She was standing with her back against a slanted wall so she was facing the floor. Her arms were bound in front of her, completely enclosed in something that felt like a pillowcase. Her elbows were apart and the backs of her hands touching so she couldn't summon any energy to free herself.

Someone shifted to her left so she finally opened her eyes. Virago was similarly trussed, her hair falling on either side of her face so it was impossible to tell if she was conscious or not. Beyond her, Beatrice saw Lasair was also present and the fact she was bald meant that Beatrice could see her eyes were open. She hissed between her teeth and Lasair turned to look at her. Virago remained still.

"Are you all right?"

"I believe so," Lasair said, "now. But before…"

Beatrice said, "Right. I remember multiple broken bones and possibly paralysis."

Lasair said, "I was thrown from the vehicle… and then I was crushed by it."

Beatrice winced. "Probably a memory you would have been better off without."

"Yes." She scanned the room, an empty space with a door in the wall across from them. There was no window, no ventilation, no chairs or tables. She rolled her shoulders to test the cloth binding her arms. It truly was similar to a pillowcase; enclosed around her hands and stretching up past her elbows. She flexed her arms but the material didn't give at all.

Beatrice had been conscious for several minutes, constantly trying the limitations of her restraints, when the door finally opened. A man in a black suit entered, shut the door behind himself, and scanned the three women hanging in front of him. The man was utterly unremarkable in style or appearance. She could have seen him a thousand times on the street or he could have been a complete stranger. He walked to the center of the room and stood with his hands clasped in front of him.

"Apologies," he said. He was American, judging from the accent. "It was easier to transport you in that state than dealing with you constantly fighting me."

"It also served to demonstrate your capabilities," Lasair said.

He smiled. "That, too."

Beatrice said, "You killed us just to prove you could bring us back to life?"

"I killed you to prove I could. I brought you back to life because I don't necessarily want you dead. Not yet, anyway."

"Who are you?" Beatrice said.

"Bao Tai Sek. Your earliest memory is waking up in the cargo hold of a ship with a man you believe to be your grandfather. You were taken to France where a young couple raised you to the best of their abilities until you ran away to London. Eventually you robbed the house of one Dorothy Boone, which led to your body being encased in stone. Lady Boone freed you and, in gratitude, you remained on as her assistant. That job quickly grew to include lover."

The Stranger moved to stand in front of Lasair. "Amanda Visser. Your earliest memory is walking through a mining camp in the Witwatersrand. You were taken in by a pair of men who told people they were brothers but were in fact lovers. They doted upon you until the Second Boer War broke out, at which point they relocated north until they ended up in Ireland. They chose someplace cold because you were always feverish. When your fathers passed away, you began taking long walks in the countryside. That's when you discovered the Brigidine Sisters and realized you were home."

He walked back to Virago, who seemed to be still unconscious. "And Emmeline Potter. Claimed by a woman who had given birth to six boys and gave up on a daughter of her own, raised in violence and revolution. She remained where she grew up and spent her entire life fighting because it's easier to be hated and feared than to convince someone to love her."

Beatrice hated Virago, but there was no need for cruelty. "Who the blazes are you?"

"I'm not important. You are." The man stepped back and indicated all three women. "Earth. Fire. Water. You only lack the air elemental to complete your number. Myself and people like me are charged with ensuring you never complete your quest. Miss Sek, you were on the right trail a few times this past year, but we pushed you onto the wrong track so you wouldn't get too close."

Virago said, "What does it matter to you if we're successful or not?"

Beatrice was surprised; she would have sworn the other woman was unconscious. She still hadn't moved or lifted her head, but she'd spoken as clearly as if she'd been awake for hours.

"We know the prophecy just as you do. The four elements unite to create a fifth: void. Do you have any idea what that means?"

Virago finally lifted her head. "It means men like you are scared and doing everything in your power to stop it. That's all I need to know."

He stepped forward. "We're scared because your success would mean the end of the world. If we must kill three women to ensure the continued survival of this planet, then I am absolutely prepared to do that."

CHAPTER FIFTEEN

"So you brought us back to life just to kill us again," Beatrice said.

"I brought you back to warn you. To inform you of how dangerous this path is, and hopefully convince you to decide against taking it. We don't want to become murderers - permanent murder, that is - unless it becomes absolutely necessary." The Stranger stepped forward and, with a wave of his hand, Virago sagged away from the wall. He grabbed her by her shoulders and turned her, gently urging her onto her knees. She struggled against him but there was little she could do with her arms bound. He kept one hand on her shoulder while he held the other up in front of her face. "I'm not going to physically harm you. I merely wish to show you a vision of the future."

Beatrice said, "If you wanted to hurt her just a little..."

Virago twisted her head to sneer at her.

"You wish to create Void without even knowing what that means. I can tell you exactly what it means: the elimination of magic in the world. Reuniting the four elementals will reestablish their dominance. That would be catastrophic for the continued survival of the human race. Since Miss Potter has proven to be the most dedicated of your trio, I thought she should be the one to bear witness to what is at stake.

Apologies, Miss Potter. This won't hurt, but it will be... uncomfortable."

Virago started to respond as he pressed his hand against his forehead. Whatever words had been on the tip of her tongue were swallowed by a gasp. She arched her back and her eyes rolled back in her head. Her body tensed as if her spine had suddenly become stone. Beatrice could see golden energy flowing between the palm of their captor's hand and Virago's face. Her eyes were wide open but the color faded, leaving the irises as disconcerting pinpricks in a field of white.

"They ma-arch. They march, so many of them in formation. Brown uniforms. Hard-faced young men. Frightened young men. Banners of red and black and white. Death. Oh god, thick clouds of smo— bodies. The ashes are bodies, bodies burnt, buried..." Tears were flooding down her face. "Prisoners. God... so ma-any of them..."

The man said, "The seeds of this have already been planted. The wheels are turning and could not be stopped even if we tried. Now..."

Virago seized roughly, her shoes kicking the floor as the energy in the man's hand shifted from golden to a sickly green. Beatrice could see Virago's biceps flexing against her bindings, straining whatever material they were made from.

"What are you doing to her?"

"Only what is necessary. Tell them what you see, Ms. Potter."

She turned her head as if trying to look away, but her eyes remained locked on his hand. Her jaw trembled and put a tremor in her words when she finally spoke.

"Bomb. A bomb. Oh, God, it's... it's ma-massive. 'Rain of ruin...' So many dead. So many." She sobbed and sagged forward, but their captor used his free hand to keep her upright.

Lasair said, "Stop this!"

"She must see it all," the man said.

Beatrice pulled at her own restraints but she was helpless to do anything but watch.

"Complete devastation." Virago's voice was raw, as if she was forcing the words out but would never speak again once she was done. "Children. Civilians."

He dropped his hand, instantly releasing the tension in

Virago's body. She slumped forward and he tenderly helped her sit up. Virago sobbed, head bowed, looking more defeated than Beatrice would have thought possible. All hint of bravado had vanished from her. The anguish on her face made it impossible to imagine it had ever worn the smug smile Beatrice had come to associate with the terrorist.

"Who would use such a weapon?" Virago whispered. "What kind of monsters will we be fighting in this war of yours?"

The man said, "I'm sorry, that was misleading. The first images... the soldiers, the flag, the camps... that was the enemy. The bomb you saw was us. That is what the side of the angels resorts to in order to finally end the conflict. Something around two hundred thousand killed, hundreds of thousands more will die in the aftermath. Both sides will resort to inhumane actions to defeat their enemies resulting in war crimes that violate every code of ethics imaginable. But with magic in the world, there will be other options. Less brutal options."

Lasair said, "How do you know any of this?"

"It's our burden." He stood and guided Virago back to the wall. She remained docile as he restrained her again. "We do everything in our power to prevent the worst possible outcome. Sometimes that means allowing less-awful things to happen."

Beatrice said, "Like the murder of three innocent women."

"Actually, I would only need to kill one of you. She would be replaced by another elemental, but that person would be a child and it would be a few decades before they were old enough to be a problem. By then, the war will be underway."

"A few decades?" Virago muttered, stunned that such horrors might be seen in her lifetime.

"But of course no one absolutely has to die. Simply agree to abandon your search for the fourth elemental. Return to your lives. Forget about each other and the prophecy. We will keep watch over you from a distance, as we always have, but if you give us no reason to harm you... we will remain unseen. The choice is yours, ladies. I'll give you a chance to discuss~"

Virago said, "We'll stop."

Beatrice looked at her. Never had she seen anyone look so utterly defeated. Virago's face was pale and drawn, though the color had returned to her eyes.

"I began this quest. I forced Miss Sek and Lasair to join me. If they attempt to continue without me, I will stop them myself."

The Stranger closed his eyes and allowed himself a small, relieved smile. "The world will not know the sacrifice you've made today, but know that you have our gratitude. Now, I would prefer not to extinguish you all again, but I can't have you knowing where we are."

"We'll go quietly," Virago said. "Bag our heads, drug us, whatever you need to do."

"Thank you, Ms. Potter. I must say, I am overjoyed to see that you've come around to our way of thinking. You'll all be returned directly to your homes. I'll prepare your transport immediately."

He turned and left the room.

Beatrice said, "I'm surprised to see you give in so completely."

"You didn't see what he showed me." She pressed her lips together and swallowed hard. "If he'd asked me to save him the trouble and end my own life, I would have. We cannot allow that reality to come to pass. We cannot bear the burden of such atrocities."

The door opened and the Stranger returned, this time flanked by three other men. They were nondescript, bland men in unremarkable clothing, and each carried a black hood. "These will be your escorts home. Thank you for your cooperation, ladies. Rest assured that you have saved millions of lives."

"I meant what I said," Virago muttered to both of her fellow elementals but looking at neither of them. "If you continue this quest, I will find out and I will end you myself. This is a vow."

One of the men slipped a hood over Beatrice's head, blocking out anything else Virago or Lasair might have said.

Getting Leola out of the burial chamber took all three of them, Dorothy and Trafalgar acting as anchors as Denny made sure the rope didn't rub against the edge of the shaft. Leola ascended by planting her feet on the curved wall and pulling herself up the rope. She moved an inch at a time, making achingly slow progress, but Dorothy knew only tragedy would come from rushing the process. Even though she could feel Amenemhat's lead increasing, she wouldn't dare put Leola's life at risk just to pursue him.

By the time Leola reached the top, she was covered with sweat and panting for breath. Denny took her hand, pulled her to safety, and let her lean against him as he walked her over to the wall. She sat down and handed Trafalgar a small wooden box about the size of a humidor. She looked past Denny at Dorothy and smiled.

"Nice to see things returned to normal while I was down there. Hello, Lady Boone."

"Hello, Miss Kidane." She handed her canteen over and indicated for Leola to drain as much of it as she needed. "Nice to see you with my own eyes once more." She looked at Trafalgar. "Hopefully the risk you took was not in vain."

Trafalgar had opened the box and withdrew the scrolls within. She skimmed the contents and nodded. "From what I can tell from an on-the-fly translation, this does indeed seem to be a collection of spells. Was there anything else in the tomb which may have fit the description?"

Leola shook her head. "Some treasures, though. Gold, statues, jewelry. Amenemhat must have had some people who still liked him even after he was executed."

"Then we shall have to assume this is it."

Denny said, "I can call for a police guard to watch the mastaba, just in case Amenemhat tries to come back."

Dorothy said, "Good idea. And best give them descriptions of all of us. We have no idea if we'll suffer another swap before all is said and done."

"Probably wise," Trafalgar said. "Better that none of us can access it than risk Amenemhat getting inside. Where do we go next?"

"The fourth tomb from Denny's investigation. He'll probably be long gone by now, but we might get lucky." She tugged at her clothes and took a moment to examine what she was wearing. Oversized trousers and a shirt that had been patched more times than it had been washed. She wasn't wearing a brassiere and suddenly doubted she'd had a bath since having her body taken in the Inkwell. "And then directly to the hotel where I can deal with a few issues of hygiene. I've never wished more for a dress than I do at this moment."

Trafalgar raised an eyebrow. "Dorothy Boone in a dress? I never thought I would see the day."

"Nor did I. But I believe I've had quite enough of men's clothing for the next little while."

"I'll be sure to snap a photograph for your parents."

They left the tomb and climbed into the car that was left. Denny directed them to the final tomb but, as predicted, Amenemhat had already been there and gone by the time they arrived. Dorothy and Trafalgar went inside and confirmed he'd been there. The false wall had been destroyed, and Dorothy moved one of the stones to reveal dust underneath it. He'd come directly to the tomb of his lover and stole the ka statue with her consciousness inside.

"What do we do now?" Trafalgar asked.

"We still have the advantage." Dorothy stood and brushed the dust off her hands and began to pace. "We have the Books of Breathing, but he might attempt to get an unwitting victim to read Henuttaui's inscription to provide her with a temporary host. Amenemhat knows we have the Books. He'll come for us, but not immediately. From what he's seen and what I presume he learned from being inside my body for the past few days, he'll know what we're capable of. He won't rush in blind. He'll regroup and come up with a plan first."

Trafalgar said, "I fear that he'll dispose of Desmond's body with haste."

Dorothy thought for a moment and then dismissed the idea. "No. Swapping bodies is just as disconcerting as you might imagine. Now more than ever he'll want a clear head. Being in Desmond's body puts him in control of someone who is strong and clever. Someone who knows how we operate. He's too valuable to just throw away."

"Then his first order of business will be securing Henuttaui. He'll want to be certain she's protected after going through all this trouble to retrieve her."

"Right." She chewed her bottom lip. "He's retreating now. Looking for a safe haven. But he won't leave us alone indefinitely. Eventually he'll come for us." She sighed and rolled her shoulders. "That's one bit of good news, at least."

"Good news?" Trafalgar said.

"Yes. If we know he's coming for us, then we can return to

the hotel and rest for a while. We'll have to be on alert, of course, but we don't have to exhaust ourselves searching all of the Sahara for him. We can set up defenses, come up with a plan, relax, take a bath. And more importantly, I can put on a bloody bra."

Trafalgar said, "Ah... well..."

"What?"

"When we left London, you were in Desmond's body. We stopped at Desmond's home so you could pack for this trip. So unless he has a predilection I'm unaware of..."

Dorothy blanched and then rolled her eyes. "Oh, crumbs. Fine. To a clothing store on the way back to the hotel."

Trafalgar chuckled and followed Dorothy out of the tomb.

Amenemhat was covered with rock dust, his muscles aching from the effort of breaking down the wall in his beloved's tomb. His new host, Desmond, was indeed physically stronger than Boone, but he lacked stamina and seemingly had no experience in hard labor. The muscles of his back were aching something fierce, and he had to keep flexing his fingers to prevent them from locking on the steering wheel. He couldn't help but feel he had made a bad exchange.

But it was worth it. He looked at the passenger seat where Henuttaui's ka statue lay cradled in his jacket. The inscription carved into the base would be enough to grant her life, but he needed someone to recite it. Even then it would only be a temporary solution before they would have to find a new host. The Books of Breathing would allow him to force Henuttaui into a host which she would then have complete control over. No bleed-through from the previous consciousness, no slow fade into oblivion.

He considered Boone a worthy candidate. She was strong and beautiful, and worthy of Henuttaui's cleverness and personality. But Miss Trafalgar... he had only seen her briefly, but her strength was evident in how she handled the rope lowering her friend into the burial chamber. She was tall and equally as beautiful to Boone, and there was something about her eyes which reminded him of his lost love. She would be nobody's second choice.

Perhaps when the time came, he would capture them both and allow Henuttaui to choose which one she would take. It was only right that she have a say in the process. It would serve a dual purpose to have them both present when his plans came to fruition. Trafalgar and Boone seemed to have a great many friends and the means to remain on his trail across continents. One of them would become his beloved's new host and the other would be killed to discourage any further pursuit.

It might have taken far longer than he would ever have imagined, but now the moment was close enough that he could almost taste it. He and his beloved would be together again, and nothing would get between them again.

CHAPTER SIXTEEN

The proprietor of the hotel seemed suspicious when Dorothy asked for a key to her room, a key he'd originally given to a man traveling alone, but that key was with Desmond's body. Leola vouched for her and insisted the circumstances were entirely proper. They retired upstairs and took a moment to regroup in the corridor. They had to be on alert, since Amenemhat now had access to Desmond's memories. Denny made the appropriate calls and assured them that the tombs of Amenemhat and Henuttaui were now being guarded around the clock.

Dorothy had bought the necessary clothing from a shop Leola recommended. She stripped out of the clothes that reeked of male sweat and old fish. She filled a basin with water so she could wash up. She submerged her hands and brought them up back up, watching as the water slipped through and around her fingers. They were unmistakably hers, the familiar knuckles and fingernails that she'd seen her entire life. After nearly a week of looking down to see shockingly large hands with their soft, uncalloused fingertips, it was like coming awake to see her own beautiful hands once more.

She closed her eyes and touched her face. She left behind streaks of water on her cheeks, her lips, and the bridge of her nose as she explored her features. No beard, no unusual topography. She moved a hand behind her ear and felt that one spot which became grimy if it wasn't properly washed, and she wet a sponge to take care of what Amenemhat had neglected. The water trailed down her neck and caught in her hair in a way she knew very well.

There was a knock on the door, a summons she considered ignoring for further exploration, but she knew it might be something important relating to Amenemhat. She was still nude save for her underwear so she wrapped a dressing gown around herself as she left the bathroom.

"Yes?"

"Lady Boone?"

Dorothy unlocked the door and smiled at Mazzi. "What, you didn't recognize my voice?"

Mazzi chuckled. "It's a bit more melodic than the last time. And you have cleaned up nicely since we last saw each other."

"I've barely cleaned up at all," Dorothy said, "but I thank you for the compliment. Is everything all right?"

"Everything is fine. I was downstairs. Leola mentioned you were back to normal but you were lacking in wardrobe. I thought I might offer you a few things you might need." She patted the bundled clothes she was holding. "Shirts, slacks, socks. I don't have a dress, but you didn't seem the sort for dresses." She chuckled and passed the bundle to Dorothy. "Well, you didn't seem the sort for dresses when we met. But I meant from your personality..."

Dorothy laughed and took the offering. "I gather your meaning. And you're right, given the option I would prefer trousers. Thank you. This is very thoughtful of you."

"*Prego.* So how does it feel to be back in your own skin?"

"Remarkable. I've been taking it for granted, but now that I've had to live without it for a while, I look forward to getting reacquainted with myself."

Mazzi raised an eyebrow. "Mm. Sounds delightful. May I watch?"

Dorothy almost laughed, but she remembered the surge of emotions when she'd woken to find Mazzi in bed with her. She stepped back out of the doorway and inclined her head.

"If you would like."

Mazzi laughed softly, but the smile didn't make it all the way to her eyes before it wavered and died. "Yeah...?"

"Come in."

Mazzi hesitated a moment and then stepped inside. Dorothy shut the door and twisted the lock as Mazzi took a seat in the room's armchair. Dorothy felt Mazzi's eyes on her as she walked to the dresser, placed the clothes on top, and then moved to sit on the foot of the bed. Mazzi had crossed one leg casually over the other, her fingers linked together over the knee. She intended to look casual, but Dorothy could see the tension in her eyes and the set of her lips. Dorothy kept her knees together and tried to look reassuring.

"Whatever is about to happen is fine. Whether that means you get up and leave in the next thirty seconds or you tear off your clothes and join me on this bed, it's fine. All right?"

Mazzi's cheeks were pinker than they'd been when she came in, but maybe that was just sunlight reflecting off the red walls. She nodded and Dorothy made herself more comfortable. She closed her eyes and ran her hands over her thighs, feeling them through the material of the dressing gown. She wanted her eyes closed for the beginning so she could forget Mazzi was there, and so Mazzi could feel unobserved to follow whatever urges she might have.

Dorothy kept her feet on the floor but pointed her toes, letting her knees fall away from each other. The slick material of her dressing gown fell away to expose her legs, so she moved her hands up. She untied the belt and pushed the two halves away, letting them fall open to reveal her underwear. Every touch was familiar, every sensation she caused something she knew well from years of experimentation. Hiding under the blankets, figuring out what felt best and when to hold back. She thought of those early explorations with a smile and gently plucked the robe off her shoulders, letting it fall down her back.

Mazzi drew in a sharp breath. Dorothy almost looked at her but stopped herself before she could open her eyes. She moved one hand up to unclasp her brassiere. It opened in the front, and she lightly dragged her fingers up and down her cleavage, up to her décolletage to her throat. Desmond hadn't been particularly brawny, but she was reminded of how it felt to be smaller, more petite in every way, almost delicate. She moved her hand down to cup her breast, pushing aside the cup of her bra and teasing the nipple with her thumb.

Mazzi shifted in the chair, causing it to groan under her. Dorothy heard clothing being adjusted and the rasp of a zipper and she smiled.

"Considering how you tried waking me up the last time you were in this room," Dorothy said, "I find it difficult to believe you're shy."

"That was before I knew how beautiful you were."

Dorothy chuckled. "Ah, fresh..."

"And... you're a woman. I talk a good game, but with a man I know exactly what to do. Which buttons to press and how to... how to dance. I know he will lead. I know I can begin the dance and he will take over. Then all I must do is follow. With a woman..."

"I understand." Dorothy opened her eyes and looked at Mazzi, who tensed with her hand just under the waistband of her pants. "It's all right. I want you to touch yourself."

Mazzi said, "You first."

Dorothy smiled and maintained eye contact as she circled her nipple with the pad of her thumb. Mazzi's throat moved as she swallowed, and Dorothy watched the tip of her tongue slip across her lips as her hand moved lower.

"I've been thinking all day about waking up with your hands on me," Dorothy said. "It's a shame that it wouldn't have happened if you had seen the real me."

"But it got us to this moment, no?" Mazzi said. "So maybe it's all for the best."

Dorothy smiled. "Perhaps."

"Don't stop."

"Talking or...?"

"Either."

Dorothy smiled and took off her bra. She was rewarded with a hitch in Mazzi's breathing. She put one hand on the mattress behind her as she dragged the other down her stomach, stretching her fingers over the crotch of her underwear before curling them back toward her palm. She sighed and let a shudder pass its way through her. That was it. That was how it felt to be aroused, to be on the verge of greater pleasure. She moved her fingers in a well-practiced dance to get the cloth out of her way so she could feel skin, teasing the outer lips with her fingers before spreading herself.

The chair creaked again as Mazzi leaned to one side.

Dorothy bent her leg and twisted at the waist to give her voyeur a better angle. She opened her eyes and saw that Mazzi's hand was hard at work inside her trousers.

"I'd like to see you," Dorothy said, "if that's not asking too much."

"See me..."

Dorothy's eyes struggled to stay open. "Your breasts would be enough."

Mazzi smiled nervously. "I think I can do that." She kept her right hand where it was, reaching up with her left to clumsily work at the buttons of her shirt. It was some heavy material that fell in on itself as the buttons were undone, but Mazzi hunched her shoulders and shrugged it out of the way. She was wearing a brassiere without a corset just as Dorothy frequently did. She loved the way it felt, the freedom of having her stomach and hips unencumbered by a stiff framework of whalebone. Mazzi tugged the tail of her shirt from her trousers.

"When I was in Desmond's body," Dorothy said, "in the plane on our trek here, I was aroused by the very idea of you. I suffered a very visible reaction to those thoughts."

"Did I make you uncomfortable?"

"Gloriously so," Dorothy said. "I wouldn't trade my femininity for anything, but I must admit having one of those at the ready whenever I needed one would be quite... useful..."

Mazzi said, "I hear they make~"

"I have one of those."

"Here?"

"In London."

Mazzi whimpered. "A pity. I would love to feel your weight on top of me, Lady Boone."

Dorothy grunted and arched her back. "Your hands on my hips. Guiding me."

"Yes. Though I doubt you would need much guidance..."

"I don't know. Sometimes it's nice to let someone else lead." She wet her lips and watched as Mazzi tossed aside her bra. Her nipples were small and dark, and Mazzi looked down to watch herself tease them to erection.

Dorothy sighed. "Quite lovely... quite, quite lovely."

"Are you sure you just want to look?"

"I want to do whatever you're comfortable with."

Mazzi took her hand from her pants and stood up,

pushing them down far enough to reveal a half-slip, then pulled them off over her boots.

"Leave the boots on," Dorothy said.

"You're not the first to make that request. I also have a scarf... a long white one."

Dorothy said, "Would you bind my hands with it?"

"If you asked politely."

Dorothy moaned low in her throat and watched as Mazzi walked toward her. She sat up straight and Mazzi took a position directly in front of her. Dorothy leaned forward and kissed Mazzi's collarbone, sliding her lips toward her shoulder. Mazzi put her free hand on the back of Dorothy's head and gently eased her lower. Dorothy kissed her way down the curve of Mazzi's chest until she could close her lips around the nipple. Mazzi made a quiet sound of approval and began stroking Dorothy's hair. Dorothy was rolling her hips against the stroking of her fingers, breathing deeply and smelling Mazzi's skin and sweat.

"I'm very close," she said against Mazzi's breast.

"Then let go." Mazzi bent down and pressed her lips to Dorothy's hair. "Find yourself in that release."

Dorothy's lip brushed the inner curve of Mazzi's breast as she pinched her clitoris between two fingers, lifting up off the mattress as she climaxed with a series of low, stifled grunts. She sagged forward and Mazzi continued stroking her hair, holding Dorothy's head against her chest.

"Do you think you could make me finish so sufficiently?"

"I believe I could do it with just a handful of words."

"Why don't you put your money where your mouth is?"

Dorothy smiled up at her. "My money is not anywhere near where my mouth is going."

Mazzi yelped in surprise as Dorothy wrapped an arm around her and twisted, pinning her to the mattress with a ferocious growl.

True to their word, Beatrice's captors delivered her back to Threadneedle Street without further harm. She was hooded for the entire journey and placed in a different car for the final leg of their journey just in case anyone happened to see the car when it dropped her off. She was helped out of the car and the hood was removed. Before her eyes had a chance to adjust to the light, the car was already at the end of the street. It was an unnecessary level of security; she had been effectively dissuaded from continuing her search for the fourth elemental. Seeing Virago shaken had been enough to convince her that no good would come from the quest.

She let herself into the townhouse and started down the hall to the kitchen. She made it halfway before she paused. Her mind was full of what Virago had told them and questions about what would happen in the future. If the war was inevitable, just how horrible would it end up being even if magic was used? She put her hand against the stairs and turned toward the parlor. Those questions could wait until another time, for now she had more pressing concerns.

Despite her distraction, she could tell something was amiss in the house. She opened the parlor door and looked inside. The curtains were drawn and everything seemed to be in order. Normally if she and Dorothy were going to be gone for a decent stretch of time, they put the house together before leaving. Beatrice hadn't had the opportunity to do that before being drawn out by Virago. Books were still lying out on the table. A teacup was forgotten on the end table.

The floor creaked. She couldn't see anything but she lashed out blindly and closed her hand around the unmistakable soft column of someone's upper arm. She heard a yelp and used it to identify the face, swinging her body around and punching the intruder square in what she hoped was the nose. She misjudged the invisible person's height and cut her knuckle on a tooth, hissing as she pressed her unseen adversary against the wall.

"Ivy Sever," she said, "my least favorite member of the Mnemosyne Society."

"Careful, Sek. You're gonna make me feel bad about coming all this way to check on you."

"I don't need you checking up on me."

"Tell that to Dorothy Boone." There was a smear of pinkish blood where Ivy's mouth would have been, bright enough to see but fading as it was exposed to the air. "She tried getting in touch with you, but there was no response. Was like you vanished into thin air. She was concerned for you. I did the decent thing and volunteered to come make sure everything was okay."

Beatrice said, "And when you found the house empty, you decided to see what treasures you might abscond with."

"Never! Okay. I may have taken some biscuits from the kitchen, and I did make some tea. Then I heard you sneaking around--"

"Sneaking around? This is my home!" The blood had faded completely. Beatrice found it difficult to carry on a conversation without a focal point. She felt as if she was arguing with the wallpaper pattern.

"A home you seemingly abandoned. You were supposed to be here recuperating. Dorothy was concerned. Rightfully so, it would seem. You look like you've been through the wringer."

Beatrice released Ivy's arm and shoved away from her. "Big talk from someone who isn't even showing her face."

"I hardly have a choice." She followed Beatrice out of the parlor. "I can report back that you're in one piece, but you know Boone's going to ask where you were and why you didn't respond to any of her attempts to contact you. She must have been desperate if she brought me in."

"That's putting it mildly."

"So? I get nothing?"

Beatrice filled a glass with water. "I'll contact her myself. I don't need you acting as a go-between and I know Lady Boone didn't intend for you to make yourself at home. Kindly go back to wherever it is you call home."

"Fine. But you owe me one."

"You did nothing to merit a favor." She turned around and scanned the room, realizing something about Ivy's invisibility. "Oh, god. Are you nude?"

Ivy chuckled but otherwise didn't answer.

Beatrice groaned and rolled her eyes. "Just get out."

She heard footsteps in the hall followed by the opening and closing of the front door. She finished her water before she went to confirm the invisible assassin had indeed left the house. She did regret worrying Dorothy and she would do everything in her power to make amends, but first she would have to come up with a story to explain her absence.

CHAPTER SEVENTEEN

Dorothy woke to find the bed empty, so she dressed and went downstairs. Trafalgar was seated at a table near a window, dressed in a beautiful orange and white gown. She was engrossed in the papyrus they'd retrieved from Amenemhat's tomb, using her left hand to keep her place as she translated into a notebook with her right hand. She looked up as Dorothy joined her and nodded her head in greeting before going back to work.

"That dress is smashing."

"Thank you. Agnes loaned it to me. She said the color flatters me more than it would her."

Dorothy said, "She's not wrong. Have you seen Mazzi?"

Trafalgar looked up, a knowing glint in her eye. "Yes, she passed through not long ago. She looked... frazzled. But happy. She asked me to pass along her apologies. It seemed as if she thought you would expect to see her upon waking."

"Well, of course. We fucked."

Trafalgar raised an eyebrow. "There was a time when a comment like that thrown out so casually would have shocked me."

"That's why I said it. Have I lost my ability to scandalize you?"

"Poor Dorothy."

"Indeed. I shall have to find another reason to bed a woman in every port we visit."

"I'm certain you'll think of something."

Dorothy scanned the work Trafalgar had already done. "Making progress?"

"Very slowly, but yes. I've confirmed these are the Books of Breathing. My hope is that if we decipher the right spell, we can use it to force Amenemhat out of his body and put Desmond back where he belongs. Otherwise we run the risk of a situation where he's effectively holding himself hostage."

"And any damage he does to Desmond's body can be remedied by jumping to a new host."

Trafalgar shook her head. "I don't think he would be able to do that again without the spells or the ka statue. He was only able to do it with you because it was your body."

"Mm. Perhaps. Let's hope Desmond doesn't suffer any lingering effects. How are you feeling?"

Dorothy said, "I'm perfectly fine. Everything in working order. Mazzi checked thoroughly." She looked for evidence she'd gotten a rise out of Trafalgar, who betrayed nothing. "There is a bit of discomfort knowing that someone was using my body for so long without my knowledge or consent. A sense of violation, I suppose. But to that end, there's a distance to whatever happened on the boat. I'm a bit sore, which indicates there was some amount of fighting done. I have bruises and scrapes I cannot source." She held up her arm to reveal a long scrape on the underside near the elbow. "I don't know what I did or who it was done to. I'll likely never know."

"And you're content with that?"

"Is it ideal? No. But I'll come to terms with it in time. My interlude with Mazzi went a long way toward reclaiming this body as my own. When she touched me, when her lips trailed up the inside~"

Trafalgar said, "Enough!"

Dorothy slapped the table and laughed. "Ha! I knew you weren't as calm as you appeared."

Trafalgar sighed heavily. "You are infinitely immature."

"Gloriously so, and may I never grow up. But on a serious note... I nearly lost my life aboard the *Skylarker*. Even if there is some sort of afterlife - and I believe Amenemhat's very presence lends credence to that theory - then I must go to it without my body. The past few days I was given a very clear look at what that might be like. I think everyone takes for granted just how precious their 'self' is. I feel reborn, and I regret being so cavalier with my life and safety in the past."

"Ah, so you'll cease taking unnecessary risks?"

"Let's not get crazy," Dorothy smiled as she took a sip of her water.

Trafalgar said, "Before we left, Threnody asked me about the body-swapping process. I think the idea intrigued her. The chance to undo the damage caused to her face, to finally leave behind the mechanics and the masks. I felt horrible dashing her hopes, but that was when I thought the effects would be temporary. Maybe with the Books..."

"What? You can find someone willing to surrender their body?"

Trafalgar put down her pencil and massaged the crease it had left in her finger from writing so long. "Is it so unthinkable?"

"I suppose not. Denny brought up the same subject when we were alone."

"Really? What would he change... no, I'm sorry. It's not my place. But that does prove my point. I'm not sure you would understand."

Dorothy said, "Why not?"

"A white woman, born and raised in privilege..."

"Sapphic."

Trafalgar acknowledged that with a twist of her wrist. "Yes, but not openly or obviously. You've had hardships. I don't mean to imply your life has been endless ease. But as an African woman in London, I must say I can see the appeal of wearing someone else's body. We all have an inner idea of what we look like, how we sound, how we appear to others. Our actual appearances don't always reflect that. I'm sure there have been occasions when you wish you were stronger or faster or... well, to be frank, male."

Dorothy considered the statement. "Not permanently, no. I suppose that is privilege, to be content with the lot I've been given in life. Are you unhappy with who you are?"

"I love who I am. I'm proud of where I'm from. But I can understand someone wishing they were seen differently by the world. These spells might give them the means."

"At the cost of someone else's body."

"Perhaps a mutually-beneficial exchange could be worked out."

Dorothy shook her head. "We cannot allow ourselves to start down that road. Jumping from one body to another for strictly cosmetic reasons? It's far too dangerous to allow something like that to become the norm. And think of the criminal potential, as Agnes pointed out! A person commits a crime and, in a matter of hours, they could jump to a new body. It's our duty to ensure these Books never get into the wrong hands. That's been the purpose of my entire career. I'm not only protecting ancient people from being forgotten, I'm protecting the modern world from things which would harm it."

"You make an excellent point," Trafalgar said. "Once everyone is back in the proper bodies, we will see that the books are properly deal with. But that begs one final question. When all is said and done and we've successfully returned Desmond to his body, what happens to Amenemhat?"

"We return him to the ka statue."

"For eternity?"

"He managed for several hundred years, by choice, I should remind you. The fact he's conscious now is an aberration. He should have died two thousand years ago. We won't be condemning him to anything by reversing the spell. We shall merely be setting things right."

Trafalgar sighed. "I find it a difficult decision, that's all. He's a person, living and breathing and aware. Sending him back to that prison seems cruel. Brutal."

"The other alternative is allowing him to live out his days in a body which doesn't belong to him, condemning an innocent soul to the statue. Amenemhat's prison is one of his own making. What's happening right now is just a brief respite from what he chose as an afterlife. He's not supposed to be alive in the here and now, as evidence by the fact he's only here by forcibly taking over the bodies of others."

"If at all possible," Trafalgar said, "we should try to convince him to go of his own accord. If nothing else, it will lessen the chances of causing injury to Desmond's body."

"That we can agree on." Dorothy sat up straighter and looked around. "I think I shall investigate to see if I can find anything to eat. All the fornicating with Mazzi has worked up a hunger."

Trafalgar sighed heavily. "If you're merely saying these things to get a reaction from me, I will simply learn to hide it better."

"But it gives me such joy."

Dorothy winked as she left the table. Trafalgar shook her head, picked up her pen, and went back to her work. She would never have admitted it out loud, but she did consider Desmond far more expendable than she considered Dorothy. He was the only person in the entire ordeal who volunteered himself for the exchange. If their non-lethal weapons and careful reasoning didn't convince Amenemhat to surrender himself to the ka statue, she feared she would be willing to resort to more terminal options.

Amenemhat abandoned the vehicle, unsure if his foes had the ability to track it or not. He kept Henuttaui close to his chest as he moved through the marketplace, ignoring the merchants and other customers trying to get his attention. He was sweating under his shirt. His body felt uncomfortable and large, too thick across the chest and oddly heavy in the thighs. The man whose body he was currently using spent much time sitting, that much was clear, and the strain of running from where he'd left the car left him exhausted after only a few minutes.

He stopped and leaned against a stone wall to catch his breath. He unwrapped the top of the ka statue held across his arms like a child and gazed into its painted eyes. It looked nothing like her, but it was almost as if he could feel her inside the carving. He pressed the pad of his thumb against the cheek and stroked it. He could imagine the feel of her skin, the slickness of her sweat and the way she shuddered when he touched her.

"Soon, my love. Very soon you shall feel the sunlight on your face, you will breathe the air once more. I vowed it so long ago, and death will not prevent me from keeping that promise."

He bent down and pressed a kiss to each of the upraised hands on the statue's head, then wrapped it up once more. He scanned the street and let his gaze pass over the crowd in search of anyone who looked like they might be searching for him. He spotted a white face in the crowd, an older man with a crown of curly white hair and black-rimmed glasses. The woman with him was also white, and looked vaguely familiar to him. His memory was jumbled after leaping out of Boone and into this new body. Everything that happened to him in London and aboard the *Bessemer* seemed like a rapidly-fading dream.

Before he could remember where he'd seen her, the man locked eyes with him. He brought his hand up to point, but Amenemhat was already running.

"Stop that man!"

The Keepings, he remembered, Leonard and Agnes. His new host knew them as well, and he'd seen the woman in the tavern. They had obviously pursued him just as Boone and Trafalgar had. How many blasted allies did this woman have? How many would he have to kill just to live in peace?

He kept the ka statue cradled close to his chest and dug in the pockets of Desmond's jacket for anything he could use against his pursuers. He found coins and folded money, a key, and a small set of small black stones. Their outer texture was rough and they had a peculiar odor to them. He hoped they might cause the Keepings to slip and fall, or perhaps one of the shoppers he shoved past would slip on them and cause a blockade. He twisted at the waist and let the balls fall.

The marketplace was too loud to hear them hit the ground, but the results were apparent even without looking over his shoulder. People shrieked, some cried out in surprise, and then he caught a whiff of sulfur wafting on the breeze. When he reached the corner he stopped and looked back. Leonard Keeping had stopped to lend aid to someone who was bent over and hacking, but Agnes had a rag wrapped around the lower half of her face and was still in pursuit. She was almost close enough to reach out and grab him.

He spun to face her, bending his knees slightly. She slammed into him and he twisted at the waist, his arms hooked under hers, and lifted her off the ground. Agnes grabbed his hair with both hands and he cried out as she pulled him down with her, both of them tumbling end-over-end. Agnes hit the ground first and shoved him to one side. He rolled and she ended up on top of him, using her leg as a kickstand to prevent further rolling. She sat up and placed her hand on the flat of his chest, holding him down.

"Amenemhat, I presume? Trafalgar told us you might look differently from the last time I saw you."

Their positions meant that Amenemhat didn't have enough leverage to sit up, her arm like a pike on his sternum. Instead he grabbed her wrist with one hand while smacking her just below her elbow with Henuttaui's statue. There was a small risk of breaking it, but the stone was exceptionally strong and her arm was under strain. Her arm bent in a gruesomely unnatural way and her face twisted into an anguished shriek behind the mask she was still wearing. Amenemhat shoved her off and got back to his feet. Agnes clutched her broken arm, too pained to continue her pursuit. He spotted a dark alleyway between two buildings and darted into it, jumping over a crate and sidestepping a puddle of some unidentified liquid on his way to a side street. He ducked into another alley, and then another, only stopping when he was positive the Keepings had been left far behind.

Desmond Tindall was unaccustomed to this amount of activity, and Amenemhat collapsed against the pale yellow brick wall, his hands shaking as he tugged at the collar of his shirt. It felt very constricting even though it wasn't buttoned. His heart was thudding against his ribs and the world spun around him. He didn't remember sitting down but eventually realized he was slumped against the wall, legs out in front of him, struggling to focus on anything.

He closed his eyes and let the sun pound down on him, making him sweat even as it dried the sweat on his cheeks and forehead. He tightened his grip on the ka statue, grateful he'd been able to keep hold of it. A shadow crossed over him and he squinted one eye open, half-expecting to find a vulture circling. Instead he saw a suspicious woman wearing a dark blue abaya and a *niqābi*. The veil left her eyes exposed, which was enough for him to determine she was considering whether he was worth the effort to step over.

"American?"

He nearly told her the truth and said he was Egyptian like her, but he knew his coloring would prevent her from believing him. "British. I just need a little water."

The woman seemed to sneer behind the brown cloth

concealing the lower half of her face. She looked over her shoulder, then in the other direction, either to determine if anyone would see her helping a British man or to see if there was anyone else to help him before he perished. Finally she sighed and held out a hand to him.

"Come with me."

He let her help him up, wavering a bit before finding his balance. She waited until he was steady and then led him inside. Once they were indoors she removed the veil by lifting it off one ear and letting it hang loosely from the other, letting it brush her cheek like a lock of hair.

"I am Ruby," she said.

"Amenemhat."

She looked over her shoulder at him. "That is a British name, is it?"

He scolded himself for the mistake. "Boone. Desmond... ah, Desmond Boone." He knew that was wrong as well, but his mind was too frazzled to correct himself again. They were in her kitchen, a cramped room that was barely large enough for a table. He lowered himself into one of the two chairs as she filled a glass and handed it to him.

"Why are you collapsing on my doorstep, Desmond Boone?"

"I was... being chased. Assaulted."

She snorted and looked away. "British. You're surprised? Or maybe it was because you stole something? What is that you're holding?"

"It's mine," he growled, glaring up at her in case she tried to take it from him.

"Hmph." She cocked a hip and watched him carefully. "Who do I have to worry about chasing you? Police? Grave robbers?"

He shook his head. "Neither, I assure you. My pursuers were dealt with. I was merely ensuring they could not pick up my trail. I underestimated my stamina and the heat."

"That could have been a deadly mistake."

It undeniably could have been. It made him curious what might happen if he had died. Would Trafalgar and Boone have found the body? Would they have been able to use the Books to return Desmond... Desmond... whatever his last name is to his proper self? What consequences would there be, placing a consciousness into a corpse?

Ruby snapped her fingers, startling him. "You looked like you were fading away. Almost dropped your treasure there."

He looked down to see the statue had almost slipped off his lap. He corrected that, lifting it and carefully placing it on the table. The cloth he'd used to swaddle it fell away to reveal its face.

"Is that a ka statue?" Ruby asked.

"You know of them?"

Ruby nodded and picked it up. Amenemhat reached to stop her, but she was too quick. She examined it carefully. She turned her head one way, then the other.

"It looks real," she said. "I've seen many fakes for the tourists. They are gaudy and ornate, but this looks like something an actual artisan may have crafted." She ran her eyes down the length of the statue and held it up to the light. "There's a carving on the base."

Amenemhat became very still. If she read the spell aloud, his beloved would be standing in front of him. Her lips moved to the shape of the words, but she gave up before making it through even one phrase. She put the statue down.

"You could probably fool someone with that for a lot of money."

"It is not for sale. And I am not a thief."

"Not many innocent men nearly kill themselves running away from something."

He ignored the comment and pulled the statue closer. "If it would be all right, I would like to remain here for a while. To recuperate from my run."

Ruby's expression revealed she didn't believe him, but she still nodded. "You will remain in this room. Drink as you need. Touch nothing but the glass without permission."

"As you wish."

She turned and went into the next room. Amenemhat watched her go. He doubted he could convince her to speak the words required to free Henuttaui from her imprisonment, but she would make a fine enough temporary host. She was, at the very least, worth the effort of trying.

CHAPTER EIGHTEEN

Dorothy leaned across the table to see the character Trafalgar was pointing at, but she couldn't come up with a translation off the top of her head. She was rubbish when it came to logographic languages. She was much more comfortable with words that meant other words. Languages like Italian, Mazzi's tongue. She'd said some very interesting things that Dorothy would love to have translated, if only she knew anyone who wouldn't blush repeating it. She chewed on her thumbnail as she considered asking Mazzi for a few lessons.

"Good lord!"

Dorothy jumped at Trafalgar's outburst, turning in the chair to see what had caused such a reaction. Leonard Keeping had just entered with an arm around Agnes' waist, even though she was clearly telling him she could walk under her own power. Her right arm was encased in plaster. Dorothy leapt up and went to them, placing a hand on Agnes' shoulder.

"What on earth happened to you?"

"Amenemhat," Leonard said. "We spotted him in the marketplace. It was... bizarre to see a friendly face looking so hostile. Although I'm sure Agnes felt the same way when Amenemhat used your body to attack her in London. Lovely to see you're... yourself again, by the way."

Dorothy said, "Lovely to be myself. Here, Agnes, sit... sit."

"I'm not an invalid. It's just my arm." Trafalgar handed her a glass of water as she sat down, and Agnes thanked her quietly before taking a drink. "He assaulted us with some foul-smelling pellets which exploded on impact."

Trafalgar said, "Threnody gave those to us. I suppose we can report back that they're effective."

"Very much so," Agnes said. "I managed to catch up with him, but the bloody bastard broke my arm. Fortunately there was a doctor in the crowd who rushed me to his clinic so he could put this on." She lifted her cast and wiggled her fingers.

Leonard said, "The crowd saw a man assaulting a woman several years his senior, so it wasn't difficult to organize a search party~"

"'Several years'?" Agnes muttered at her husband.

"~to scour the area for him. But he must have found some shelter."

Dorothy said, "I hate to say this, but Desmond doesn't have the constitution for long bursts of physical activity. He couldn't have gotten very far."

"That area is like a maze," Leonard said. "He could have ducked into any number of empty buildings or shops."

"It's a pity Beatrice isn't here," Trafalgar said. "There might be more arcane means she could employ to track down our quarry."

Dorothy said, "That reminds me. I wanted to try getting in touch with her again. She wouldn't go this long without contact. Hopefully Ivy Sever has news." She put a hand on Agnes' shoulder again. "I hope you'll forgive me for the part I played in this injury, Agnes."

Agnes smiled. "You would do the same for me. Now go. Give Beatrice my love."

"I will. And any expenses you've made on this journey will be completely taken care of when we get back, I assure you."

"All a part of membership in the Mnemosyne Society," Leonard said. "Think ahead to months or years from now when Agnes and I enlist you in some quest. How would you respond if we offered to reimburse you?"

Dorothy sighed. "I would say that the adventure was worth the expense. But you still have my gratitude, both of you. And if you require any assistance while you're recuperating, you know where to find me."

"Indeed I do. Now go! Beatrice must be anxiously awaiting your summons." Dorothy nodded and departed for the front desk. Agnes watched her go and then turned to Trafalgar. "How has she been? Any ill effects?"

Trafalgar shook her head, an indication of reservations rather than negativity. "It's hard to be certain. She seems like the Lady Boone we've all come to enjoy, but I can tell the experience is more harrowing than she wishes to admit. We've been working on the Books of Breathing translations and I've been using it as a pretense to test her memory and cognition. She occasionally has difficulty shifting from one topic to the next. I'll ask her a question when she's in the midst of translating something and it takes her a moment to catch up. I'm not even sure she's aware it's happening."

Leonard said, "She's been through quite a singular ordeal, one which put tremendous strain on her mentally and physically. We may never know how extensive the damage was, or what the long-term effects might be. She may need a few solid nights of rest to be herself again. Or it might be years before we see the full ramifications of having her consciousness passed around like bad penny."

Trafalgar said, "The only thing we can be sure of is that there are no experts in this sort of affliction. There are no symptoms to watch for, no physician who can examine her for clues. We shall simply have to keep our eyes on her for the time being."

"Agreed," Leonard said.

Dorothy returned a minute or so later looking much relieved. "Ivy sent a telegram. Beatrice has returned home, safe and sound but looking 'weathered,' whatever that might mean. I thought of calling her directly, but I don't want to disturb her if she's actually resting."

Trafalgar said, "That's splendid news, Dorothy. I'm glad she's safe."

"I am a bit curious where she might have been, but that can wait. For now I can put my mind to ease about her and focus on Amenemhat."

"I am of the opinion that nothing should change," Trafalgar said. "We would be squandering our time hunting him, exhausting ourselves in the heat while he rested and relaxed in whatever spider hole he's taken as his shelter. We should remain here and continue working on the Books. They are the only weapon against him we can count on."

Leonard nodded. "Well said. I agree with Miss Trafalgar."

Agnes said, "So long as I can get in a few licks once he shows up. I owe him a broken bone or two, just to even the score."

Leonard said, "I'll stay out of your way when the time comes, love."

Dorothy looked at Trafalgar and gestured at the table where they'd been working. "Shall we?"

"After you, Lady Boone."

Amenemhat wandered Ruby's kitchen, examining the cabinets as he pondered his next move. She had a staggering amount of food; bread, butter, cabbage, cheese, flour, and cornmeal. He found a tin of sardines in olive oil, one of which he ate but found unbearably salty. Fruit and meat in such quantities were normally reserved for the elites. He had seen pharaohs buried with smaller stores than what Ruby had socked away in her small home.

She returned to find him examining a bag of navy beans. She had changed into a lighter robe, her hair now uncovered and the veil gone.

"Are you hungry? I could perhaps make you a small something to eat."

"Is it not scandalous for you to entertain a man in your home?"

Ruby opened a cabinet and withdrew a pan. "I have better things to do than worry about what people think about me." She stood in front of the oven. "What about you? Are you ready to tell me exactly who I'm harboring in my home?"

"There are people hunting me. My beloved, she needs my help. My foes wish to prevent me from doing what must be done to save her life."

"Why would they do such a thing?"

"They do not care about her life. They believe she deserved to be lost forever."

Ruby frowned at him. "They sound beastly."

"You have no idea the lengths to which they have already gone to stop me."

"What can be done to help?"

Amenemhat thought before answering. He hadn't considered the possibility of an ally, especially not one with access to benefits of the modern world. If Trafalgar and Boone could bring an army, then he should at least make use of a lieutenant.

"Do you have access to transport?"

"I can get a car if that is what you need. Where do you think I'll be taking you?"

"I must get to Thebes."

She stared at him for a long moment and then said, "Do you mean Luxor? That's over six hundred kilometers!"

"Please. It is vital. Unless... does anything of the ancient city remain?"

Ruby said, "In Luxor? The entire city is basically a ruin. Everywhere you look, there is a temple."

Hopefully that meant there was a chance of finding one of Amun's temples. Performing the ritual there would not only bless his endeavor, it would eliminate the need for the Books. The power of his god would be enough to lock Henuttaui into a new host. He could even secure his place in Desmond Tindall's body at the same time. He tapped his fingers on the table and stood up. Ruby backed away from him but didn't retreat. She was strong, brave. She was also beautiful and Egyptian. He had resigned himself to finding a Caucasian host, but perhaps everything would work out. Perhaps Amun was still smiling on him after so much time.

"Please, Ruby. If I can get to Thebes... o-or Luxor, you called it? If I can get there, my beloved will be saved." And best of all, he neglected to add, Trafalgar and Boone would be unaware of his plan. He would leave them hundreds of kilometers behind thinking he was still coming after the Books. By the time they figured out the truth it would be too late for them to do anything but surrender.

Ruby said, "What's her name? Your beloved."

"Hen... ah..." He realized he could not give her true name, but he hadn't thought of anything to say instead. Fortunately, Ruby saved him.

"Hannah. It's a good name. For Hannah, I will see what I can do."

He smiled and gripped her upper arms, perhaps harder

than necessary, but he couldn't contain himself. "Thank you, Ruby. You have saved both of our lives."

Dorothy's mind wandered. She was no stranger to a short attention span, but now she couldn't help but wonder if it was due to the translation work or if it was a deeper affliction. Had something gone awry during one of her 'swaps'? When she went from herself into the statue, or from the statue to Desmond, or from Desmond back to herself? That was a long distance for a soul to travel, and it stood to reason not all of it survived the journey. Were there pieces of her left in the statue? Did shreds of Amenemhat survive in her psyche, waiting to reveal themselves?

"Dorothy."

She looked up, looked down at her pen, then shook her head. "I apologize. Was I tapping the pen on the table again?"

"On the contrary. I don't think you've moved in the past five minutes. Why don't you go upstairs to rest?"

"We're on a bit of a timetable."

"And you've been through an extraordinary trauma. In fact, having your mind ripped out of your body not once but thrice is more alarming than whatever concussion Beatrice may have suffered. Go upstairs, get some rest, and let me work on this. When you wake up, you can take over while I rest. It's one of the benefits of working with a partner."

Dorothy put down her pen. "Are you sure you don't need my help?"

Trafalgar's smile was patronizing. "I would hardly classify what you're doing here as 'helpful.' I would much prefer a rested Dorothy in a few hours to what you are right now."

"Very well. If you insist on insulting me."

"I do."

Dorothy stuck her tongue out and stood.

"If Mazzi comes by, I'll be sure to send her up."

"I thought you wanted me rested."

"There are many kinds of rest," Trafalgar said.

Dorothy chuckled. "Good luck with the Books."

"Sleep well."

Ruby had no idea what she was doing, or what had possessed her to agree to such madness. It was over six hundred kilometers to Luxor with a crazed British man who seemed barely coherent at the best of times and dangerously erratic the rest of the time. There was something not right about his eyes, the way he spoke, the way he moved. She watched him from the corner of her eye while she'd cooked him a meal and observed myriad peculiarities. He stared at the icebox and oven as if he'd never seen them before. He poked and probed the bread like an alien being presented with something new and strange. And sometimes he would just stare at his hands. She'd even seen him touching his face in a way that suggested he wasn't sure what he looked like.

She'd heard of people losing their memory, but why not admit the truth if that was the case? Surely pity would be better than suspicion.

Of course maybe she was wrong, because despite her suspicions she was trying to help him. There was no chance her car would make the trip to Luxor and back, even if she was willing to make the drive. Hamid owned a bus, but she doubted he would loan it to her even if she explained why she needed it. And how could she? She could barely explain it to herself. He would call her mad, and rightfully so. Perhaps she should just find a revolutionary and tell them about the strange British man hiding in her home. They would deal with the problem for her.

But then she remembered Osman. She had seen his life fade, the blood seeping into his shirt from the horrible wound in his throat. She would have given anything to bring him back, to save him, even if it meant taking the bullet herself. If Desmond Boone had a chance of saving his beloved with her help, then she couldn't bring herself to deny him.

There was still the small matter of practicality. She prided herself on her imagination, making every *nekla* count when buying groceries and finding ways to wash her clothes without paying for water. She doubted there was any hope of finding safe, quick transport to the town Desmond wanted to visit. Perhaps she wouldn't have to follow-through after all. If she went back and told him it was simply impossible, he would have to understand. And her conscience would be clear.

She didn't know if she was pleased or distressed when she spotted the opportunity sitting on a service road just outside of town. She tried to ignore it, but the sun kept catching the metal and glinting in her eye as if one of those dead, ancient gods was trying to send her a hint.

Finally, as night was falling, she surrendered and drove to where the impossibly convenient machine was waiting. She got out of her car and found the pilot, explaining the situation to the best of her ability. She mentioned the strange British man, his quest to save a lover who was in danger, the foes he claimed were around every corner, and the queer little statue which never strayed far from his reach.

When she finished, she clutched her hands together in front of her and watched the pilot's face carefully. "Well?" she asked. "Is there any chance you can help?"

Isidora Mazzi smiled as she scanned the horizon, one hand fisted on her hip as she rested the other on the side of her plane. "I believe there's something I can do to help you," she said, "but first I need to speak with some friends of mine."

Chapter Nineteen

Dorothy's head was pillowed by her hands, though she definitely was not asleep. She had gotten upstairs to discover the Keepings asleep in her bed. She remembered offering them use of her room and went back down, now completely concerned about the potential damage to her memory. Sitting down again, she had put her head down on the table and went through everything she thought she should know. The names of her parents and brothers, the rooms of the house in which she'd grown up, the name of her loyal kitten. Her grandmother. She listed as many of her quests as she could recall, as close to chronologically as she could muster.

So while it may have looked like she was asleep, she would have adamantly denied that fact. She was not the sort to simply doze while there was work to be done. And yet, when she blinked open her eyes to find Mazzi standing over her, the pilot's body language indicated she'd been there for quite some time. Trafalgar had also put down her pen and was in the process of packing everything up.

Dorothy sat up straight and flattened her hands where her head had just been. "Hello."

"I think you drifted off," Mazzi said.

Dorothy shook her head. "No, I was awake."

"Of course you were," Trafalgar said. "So you heard Mazzi

telling me... telling *us*... that her plane was hired to fly Amenemhat to Luxor."

Dorothy looked at Mazzi. "He contacted you?"

Mazzi shook her head. "I was approached by a woman named Ruby. Initially I believed she was the, ah, the woman. You said there was a woman your enemy was trying to revive..."

"Henuttaui," Trafalgar said.

"Right. But she seemed like a normal person. I think she is just, ah, someone who is trying to help. From what she told me, she believed Amenemhat is a British man named Desmond who is attempting to escape his enemies. She implored me to help. She said it was a matter of love."

Dorothy said, "So either Henuttaui is a master manipulator, or she's an innocent. What's our plan?"

"I told her I had another client going out tonight, so I couldn't take her before tomorrow morning. My baby can get you there in four hours if I push her. Then four hours back here to pick up Amenemhat."

"Your plane handle that kind of exertion?

Mazzi shrugged. "We're going to find out. This trip has been the best trial I could have hoped to give the old bird. I'm willing to give it a chance."

"Then so am I," Dorothy said. "Although I wonder if we might save ourselves some time and simply wait until morning and ambush him at the plane. We know he will be there."

Trafalgar said, "And we know he will most likely be with this Ruby woman. If we make a move against him, he could use her as a hostage. And once he's aboard the plane, we'd have no hope of getting to Luxor before he did. This gives us the opportunity to corner him in a place where he'll have no escape. We covered all of this while you were listening intently with your eyes closed. I'm shocked you don't remember."

"Shush," Dorothy said. Of course this Ruby woman made an ambush untenable. She should never have brought up the possibility. God, how badly damaged was her mind? "We'll have to leave immediately. And it doesn't give you much chance to sleep."

"I slept this afternoon." She winked at Dorothy and stood up, pushing her chair back under the table with the side of her foot. "Let me just grab something to eat while we're in the air and we'll be off."

Dorothy said, "I do wish Denny was here. If everything works out in our favor, we may not have cause to come back to Cairo, and I would like to say goodbye to him before we left."

Trafalgar sighed. "Okay, we can no longer even pretend you were awake. Denny is here. I required a few references and he was kind enough to bring them by from the library. There's a little restaurant next door and he said he was going to have dinner. That's where Mazzi is going right now."

"Oh. I'll..."

"Go. I can wait. But here..." She opened her bag and handed two large books to her. "Return these to him."

Dorothy jogged to catch up with Mazzi, who led her to the restaurant. Denny was sitting alone near the counter, leaning away from the food on his plate to read the book he had lying open on the table. He looked up when Dorothy entered and smiled brightly. He waved her over and marked his place in the book with a ribbon.

"I'm almost finished eating. Otherwise I would ask you to join me."

"That's all right, I'm not staying." She sat across from him. "Trafalgar wanted me to return these, with her thanks. We're about to leave for Luxor, and I don't know if we'll be returning to Cairo before going home. If that is the case, I wanted to say goodbye to you. It's been an extraordinary pleasure meeting you, Mr. Razek. What we shared was... extraordinarily unique, which might sound a bit repetitive, but it deserves to be said twice. I never thought I would experience anything like that. You gave me an experience that cannot be duplicated."

He pushed his glasses up with the knuckle of one finger. "Well... thank you very much, Lady Boone, but I should be thanking you. I've never been so bold as I was with you. I felt safe from ridicule or shame because of how you reacted to... to who I am. I appreciated that so much. And what happened between us in the tomb? As marvelous as that was, it was second to your attitude. I don't know if you understood what that meant to me." He held his hand across the table. "I hope we get to work together again one day."

Dorothy shook his hand. "Barring that, I hope we get to spend any time together, be it business or personal. You're a valuable asset, Denny Razek, and a person I would like to get to know better. And perhaps next time I shall give you and Desmond a proper introduction."

He chuckled. "Be well, Lady Boone. Good luck with your foe."

She stood and went to where Mazzi was waiting for her food.

Amenemhat stared into the eyes of Henuttaui's statue. Ruby had gone to bed, reluctantly trusting him to behave himself in her home. There was nothing for him to steal and there was no benefit in harming her. She was the only one who knew where to find the pilot with whom she'd made her arrangements. His only chance of getting to Luxor was Ruby's continued well-being, which turned him from potentially dangerous into a sort of guardian. He planned to stay awake the entire night. He doubted he could relax enough to sleep, and he didn't want to give Desmond Tindall's lingering subconscious a chance to assert itself in dreams.

He thought back to memories of his own life to strengthen the hold on his mind. Searing days when the sun seemed to be impossible to avoid, nights when the chill was almost unbearable even when bundled in every sheet he could find. But even on those coldest nights he'd found warmth when his beloved would come to him. He remembered the night he told her they'd been discovered. His heart was pounding in his chest, fear gripping him in its icy talons as she placed his head against her chest and told him everything would be fine.

"I will find a way for us to be together," he swore to her then, "either in this life or the next."

Henuttaui wept when she cupped his face. "Do not make me wait too long, my love."

There were tears in his eyes now, shame at taking so long to fulfill his promise and joy at being so close to his reward. He stood and walked to the window to look outside, wishing they were underway at that very moment. Ruby assured him that waiting until morning would get them to Luxor much faster than if they traveled by car. He couldn't help but feel like time was slipping through their fingers. Another few hours, another day. How long would he have to wait?

Meanwhile, Trafalgar and Boone were out there somewhere. Were they coming for him? Were they destroying the Books of Breathing? No. They would never do that while he was still occupying their friend. He reached up and touched his face. At the moment, Desmond Tindall was his hostage and his insurance. So long as he wore their friend's face, they would pull their punches. That would be their ultimate downfall.

Leola was waiting for them at the plane. Trafalgar smiled as she approached and pulled her old friend into a hug. "I was afraid I would not get a chance to say goodbye."

"I had the same fear. I knew your schedule may not allow it, but Mazzi told me you were setting off tonight and I had the time to wait." She squeezed Trafalgar tightly. "I could not have this life without your assistance. Everything you showed me in our travels, the opportunities you afforded me, the education I gained without even knowing I was learning. I'll be forever grateful to you, Trafalgar."

"I've not had many friends, so I treasure the ones I do have. No matter how far away they might move. You're my family, Leola. Thank you for everything you've done for me."

Mazzi and Dorothy had been giving them space for their farewell and now moved closer. Dorothy was already wearing her leather flight cap and goggles, lifting her chin to tighten the strap along her jawline. She hugged Leola as well, thanking her for everything she'd done for them since their arrival in Egypt. "Our mission would have been utterly impossible without you. Thank you."

"I apologize for all the times I got in your way before you and Trafalgar became allies."

Dorothy laughed. "Don't be. You provided me with a challenge. That's something that is always welcome. But I will admit that I'm grateful we're now on the same side."

Leola winked at her and wished Mazzi luck on her flight.

"Everyone aboard who is going aboard. Next stop, Luxor! Four hours from now."

"Is that speed truly safe?" Dorothy asked as she climbed the side of the ship.

"Perfectly!" Mazzi assured her.

Dorothy had been seated in the center for their flight out since, being male, she'd been the heaviest of the three. Now Trafalgar had the weight advantage, so she was in the center.

Dorothy was quietly grateful for that; even in the dark she didn't trust herself to ignore the distraction of Mazzi's neck. Not now that she was intimate in its taste and how it felt against her lips...

Mazzi settled into the cockpit. "And if it's not, I'll feel a shimmy in the hull long before it becomes an insurmountable problem. I can adjust enough to keep her in the air if that happens."

"And if there's a catastrophic failure for which you cannot correct?" Trafalgar asked.

"I'm confident there will be places between here and there that aren't a barren wasteland. Might be a bit difficult to find them in the dark, but don't worry. I'll do my best not to strand us in the desert."

Dorothy said, "Confident but not certain...? You *have* been to Luxor before, haven't you?"

Mazzi laughed. "I've never been to Egypt before! But I have a map."

Trafalgar twisted in her seat to look at Dorothy, who shrugged and made sure the harness holding her to the seat was snug. Leola backed away from the plane as Mazzi started up the engines. She looked back to make sure they were snapped in.

"You ladies ready?"

"As we'll ever be," Trafalgar said.

"Good enough for me!"

The plane lurched and Dorothy gripped the edge of her seat. She didn't know much about the future of aviation, but there was one advancement she knew had to be right around the corner. The skies would belong to the first person who included enclosed compartments on their planes. She squeezed her eyes shut and ignored the wind on her face as the plane lifted off the road into the pitch black night.

Chapter Twenty

Beatrice tried to sleep but found she couldn't. She tried going to sleep in Dorothy's bed but even the familiar blankets and lingering scent of Dorothy's perfume couldn't calm her mind. The lingering effects of her concussion were completely healed, and she couldn't help but wonder if her resurrection had something to do with it. She tried putting everything out of her mind, the way their captor ordered, but there was just too much weighing on her to completely erase it all. She pressed her face into the pillow, eyes squeezed tightly closed, but her mind refused to slow down. It conjured up memories of Dorothy. The taste of her, the smells, the way her lips moved when she dreamed.

It was close to three in the morning when she gave up. She went into the bathroom and took off her pajamas, laying them over the rack next to Dorothy's tub. Dorothy liked to consider herself a modern woman, but she was very influenced by her grandmother's Victorian tastes. The four-poster bed, the claw-footed tub, and the full-length mirror positioned next to the sink. Beatrice had seen herself in that mirror a great many times, both alone and with Dorothy on those glorious occasions they bathed together.

Now she angled the mirror and turned her back to it. She twisted her head so she could see the tattoo drawn onto her back. It was a tree with the trunk stretching from just below her shoulder blades down to just above her ass. The bare branches spread like skeletal fingers across her shoulders. If she let her hair grow long, it looked like the tree had sprouted leaves, but she usually tried to keep it at a more manageable length.

There was no evidence of the damage she'd sustained in the crash. She remembered the pain, though. She would never forget that horrible and sharp sensation. She'd known she was dead. There was no doubt in her mind that there would be no recovering. Now she was back and she was alive. She was in a room she thought she would never see again. There was a row of creams and lotions lined up next to the small vanity and she picked up one bottle at random. She unscrewed it and smelled the contents.

Dorothy on a sunny day, eyes shaded by the wide brim of a hat, standing on the banks of the Thames. She had been wearing a blouse with large shoulders and long sleeves. She'd been wearing gloves and, when she slipped them off for the walk home, her palm had felt slightly clammy. Beatrice had waited until she was certain no one was paying attention to them and brought the hand up to kiss the knuckles.

Lying on the field in Wales, she'd resigned herself to never seeing Dorothy again. Never touching her, never hearing her voice. Now, thanks to Ivy Sever, she knew Dorothy was back in the right body again. All she had to do was finish the business with Amenemhat so she could come home and be properly reunited. She wished she had gone with her, concussion be damned. Dorothy needed her. Trafalgar needed her.

At the very least, staying behind had proven to her that the quest to find the other elementals was better left forgotten. She'd wasted too much time and neglected her duties as Dorothy's majordomo. She could move on from trying to discover her past. If Virago's vision was to be trusted, that way only led to death and destruction. If it meant saving the world, she could live with her ignorance.

But still... she wondered. She drew energy to her, feeling it seep through the air and gather around her fingers like a static charge. She could see the pale blue glow in the mirror as the power continued to grow. She rolled her shoulders and took a slow, steady breath. She gathered more power to herself, holding her arms out to either side and curling her hands up as if she was trying to catch rain. The tingling moved up through her arms and she watched as the ink in her tattoo began glowing. It was a pale color at first but steadily became brighter.

It was harder to breathe now, but she continued drawing power. Her arms were shaking. Her chest was constricted but she still managed to inhale and exhale. Shallow breaths and sweat on her upper lip. Her entire body was trembling now, but the tattoo was bright enough to light the entire room. People could likely see it from the street, an unnatural azure shine coming from the upper floor of the peculiar townhouse tucked among financial institutions of Threadneedle Street.

"Burn," she whispered. The skin around the tattoo stung. "Burn," she said again, baring her teeth as she focused her energy on the design. The tattoo seemed alive in the mirror now, the reflection of her body harder to see as the tree seemed deeper, sharper. Now she could feel the pain deeper inside, like swallowing some hot liquid and feeling it burn all the way down. Pain blossomed inside of her but still she pushed. She wanted to burn the ink away, wanted to be done with the elemental inside of her. She felt something wet on her lip and knew her nose was bleeding, but she wasn't concerned until she felt the same moisture on her cheeks.

She released her hold on the magic and let it spill from her. The effect was almost as painful as holding onto it, and she screamed as her body seemed to be engulfed in flame. The walls and floor shook violently and only then did she realized she'd been hovering a few centimeters off the ground. She put one hand out against the wall to catch herself as she collapsed, but she still must have lost consciousness for a brief time. Her next memory was lying on the floor, blood crusted on her face, and pushed herself up with shaky arms. She wet a washcloth and cleaned away the blood, still trembling and trying to catch her breath.

So it would seem she couldn't force the power out of herself. She couldn't explore its origins to make peace with what she was. So what the hell was she supposed to do?

Her introspection was shattered by the sound of something on the ground floor. She closed her eyes and slumped against the basin. Three intruders in the past week.

Dorothy would have her hide when she found out what a pisspoor job she'd been doing of watching over the place. She grumbled and got to her feet, passing through Dorothy's bedroom to grab a dress shirt before she went to investigate.

Virago was standing in the front hall, the door standing open behind her. She wore a black cloak with the hood up to cover her face, but there was enough visible to confirm it was her.

Beatrice grimaced as she descended the stairs. "I thought you agreed to cease your quest for the other elementals."

"I did. But I spent the entire trip home thinking. And I could not shake those images... those horrors he showed to me."

She brought her hand up to her temple. Beatrice was on the same level with her now and could see her skin was ashen, revealing dark shadows under her eyes. It had only been a few hours; the trauma must have been tremendous to have such marked physical effects so quickly. She stunk vaguely of smoke, as if she had just stubbed out a cigar on the front stoop. Virago raised her eyes to meet Beatrice's gaze.

"So why are you here?"

"I can't... be certain that I've fully conveyed the horrors I've seen."

"Trust me," Beatrice said, "you got your point across very well. You don't have to worry about me following any further leads."

Virago said, "But that isn't enough. Your word isn't enough. As I said before our abduction, we have been drawn to each other for our entire lives. You and I encountered each other purely by accident. Who is to say that won't happen again? One of Lady Boone's quests takes her to Kildare and you encounter Lasair? What if the air elemental happens to be there when you arrive? We cannot take the risk."

Beatrice narrowed her gaze. "What have you done?"

"I've just come from Kildare," Virago said. "You would be surprised at how quickly you can douse an eternal flame if you use enough water. She burned... so brightly. But when she ran out of oxygen she finally had no choice but to surrender."

"You killed her."

"For the sake of the world. And when I'm finished, I will seclude myself until our successors come of age and I will extinguish them as well. I do wish there was another way, Beatrice. I've come to respect you quite a lot in our short acquaintance." She brought her hands up and flicked her fingers.

Beatrice opened her mouth to respond but water poured out over her lips. She brought her hand up to try catching the flow, but there was too much of it. She gagged and coughed, choking on it. She backed away from Virago, who followed her and flicked her fingers again. More water filled Beatrice's mouth. She couldn't draw breath, couldn't do anything but try to swallow as much as possible, but it was like trying to drink the ocean.

"It will be quick," Virago said dispassionately. "Just like going to sleep."

Beatrice remembered holding energy just a few moments earlier, how it felt like her lungs were going to be squeezed into raisins. She pulled that energy back and let it flow up her arms, over her shoulders and into her throat. She opened her mouth as wide as she could and expelled it like dragon's breath, forcing out whatever Virago was using to manifest the water on her tongue back at her. Virago was weakened by exhaustion and easily knocked off her feet, stumbling back into the staircase she had pinned Beatrice to during her first visit.

"You're not thinking clearly." She wiped the back of her hand across her mouth. "We've never been the best of friends, but I don't want you to suffer."

"Then don't fight back when I stuff you full of the Thames."

Beatrice braced for the blow but was still unprepared for the strength behind it. She was lifted off her feet and carried through the window, arms up to protect her face from the shattered glass. Instinct saved her by putting up a cushion of energy between her and the ground. It gave her something to bounce gently off of and she rolled onto her hands and knees as Virago stalked out of the house. Her nose was bleeding, her eyes red with bloody tears. She held her hands out to the side, the fingers wrapped in a web of crackling energy.

"All of your friends," she said, "will die if we are allowed to survive. I'm only doing this to save them. Don't be blind."

"You're not going to stop, are you?"

"When you and the other elemental are dead, I will go

into hiding until the others come of age. The void must not be allowed to happen."

Beatrice closed her eyes. Virago was an evil woman, a terrorist, a murderer many times over, but she still wished there was another way. She planted her hands on the street and summoned energy up through the stone. She reached deep into the bedrock, the very frame of the planet, and drew it to her. She was an earth elemental, and she could access more of it than the average practitioner. Beatrice opened her eyes to see Virago pulling back for another magical blow.

"I'm sorry."

Two columns of stone erupted from the street and twisted around Virago's body. Beatrice bared her teeth and twisted her hands. The rocky snakes mimicked her movements and twined themselves around Virago until she was unable to move. Only her head was exposed when Beatrice was finished.

"You can't keep me trapped like this forever."

"I don't intend to. I am so very sorry, Virago. It's not in my nature to murder anyone if I can avoid it, but you've made it very clear you will not be dissuaded. This is the only way to stop you."

Beatrice closed her hand into a fist. Virago's eyes widened in surprise and pain as the stone compressed and shattered her bones. She coughed up blood, head lolling to one side as Beatrice continued squeezing. The space her body occupied within the twisted stone became even smaller. Beatrice was trembling as she brought up her other hand, closed it around the fist, and sent a second wave of magical energy into the trap. Beatrice's skin was slick with sweat, her feet planted far apart to brace herself as she put her hand on top of her fist and pushed down.

The stone was crushed, flattened back into the street and taking the remnants of Virago's corpse down with it. She stood up, her knees threatening to buckle, and she was very aware of the fact she was naked save for a sloppily-buttoned blouse. She looked in either direction for evidence anyone was seeing her scandalous display or had witnessed her brutal murder, but the street was blessedly empty at this hour. She took a moment to steady her breathing and walked back into the house.

She would have to see about getting the window fixed before Dorothy got back from Egypt. But for the time being she would cover it with a shield of energy and work on a more permanent solution later. The only thing she could even consider doing now was finding somewhere soft to stretch out and fall asleep for the rest of the night.

CHAPTER TWENTY-ONE

Dorothy tilted to look over the side of the plane as they approached Luxor, watching the massive spread of ruins pass by underneath them. Mazzi found a place to land near the Precinct of Amun-Re, the place Trafalgar deemed to be where Amenemhat was most likely to visit first. "The sacred lake," she explained once they were on the ground. "Priests used the water to purify themselves before performing any rituals in the temple. Given everything he's been through since he was last in the presence of his god, there's no chance he'll skip this part."

"Jumping through multiple bodies, living in a statue for thousands of years," Dorothy mused. "Yes, I do believe I'd want to wash up after that as well." She turned and extended her hand to Mazzi. "Isidora, I also believe this entire endeavor would be ending much differently without your assistance. Thank you for everything you've done for us, and for the marathon flight on which you're embarking."

Mazzi shook Dorothy's hand. "Happy to do my part, ladies. You take care of each other. Get your pal's body back. I'm mighty glad Agnes introduced us."

"As am I."

Mazzi looked at the timepiece on her instrument panel. "I'll do my best to be lazy on the flight back, but I don't want him getting suspicious. I will fly over the temple so you'll have warning when he's nearby. Try to listen for me and stay out of sight after dawn."

"We will. Normally I'd say godspeed, but in this case, I'll settle for safe travels."

"And to you, now and in the future." Mazzi touched two fingers to her brow and saluted. "Look me up next time you need to go a long way in a hurry. I'll be there."

Dorothy said, "And if I don't need to go anywhere, but I still wish to... arrive...?"

Mazzi's grin became wicked. "Then definitely call me, ginger."

Dorothy stepped away from the plane and watched as Mazzi began taxiing. She would skip over to the nearest airfield - probably the airship docks on the banks of the Nile - to fuel up before going back to Giza for the second leg of her journey. Trafalgar waved goodbye as the plane lifted off again. She picked up the bag with her books and slung the strap across her shoulder as Dorothy did the same. They started walking toward the temple ruins.

When the buzz of the plane's engine faded and left only the night's silence behind, Trafalgar looked at Dorothy. "The woman seems absolutely smitten with you."

"I have that effect on women."

"Hm. Has that ever become an issue? Anyone who didn't quite adhere to your casual view on relationships?"

Dorothy said, "There have been a few who needed to be let down easy. But for the most part, the women I spend time with aren't looking for a relationship. How would that even be possible? We take what we're allowed... fleeting encounters and a brief reassurance that we're not always as alone as we feel."

"Hm. A bit more bleak than I expected when I posed the question."

"Sorry."

"No, I appreciate the honesty."

Dorothy said, "You'll get nothing else from me, if I can help it."

"You can expect the same."

Dorothy stopped and looked ahead. The moonlight was strong enough for them to see the pylons standing on either side of the entrance. The statues were positively massive; Trafalgar was completely dwarfed by them, one of the few times Dorothy could say she'd ever thought of her friend as looking small. The walls still looked remarkably intact, with only a handful of mud bricks broken or scattered around in the sand. Compared to the relative mediocrity of the Sphinx, Dorothy couldn't help but be impressed.

"Now *this* is more like it. Apparently the artisans of Thebes knew how to build a temple."

"Artisans...?" Trafalgar said.

Dorothy said, "Ah. Yes. The, ah..."

Trafalgar touched her arm. "Don't fret about it. Come on. It's a long flight but we'll be working in the dark. I'm certain Amenemhat will be here before we know it. No sense in wasting time."

"Agreed. Lead on."

Dorothy adjusted the strap on her shoulder and followed Trafalgar up the steps into the temple. "Have you given more thought to the plan?"

"I did little else on the flight. It's not as if we had much of a view. When Amenemhat arrives, we'll separate him from the woman he's traveling with. We must keep her safe at all cost. As far as we know, she's an innocent in all of this."

"Agreed." They stopped inside the walls in an avenue flanked on either side by stone sphinxes. Ahead they could see immense stone columns which rivaled the heights of buildings in London. "This is spectacular. It's almost a shame this has all been thoroughly catalogued. I would love to spend a weekend simply exploring here. How old do you suppose those columns are?"

"Roughly two decades."

Dorothy frowned. "What?"

"Ground water caused a collapse just before the turn of the century. Eleven of them fell like dominoes. Georges Legrain supervised their reconstruction." She swept her torch across the space. "Currently they're working to reinforce the rest so it won't happen again in the future."

"When we return home, you're telling me everything you know about these ruins."

"Everything? That could take a very long time."

Dorothy shrugged. "I'm sure we'll have many long nights

to fill if you're going to be moving in."

Trafalgar aimed her light at Dorothy's face. "Is that an official invitation?"

Dorothy held up her hand to block the light. "Oy, how many invitations do you need? Miss Trafalgar, I have a spare room. I would be overjoyed if you filled it with your things and slept there on a regular basis. We work together often enough and spend enough hours brainstorming that it's a waste of your time to keep trekking back across the river to your home. And while I should consider you as just another member of the Mnemosyne Society, you are in fact its co-founder, and I would be lost without you. Please. Move in."

"Very well," Trafalgar said. "I'll consider it."

"Oh, for bloody—"

Trafalgar snickered and faced forward again. "We pass through this hall, then move south into the first court. The sacred lake is just beyond there. We'll set up and look for opportunities to lay a trap for Amenemhat when he arrives."

Dorothy reached into her pack and touched the ka statue, confirming it was still safely tucked away. She had to keep reminding herself that Desmond was actually inside it, his essence or soul or whatever it was that made him who he was. She would have a hard time believing it was even possible if it hadn't happened to her. She didn't remember anything from her time inside the statue, a prison from which Desmond had thankfully freed her, but she'd definitely been somewhere while Amenemhat was occupying her body.

Up ahead, Trafalgar paused to examine the columns before she went right. Dorothy followed.

"Can I make a confession?"

"Is now the proper time?"

"We have all night. I'd rather not spend it entirely silent."

Trafalgar said, "True."

"My grasp of Egyptian history is... sketchy at best. I know the general details, and I can translate if I have enough resources, but when it comes to the finer details, like the location of this temple, I'm a novice. When you asked for my help with the ka statue, I was honored. And I felt... superior. It was wrong of me. I should have acknowledged that this is your area of expertise."

Trafalgar looked back at her. "I'm surprised to hear you

admit inadequacy so freely."

"I wouldn't do it with just anyone. Our partnership is about strengthening one another's weaknesses. We can't do that if we keep them secret."

"Logical." She started walking again.

Dorothy moved to walk beside her. "So...?"

"So?"

"Your weaknesses...?"

"Oh. Hm... I don't like dogs."

Dorothy rolled her eyes. "That's hardly comparable."

"Well, it's a weakness."

"I'll try to keep it in mind for future reference."

They arrived at the sacred lake. The night sky was reflected in the still water, and Dorothy stood for a moment to take in the size it. She had expected a small, ornamental basin but this truly did earn the title of 'lake.' Dorothy shook her head at the monumental scope of the temple.

"This is unbelievable. It's the size of a full city!"

Trafalgar said, "The ancient Egyptians weren't exactly known for their subtlety." She slipped the bag from her shoulder and sat it down. "We have a lot of space here. The size will give us plenty of options for concealment."

"It also gives him a lot of options for entry points. It won't do us much good if we're concealed here and he enters from the north."

Trafalgar said, "Mm. You have a point. If Beatrice was here, we could at least cover three of the potential entrances. But I suspect he would enter the same way we did. He has no reason to suspect anyone will be here waiting for him, and he'll be inclined to enter through the main gate out of reverence for the grounds."

Dorothy said, "You do seem to be in your element here."

"I enjoy Egyptology. That's probably why Leola sent me the ka statue in the first place."

Dorothy took off her jacket, draping it across a nearby stone so she could roll up her sleeves. "If I could make a suggestion...?"

Trafalgar nodded. "Of course."

"Abandon this hobby before she sends us anything else."

Trafalgar chuckled under her breath and set about preparing for Amenemhat's arrival.

They set up near the main entrance, with Dorothy to the north and Trafalgar at the south. They would wait for Amenemhat to enter, then cut off his exit. If he did enter from one of the other access points, they could easily conceal themselves behind plinths and columns until they were behind him. Dorothy assumed he would enter the pool alone, leaving his hostage at the top of the stone steps leading down to the water. That would also give them the high ground. Trafalgar believed she could recite the correct passage from the Books of Breathing before Amenemhat could ascend the steps, which meant he would be safely back inside the statue while Desmond was returned to his body. Dorothy had the strobe gun Threnody gave them, with which she could hopefully paralyze their foe long enough for the spell to take effect.

The hostage would be safe and their foe vanquished without a fight. It was the ideal solution, so Dorothy was confident there would be any number of wrenches thrown into the plan.

Once everything was ready, Dorothy figured they still had two hours until Mazzi returned. They used their packs and jackets to create padding against the stone walls and settled in to get a little rest. Dorothy stretched her feet out in front of her and looked up at the night sky. She'd agreed to take the first shift listening for the plane, but Trafalgar was still fidgeting enough that she knew she was still awake.

Finally she said, "Is there something on your mind?"

"Yes, actually. Say everything goes well. Desmond is safely returned to his body, and the spirits are returned to the statues. What happens then?"

"We go home." She realized what Trafalgar was asking. "But you mean to say what happens with the statues containing two human spirits."

Trafalgar nodded. "We discussed it already, but we didn't come to a satisfactory conclusion. And I can't think of an attractive option. Either we store them somewhere in your archives, in which case we've essentially imprisoned them, or we destroy the statues which feels like cold-blooded murder. It's not as if they can defend themselves."

Dorothy considered the question carefully before she answered. "I still believe destroying the statue would be the only proper course of action. Speaking as someone who very recently was stuck inside one of them, if anything happened to my body, I would prefer to simply be released to whatever is supposed to come after."

"So you believe in the afterlife?"

"Of course. After all of this, how can you not? You saw someone else in my body, and you saw me in Desmond's. That's proof we aren't just random consciousness inhabiting meaty bodies. There's something that makes us who we are. That must go somewhere when we die, otherwise Amenemhat wouldn't be able to transfer it into the statue where it survived for all these centuries. Amenemhat and Henuttaui should have passed on back then. Destroying the statues wouldn't be killing them. They were killed long before either of us were born. There *is* a third alternative. We allow them to inhabit someone's body. Find someone who is suicidal, perhaps, or a patient who is unlikely to recover from their illness."

Trafalgar said, "Hardly ideal."

"Mm. I wouldn't have wanted that. If Beatrice could create a golem or Threnody could construct some sort of automaton, it would still be a horrifying and unnatural extension of life."

"And Agnes' fear of a despot gaining the ability," Trafalgar said. "The charter of the Mnemosyne Society. To protect the ancient world from modern society..."

"And protect modern society from the ancient world." Dorothy drew her legs up and rested her arms across her knees. "I'm not sure we're doing a very good job of it."

Trafalgar said, "I disagree. I believe Amenemhat would eventually have been awoken no matter what we did. Whether it was fate or happenstance that it occurred now, and that you were the one whose body was stolen, we can't be sure. But imagine how terrible it would have been if Leola read the words. Amenemhat would have awoken Henuttaui by stealing someone else's body and we would have no idea it even happened. Even though the event was certainly traumatic for you, I'm grateful it happened now, in this manner."

Dorothy said, "And I'm grateful it happened in the presence of the Society. They're certainly coming together as a team. There's certainly no one else I would have wanted as my saviors."

"Mm-hmm." Trafalgar rested her head against the pillar.

"Rest. I'll wake you in an hour or so."

Trafalgar's eyes snapped open. "You're the one who should rest."

"I slept on the plane." Cat-napped, really. "You were squeezed into the seat again. Now that you can stretch out comfortably, you should take advantage of it."

Trafalgar nodded, eyes already closed. Dorothy crossed her arms over her chest against the cold of the night and tilted her head back to continue watching the stars. She had no intention of waking Trafalgar; she deserved the rest after spending so much time on the translations. Besides, Dorothy really was still coming to terms with the time she'd spent in the statue. It was hardly any time at all, especially compared to how long Desmond had spent in it, but she was reluctant to abandon consciousness when there was so much to appreciate happening overhead.

Chapter Twenty-Two

Trafalgar was understandably irritated when she woke and discovered it was already dawn, but she couldn't be too angry about getting some rest. They were going through Dorothy's pack in search of a suitable breakfast when they heard the engine of Mazzi's plane coming in from the north. They took cover in a position that allowed them to see the *Valkyrie* when it passed over the ruins. Mazzi dipped the wings, starboard and then port, before she cut to the east.

"Here we go," Dorothy said.

Trafalgar nodded.

They didn't know where Mazzi would land or how long it would take Amenemhat to get from that point to the temple, but time was short. They made sure to eliminate any signs of their presence from view and positioned themselves where they wouldn't be seen from the main entrance. Dorothy had checked the strobe gun in the night, just to ensure the weapon worked, and just seeing the beam of it hurt her eyes. She couldn't imagine being targeted by the thing. She checked to make sure it was on, then held it against her thigh and settled in to wait.

Amenemhat's attempts to stay awake and therefore prevent any of Desmond's memories from creeping in as dreams had failed. The only thing that kept him awake on the airplane was sheer terror at what he was experiencing. Ruby and the pilot both seemed completely at ease with the prospect of rising into the air and flying hundreds of kilometers in a metal canister which was barely large enough to fit all three of them. He tried not to look over the edge at the terrain, or at the horizon which was changing much too rapidly for his tastes.

He had to focus. He gripped the ka statue with both hands; it hadn't left his sight all day. He could almost hear Henuttaui calling to him from within the stone. He watched the back of the pilot's head. She seemed wary of him, suspicious. There was something in the clipped way she spoke that made him feel as if she knew who he really was. But no. That was just his paranoia creeping in. He was sweating more than the temperature could account for; he was starting to believe that Desmond... Desmond... Tin-something... that the body was rejecting him. Perhaps playing vessel to two alien essences was too many for one body to cope with. It was no matter. He didn't care what happened to Desmond Boone... Desmond... T-Tindall's... body when he was finished with it.

The pilot twisted to look at him, then pointed down. He risked a glance and, despite a lurch of fear when he saw how far away the ground was, he was also thrilled to see his temple. The glorious Precinct of Amun-Re of the Karnak Temple. It was surrounded by modernity, blocks of city streets clustered around the ancient site, but the Nile still ran sure and strong alongside. And despite the obvious decay, he could see the temple was still revered.

"They remember you, Lord," he whispered, though the wind caught his words as soon as they passed his lips. He settled back in his seat and closed his eyes.

If Amun was remembered, then his spells would work. He just needed faith. He began muttering the words under his breath as the pilot began her descent.

Dorothy had a crimson scarf wrapped around the lower half of her face, knowing that if she didn't, the stone dust swirling through the temple ruins would cause her to sneeze at an inopportune moment. She was crouched by one of the columns with the strobe gun gripped in her hand. She would occasionally stand up to prevent her legs from falling asleep or cramping when their foe arrived. Trafalgar was several meters away behind another column, barely visible from Dorothy's position. She seemed to have found a comfortable position which didn't require frequent shifting.

"It sounded as if they landed nearby," Dorothy said. "So it shouldn't be much of a wait."

"Here's hoping."

It was close to twenty minutes before they heard movement in the forecourt. Their theory that he would use the main entrance had proven correct. They both retreated farther around their columns to be certain they were completely out of sight, but Dorothy craned her neck forward so she could see when Amenemhat entered. The woman hostage was first, of course. She was dressed casually in a white blouse and off-white slacks. She was wearing makeup, her hair was pinned out of her face, and she slowed down to scan the frescoes as she came though the doorway.

Dorothy was relieved to see she wasn't acting terrorized, but there was also the concern that she didn't understand how much danger she was in.

Amenemhat entered behind her. Dorothy thought her body was in rough shape after being possessed, but it was nothing compared to the treatment Desmond seemed to have faced. He looked pale and exhausted, bags under his eyes and hair unkempt. His skin shone with sweat that had darkened the collar of his shirt, which it appeared hadn't been changed since Dorothy was occupying the body.

She blinked at that thought. *What a peculiar life I lead.*

Amenemhat moved past the woman and nudged her to continue. "There will be plenty of time to gawk later, Ruby." He spoke with a thick accent that made him sound like a stranger. The woman, Ruby, walked behind him toward the sacred lake. Dorothy was frustrated that the hostage was now between her and Amenemhat, but that might make it easier to separate them. She looked to Trafalgar, who gave a nod, and they both stepped out from behind the columns. They fell into step behind Amenemhat and Ruby.

"I believe that's far enough, Priest," Dorothy said.

Amenemhat and Ruby both turned, both startled by the sudden command. His anger quickly turned to rage.

"You again? What sort of demon are you?"

"No demon," Dorothy said, "just a clever woman. Miss... Ruby, is it? Please step toward us. You've no idea how dangerous this man is."

Ruby looked between them and Amenemhat. "I've got some idea. But you, I don't know at all. For all I know, you're the people trying to keep him from saving the woman he loves."

Amenemhat said, "Yes! Yes, these women are attempting to stop me from saving Hannah."

Dorothy said, "What he's told you are lies. His name is Amenemhat, a High Priest from ancient Egypt whose spirit is inhabiting the body of my good friend, Desmond Tindall."

"He said his name was Desmond Boone."

"He was confused. I'm Boone. The Lady Dorothy Boone. This is Miss Trafalgar. We are simply trying to put things right."

Amenemhat said, "Ruby, this is madness."

"Then why are we standing in an ancient temple? What was the purpose of his visit here?"

Ruby hesitated. "He... he said there was... there was something he needed to do. In order to ensure his success."

Dorothy risked taking a step closer. "Ruby, I want you to think carefully about this. The man who brought you here is hijacking my friend's body. His stated mission is to rescue his beloved, who I can swear to you is also residing in a small, carved statue."

"The statue..." Ruby muttered, looking at the tightly-wrapped parcel in Amenemhat's hands.

"If you put those facts together, what do you believe he intends to do? Why would he bother bringing you all this way unless he had a use for you?"

Ruby now moved quickly toward Dorothy, looking at Amenemhat as if he'd sprouted horns. He didn't bother disguising his rage as he reached under his jacket and fished out a revolver.

"I only require one body, Lady Dorothy Boone!"

Trafalgar, Dorothy, and Ruby all moved at once. Ruby ducked, Trafalgar threw herself forward to grab the woman's hand to pull her out of the way, twisting so that she was between the erstwhile hostage and Amenemhat's weapon.

Dorothy turned sideways to present a smaller target as she brought up the strobe gun, aiming it at Amenemhat's face. He flinched and fired, the bullet going wide as he cried out in surprise. Trafalgar got Ruby to safety behind one of the columns and withdrew the ravdi fighting sticks Threnody had given to her.

"Get Desmond's statue!" Trafalgar said.

Dorothy ran to the bag as Trafalgar rushed Amenemhat. She grabbed his arm, twisting him so he couldn't stop Dorothy. He swung at her midsection, a blow she easily sidestepped as she brought the butt of her ravdi stick down on his temple. He dropped to one knee and threw his weight against her. Trafalgar wrapped her arms around his torso and lifted just enough for his feet to leave the ground, then let him go. He dropped hard and she put a knee in the middle of his back.

"Dorothy!"

"I have the statue!"

Trafalgar reached out for it, but Amenemhat bucked her off. He got back to his feet, grabbed the statue he'd dropped, and made a run for the pool. Trafalgar pursued with Dorothy right behind her. When she got close enough, Trafalgar could hear Amenemhat speaking the spell on the base of Henuttaui's statue and realized he intended to use her as a host. She threw herself at him, grabbed the collar of his shirt, and pulled him toward her. She clapped a hand over his mouth to stop him from speaking. He bit down on her ring finger hard enough to draw blood, and she cried out. Their legs tangled together and they began stumbling toward the sacred lake.

Dorothy saw what was happening but feared she was too far away to stop it. Amenemhat's foot hit the edge of the lake and he began to fall. His grip on Trafalgar's shoulder tightened and Dorothy could see that he intended to pull her down with him. She drew from reserves she didn't realize she had, hooked her hands under Trafalgar's arms, and twisted to the left. Their combined weight broke Amenemhat's hold. His fingers slipped off the material of Trafalgar's dress and he went over the edge with a final desperate flailing of his arms.

Dorothy hit the ground and Trafalgar landed hard on top of her. The wind was knocked from Dorothy's lungs and she alternated between coughs and gasping until Trafalgar pushed herself off.

"Thank you, Dorothy."

"It was my turn," Dorothy managed to croak, sitting up with a hand against her chest. The adrenaline had worn off and she realized what had happened. "Oh, good lord, no... Desmond."

She and Trafalgar got to their feet and ran to the edge of the sacred lake. Though it was clear what awaited them at the bottom of the stairs, they both descended in the hopes there was still a life to be saved. The body was sprawled on the stone, his back grotesquely bent over a stone. A creeping blossom of blood was spreading across his shirt. His eyes were open and staring blindly as Dorothy dropped to her knees next to him.

"Des... no, please..."

Trafalgar spotted Henuttaui's ka statue laying on the ground nearby, shattered into several pieces. She picked up the largest piece but it seemed clear to her that there was no hope for freeing the soul that had been trapped inside of it for so long. But that was hardly worth worrying about at the moment. Dorothy had one hand under Desmond's head, her fingers smeared red with his blood, and her other hand was touching his chest for signs of life.

"Dorothy..."

"No... it's... the statue. We can repair the damage to his body and put him back inside. The body is just broken. Amenemhat... he's... he died. He's gone. If we hurry, we can just fix him and put him right." She was sobbing openly now. "He can't die. He can't die for me. Not like this."

Trafalgar knelt and put a hand on Dorothy's shoulder. "I'm sorry."

"Don't say that. Don't say that as if this is over."

"Dorothy..."

"We'll think of something, Des," she whispered, still sobbing. "We'll figure something out."

Above them, Ruby had moved closer to the edge of the lake to see what had happened. She put a hand over her mouth when she saw Desmond's body. After a moment she turned, barely stifling a scream as she ran from the temple ruins.

CHAPTER TWENTY-THREE

It quickly became apparent that Dorothy was in shock, so Trafalgar took control of the situation. She escorted Dorothy back up the steps and sat her next to one of the columns. "Stay here," she said. "I'll take care of it. Just stay here." Dorothy drew her knees in close and covered her face with both hands. Trafalgar went back to Desmond's body. She took a knee beside him and rested a hand on his shoulder. She hadn't known Desmond very well, but she knew he was a good man. He cared deeply for Dorothy and did everything in his power to keep her safe. Their relationship was unusual, but Trafalgar often felt it was more meaningful than some true marriages she'd seen. They respected each other to a degree that seemed more than just friendship. They loved each other.

"I'm sorry, Desmond," she whispered. "You deserved much better than this, my friend."

It was nearly an hour later when Ruby returned with the local police. Trafalgar did her best to explain what happened without mentioning body-stealing ancient priests or ka statues. Ruby, for her part, remained silent. It was clear that she didn't want to become even deeper entrenched in whatever the hell was happening with these crazy people. The police did a cursory examination and determined the death was consistent with an accidental fall, so Dorothy and Trafalgar managed to avoid being taken into custody.

When an officer expressed concern for Dorothy's state, Trafalgar remembered their public story. "They were engaged to be married."

The man offered his condolences as Desmond's body was taken from the pit by their undertaker. Trafalgar crouched in front of Dorothy and put a hand on top of hers. Dorothy's gaze shifted from the random spot in the air and focused on her friend's face.

"We need to go."

"Desmond..."

"They have him."

"No. *Desmond...*"

Trafalgar realized she meant the ka statue. It was lying nearby, and Trafalgar picked it up and placed it in her bag. Desmond's consciousness was still inside the statue. Theoretically, it could be transferred to another body, but Trafalgar couldn't fathom the moral consequences of doing such a thing. She also recovered the fragments of Henuttaui's statue, just in case there was any power left in it. She went back to Dorothy and touched her hand.

"Come on, Dorothy. It's over."

Dorothy wiped the back of her hand across her cheeks and extended the other to Trafalgar. "Help me up."

Trafalgar also offered her shoulder, letting Dorothy lean on her as they exited the temple. Trafalgar was already plotting how they would get home. They would have to charter an airship if they intended to bring Desmond along with them, and she assumed he would have wanted to be buried in his home country. She would have Mazzi fly Ruby home and then they would return to London. She just hoped when the dust settled, there would be some way to salvage Dorothy's resolve.

Dorothy retreated to her stateroom aboard the airship and remained there for the majority of their flight. Trafalgar spent her time on the promenade. She read and watched the European countryside pass by below. She tried to make sense of the mission they'd just completed. They stopped Amenemhat and gained the Books of Breathing. It was a powerful set of spells judging from what she'd already translated, and keeping it out of the wrong hands was a victory. But no one had been searching for the Books. There were no rumors about them, no imminent threat of discovery. She felt that their reward, no matter how valuable, was miniscule compared to what it cost them.

She made sure the airship crew took food to Dorothy's room, and most days some of it actually disappeared. On the final day of their journey, when they passed over the coast of France, Trafalgar knocked on the door and let herself in. Dorothy was sitting cross-legged in the window seat, dressed in a lightweight cotton blouse and matching slacks. She was barefoot, no makeup, her hair unwashed. She looked much as she must have as a child, and Trafalgar was startled by the transformation. She said nothing, just moved a chair closer and took a seat.

"I've lost people before, of course," Dorothy finally said, as if beginning the conversation in the middle. "My brother. My grandmother. I've never dealt well with death, Trafalgar. And never someone..." She looked down at her hands. "I loved him. I loved him more than I ever bothered to say aloud. He was so kind and generous. He cared for me. He did everything in his power to protect me, and I got him killed."

Trafalgar said, "You had nothing to do with it."

"He should never have been there."

"It was his choice. To save your life."

Dorothy turned toward the window. The setting sun reflected off the tears caught in the corner of her eyes. "Fat load of good it did him..."

Trafalgar moved to sit across from Dorothy in the window. "He loved you, too. You know that. He knew the risks and accepted that he might not return from this adventure. In his eyes, the reward was worth the danger." She put her hand on Dorothy's. "You stopped Amenemhat. You prevented the Books of Breathing from falling into the wrong hands. He would consider that a worthwhile cause."

"I appreciate what you're trying to do. But I don't want to feel better. Not yet."

"Of course. I understand. I'll leave you to yourself." She stood and went to the door.

Dorothy said, "Trafalgar... were you the one telling the staff to send me food?"

"I was."

"Thank you."

Trafalgar said, "You're welcome. I'll come find you when we're preparing to land."

Dorothy nodded, already looking out the window again. Trafalgar closed the door quietly behind her as she left.

A few hours later, Dorothy joined Trafalgar at the gangway. Her hair was done, as was her makeup, and she'd changed into a more familiar blouse and pants combo. She ignored Trafalgar's look and explained, "I don't want Beatrice to fret over me, that's all."

"Of course. Very kind of you."

"I can't wait to see her again. To hold her." She worried her thumbnail. "Thank you again. For... for being there. Or rather for not being there. Someone else may have crowded me or forced me to talk when I wasn't ready. Thank you for giving me space."

"You're more than welcome, Dorothy. The truth is, Adeline was killed by a bullet intended for me. I didn't have the opportunity to mourn properly when it happened. I know how important Desmond was to you. I know you'll need time. It's my job as your partner to make it easy."

Dorothy nodded. The ship docked and they carried their bags out. Trafalgar had arranged for Desmond's body to be transferred to a funeral home so Dorothy wouldn't have to deal with it. She escorted Dorothy off the ship and summoned a cab to take them home. She supposed she would have to start thinking of the Threadneedle residence as home now. The London weather was a shock after spending so long in the desert, and Trafalgar found herself wishing for her leather duster. A few drops of rain fell onto the window of the cab and she smiled, realizing that it was without a doubt her home.

As they pulled away from the Rookery, Dorothy surprised her by sliding across the street and laying her head on her shoulder. "I'm glad you were there, Trafalgar. I was absolutely helpless after... hm. Thank you for taking care of everything. For taking care of me."

"You're more than welcome. I'm honored to call you my friend."

Beatrice came outside when the cab arrived. Dorothy looked up at her as she exited the car and her posture immediately corrected itself. A line of worry appeared between her eyebrows.

"Trix? What happened?"

Trafalgar had noticed nothing different about the majordomo - same starched uniform, same rigid posture - but her face shuddered at Dorothy's question. Her eyes darted toward Trafalgar and her shoulders sagged just a fraction.

"Nothing that can't wait. I got your telegram this morning. I'm so sorry."

Dorothy pressed her lips together in a firm line, nodded to acknowledge Beatrice's sympathy, and looked at the bags in the back of the cab. "Our bags..."

"I'll take care of them. You two have much to discuss, it would seem. Go on."

"Are you sure?"

Trafalgar nodded. "Go."

Dorothy put a hand on Trafalgar's bicep and squeezed before she went up the steps into Beatrice's embrace. Trafalgar unloaded the luggage and took it into the house, while Dorothy and Beatrice disappeared upstairs. She had no idea what trauma Beatrice was working through, but she knew that her presence would only get in the way of their healing. She stayed only long enough to change into something more casual and less sandblasted before she took the Books of Breathing and slipped out of the house.

She walked to the Inkwell and called the rest of the Mnemosyne Society to meet her there. The Keepings were still making their way home from Egypt, having elected to take a ship so Agnes could recuperate. Cecil arrived looking mostly healed from his encounter with Amenemhat. When everyone had arrived - including Ivy Sever, wearing her costume and mask so everyone could see her - Trafalgar explained what had happened in Luxor.

"Dorothy will understandably need some time to process her loss. In the meantime, it's up to us to decide what will be done with these."

She had placed the Books of Breathing and remaining ka statue on the table, and now every eye was drawn to the stone holding Desmond's spirit.

Abraham said, "Desmond's really... in that?"

"What remains of him, yes. You saw as clearly as I did,

there is some sort of transfer that takes place. The woman who attacked you in this very room was not Dorothy Boone. The man I traveled to Egypt with was. I won't pretend to understand it, but now we're presented with the problem of... well, of how to proceed. Desmond has no body but he still exists. He could continue his life... albeit with one rather major caveat. The question is whether we have the right."

Cora said, "Do we have the right not to? Desmond understood the risk, but if there's a chance to at least let him know what happened..."

Cecil said, "So someone lets Des borrow their body, we tell him 'sorry, mate, you took a tumble and now you're dead, so kindly give Abraham his body back so we can off ya nice and proper'?"

"Why is it my body?"

Cora rolled her eyes. "It was just an example, Abe. Leave the man alone." To Trafalgar, she said, "He brings up a good point. It would be like waking him up to let him know he was about to die in his sleep. The man's body is gone, turned to ash and ready to be spread."

Ivy said, "So we just leave him in the statue? Or break the statue so no one can free him?"

Trafalgar said, "I examined the Books on our return voyage. I believe I can free the spirit to whatever is coming next."

"I believe that would be the kindest course of action," Cora said. "As much as I would like the opportunity to say goodbye to Desmond, and as I'm sure Dorothy would appreciate the chance, it would be the kindest thing for him."

"The most important thing," Abraham said, "is ensuring the Books are kept safe and secret. Can you imagine this getting into the hands of a king? Forget abdication, just leap into a new body and keep things going indefinitely."

"We should burn them," Ivy said.

Cecil said, "Well, that's a bit drastic."

"None of you are planning to use it, are you?" Ivy asked.

Trafalgar raised an eyebrow at the invisible woman. "You're not planning to use it? Forgive me, but given your current state..."

"I've come to terms with it," Ivy said. "Gotten very used to it. To be honest, I'd be miserable if I knew people could see me all the time. Things like this don't stay buried for long. People are going to find out what it can do and they're going to come after it."

Cecil said, "It's a historical artifact. Who are we to say the world doesn't deserve to have it?"

"We're the Mnemosyne Society," Trafalgar said. "The people gathering in this room are the best of the best at what we do. No one person should be trusted with the decision, but I trust the combined intelligence in this room will be enough to arrive at the correct solution."

"Perhaps we should wait until we're all here," Cora said. "Dorothy and the Keepings deserve a vote."

"Doesn't matter if we have a consensus right now." Cecil stood up. "I say we destroy it. Nothing good can come from something that powerful. Look at what happened to Desmond. Someone finds the spells and suddenly everyone else in the world just becomes a new suit of clothes to put on. Coppers would never be able to catch anyone."

Cora said, "We can't be hasty. This is a valuable historical document. Perhaps we separate the pieces... each of us keeps a portion so no single spell is complete."

Trafalgar shook her head. "I believe that would still be too tempting. Either for a thief, or for one of us. If I were to come down with a fatal illness, or if Abraham lost a limb during one of his adventures."

"Why am I always the example?"

"If Dorothy lost a limb." Trafalgar rolled her eyes. "The temptation to make ourselves whole again might be too much to resist. We are only human. When I say we can't allow this to fall into the wrong hands, that includes our own."

Cora clucked her tongue. "It seems a shame. All that power..."

"You know what's been said about power," Ivy said.

"Mm," Cora agreed, nodding her head. "Then I vote for its destruction."

Abraham and Cecil agreed, as did Cora and Ivy.

Trafalgar said, "Then it's settled. The Books will be destroyed. But we will wait for Dorothy to do it herself." She looked at the ka statue. "She needs to make the decision for herself. We can't take away her only opportunity to free Desmond."

Cecil said, "You're positive she'll come to the same decision we did?"

The question was posed to Trafalgar, but it was Cora who answered. "She will. It's the right thing to do, it's what she would want in his place, and it's the only moral option. It's going to break her heart, but she'll do it." She looked at Trafalgar. "Where is she now?"

"Home. Resting."

Cora nodded. "I'll come by and see her in a few days."

"She would like that." Trafalgar picked up the statue. "In the meantime, I'll find somewhere to keep this safe."

She looked at the statue, its crude lines and gaudy paint job. It felt like normal stone, but her experiences in the past week convinced her that Desmond Tindall was somehow trapped within.

"I'm sorry, Desmond. Truly I am."

She didn't know what else to say, what else could be done. There was no justice to be had, because Amenemhat died with Desmond's body. There were no promises to be made because their only option was to destroy the statue, which was a death sentence for him. All she could do was apologize and hope that he'd truly made peace before he offered to trade places with Dorothy.

CHAPTER TWENTY-FOUR

Dorothy and Beatrice drew a bath for each other, dividing the work so neither of them acted subservient to the other. Beatrice got the water to the right temperature while Dorothy laid out the towels and lotions. The time she'd spent in the desert plus the neglect from the time Amenemhat had spent occupying her body made her crave the utmost pampering. When the bath was ready, she and Beatrice settled at opposite ends of the tub. Dorothy massaged Beatrice's feet and Beatrice shaved Dorothy's legs. As she worked, she explained everything about the past few days, which led to her divulging her entire quest to find the other elementals.

Dorothy listened with growing alarm, but she didn't rise up out of the water until Beatrice admitted to killing Virago. "Here? In the street below?"

Beatrice nodded. "It was possibly the most brutal thing I've ever done. Since then, whenever I try to sleep, I see her face."

"Understandable." She considered for a moment and then said, "Did I ever tell you the moment I discovered my grandmother was a killer?"

"No."

"I was still living at home with my parents. I must have been... I don't recall, ten or eleven. I came home and found

Grandmother sitting at our kitchen table. She had a glass of my father's whiskey in front of her. I'd never seen a woman drink something so powerful, and she just threw it back like milk. No one else was home and I was always happy to see her, but there was something different about this visit. She warned me not to tell anyone she was there. She had blood on her clothes. I took her into the basement and helped her clean up. She told me she'd encountered a bad man who wanted to hurt many people. Though she wasn't in physical danger, she had the strength to stand for those who were weaker.

"You have great power, Beatrice. Your magic makes you a force to be reckoned with. There are people in this world with similar power who would use it against people who can't fight back. What you did was necessary. What we do is necessary." Her voice trailed off and she looked down at the razor on the edge of the bath. There was just a small ribbon of blood on its keen edge, a hint of evidence where Beatrice's fingers slipped. "No matter how much it hurts us, we must use our power - whether it be magic or intelligence - to protect the world. The nightmares and the sadness are just the price we must pay."

Beatrice leaned forward and brushed her hand across Dorothy's cheek. "When the time comes... when do what must be done for Desmond... if you need me to do it for you..."

"No. It's something I must do for myself. But thank you."

She closed the distance between them and kissed Beatrice's lips. Beatrice turned her head, using her tongue to tease Dorothy's mouth open a little wider, her hand moving under the water to slide higher up the inside length of Dorothy's thigh. Their combined moan echoed off the tile and porcelain, and Dorothy let her hands move to Beatrice's chest, teasing the nipples as she lifted her hips up to press against Beatrice's wandering fingers.

"Tell me I'm a good person."

Dorothy moved her lips to the shell of Beatrice's ear. "If you move your middle finger in a circular fashion, I will begin a religion in your name."

"I'm serious."

"So am I." She kissed back down to the corner of Beatrice's lips. "Finish me off, Trix... I'm close." She closed her eyes and relaxed her body, cheek-to-cheek with the woman she loved, and exhaled slowly. She held on to Beatrice and moved higher on her lap. Beatrice adjusted the position of her arms and cupped her hand against the hair between Dorothy's legs.

"Were you with someone else?"

"Yes," Dorothy's word was a breathless exhale. "She was inexperienced. Curious and... eager... Tentative at first. So slow." She sighed. "She used her tongue and fingers. I taught her things. I taught her... how to please another woman. And she was so clever when she gained her confidence."

Beatrice kissed Dorothy's neck. "Say nice things about me now."

Dorothy swallowed, eyes still closed. "You came into my life as a thief. You stayed because you felt you owed me a debt for saving your life, which means you cherish life. You know it's something valuable, and you wouldn't take it from anyone without cause. Beatrice, you are not just a good person, you are a person I trust implicitly. If you tell me that you killed Virago because you had no choice, I would carve it in stone." She flickered her tongue against Beatrice's mouth, initiating another kiss as she climaxed. When they parted, Dorothy brushed a stray curl away from Beatrice's face. "Hell. If you said you had to kill *me* because you'd exhausted all other options, I might be tempted to hand you a knife and show you my throat."

"I love you, Dorothy."

"And I, you. Come on... we'll be much more comfortable finishing this in bed."

They got out of the tub and toweled each other off before retiring. Dorothy spent a long while teasing Beatrice before letting her orgasm. Beatrice slapped a hand against the headboard, dug her heels into the mattress, and growled Dorothy's name with such ferocity that, for a moment, she was afraid she'd injured her. She looked up, gently brushed the pad of her thumb across her bottom lip, and carefully watched Beatrice's face for signs of more pain than pleasure. When her features relaxed, Dorothy slid up her body and rested her cheek against the smooth skin between Beatrice's breasts.

"You are a good person, Beatrice Sek. Don't let anyone tell you differently. Not even yourself."

"The same goes for you."

"Whatever needs to be done with Desmond... whatever is decided... I know that I must be the one to do it. But I need you there."

Beatrice kissed the top of Dorothy's head. "Of course, my love."

Dorothy let the tension evaporate from her muscles, her arms around Beatrice, and felt sleep begin to take her. Though she feared the dreams that awaited her on the other side, she didn't fight when it finally took her.

Desmond's remains were cremated and returned to Dorothy, who placed them on her desk as she made arrangements. A week after the Keepings returned from Egypt, the entire Mnemosyne Society gathered for drinks at the Inkwell in Desmond's honor. Those who knew him best shared stories for the benefit of those who didn't, though Dorothy balked at leaving out some of the best details simply because it would require telling everyone about his sexuality. Not every member of the society was aware of their unique relationship. Some of them thought she was mourning a lover, not a friend, and that made it difficult for her to gauge the appropriate response to their condolences.

The following morning, they boarded a train to Newcastle, and from there they would take cars to the small coastal town of South Shields. Desmond had been born there and once mentioned it was where he would like to be laid to rest. Dorothy held the urn for the entire trip, gazing out the window at the countryside passing them by. Beatrice sat beside her with Trafalgar across the aisle, and both knew Dorothy well enough not to attempt any conversation. Trafalgar had a copy of the Books open on her lap so she could prepare for the ceremony.

Beatrice drove one car, Leonard drove the other, and they gathered on a rocky outcropping just beyond the breakwater. The wind was light but with enough power for their purposes. Dorothy walked along the short ledge of stone until she reached a set of steps which would take her down to the water. The rest of the group remained on higher ground, lined up single-file at the edge as Dorothy navigated the rocky shore.

"Well, Des, here we are," she said under her breath, feeling the cold of the metal through her gloves. "We protected one another for a very long time. I was hardly subtle in my romantic dalliances and, had I been found out, you would've become a laughingstock. But I suppose we protected each other with our little lie. It was easy to pretend I loved you, Des, because you were... a good man. An honorable man. I very literally owe you my life, and I'll never forget what you did for me. Goodbye, Desmond."

She turned and nodded to Trafalgar, who brought the ka statue down with her. She placed it on a stone and stepped back to stand beside Dorothy. She folded her hands behind her back and waited until Dorothy gave the nod to begin. Trafalgar lifted her chin and spoke with a clear, calm voice. She recited the spell from the Books of Breathing, an unbinding which would release Desmond's spirit without forcing it into a new body.

When she finished speaking, Dorothy uncapped the urn. Within was a second water-soluble vessel which she removed. She stepped over the stones, crouched, and waited until the waves began moving back out before placing it on the surface. She reached into her pocket and withdrew the flowers Cora had destemmed and prepared for the event. She wanted Desmond's final voyage to be beautiful, so the petals were a veritable rainbow of white, purple, yellow, and blue. She released them to float away with the ashes, which were already beginning to trickle out through the dissolving material of the bag.

Dorothy picked up the ka statue and examined it carefully. It felt the same, the texture and the weight, but she couldn't deny there was something different about it. The entire time it had been in her presence, it felt fragile and precious. Now it just seemed like another artifact. Priceless, but at the same time too dangerous to risk falling into the wrong hands.

"You're certain he's gone?"

"As certain as I can be in this situation. We've never exactly been through this before, but the spell was clear. He's been released to whatever comes next." Trafalgar looked down at her. "I can do it, if you prefer."

Dorothy shook her head. "No. I can feel he's gone, I just needed your confirmation. I'm just loath to destroy something so ancient." She sighed and then lifted the statue, bringing it down hard on the stone in front of her. It shattered into more pieces than she could count, more than could ever be reconstructed. They hadn't been able to find out what gave the stone its unique properties, the ability to retain a soul, but it seemed prudent to ensure it wasn't left where just anyone could find it. She gathered the largest pieces so she could dispose of them elsewhere. She didn't want Amenemhat's statue sharing an eternal resting place with any part of Desmond.

She stood next to Trafalgar and looked out over the water. Trafalgar said, "I suppose now you'll have to play the widow."

"It shouldn't be too difficult. I plan to grieve Desmond as much as any wife would."

"Perhaps not as deeply as Victoria."

Dorothy managed a smile. "Well, perhaps not."

Trafalgar touched Dorothy's arm. "I'll miss him as well." She took a deep breath and let it out slowly. "Would you like us to leave you alone for a bit?"

"No..." Dorothy turned around and looked at the group lined up on the wall behind them. Cecil, Cora, Abraham, Leonard, Agnes, Ivy, Beatrice. The people she had brought together, the people who were learning to work as a single unit for the greater good. They were all honorable people, same as Desmond, and they were all so willing to through themselves into danger that Agnes was still favoring her still-healing arm. There was every chance that one day she would be back on a beach like this, saying goodbye to another friend. There was an equally good chance that one of them would come back to release her spirit or Trafalgar's. They all knew this and yet, there they stood. Former rivals turned reluctant friends and now... a true society.

"No," Dorothy said again, "we should start back. There's much work to be done."

Trafalgar nodded and started back toward the steps. Dorothy looked out at the water one last time, the flowers having spread out to cover a larger portion of the inlet.

"Godspeed, Des."

The wind tossed a stray hair across her face and she smiled, swept it away, and hurried to catch up with Trafalgar.

TRAFALGAR & BOONE

WILL RETURN IN

TRAFALGAR & BOONE

AND THE

CHILDREN OF THE BURNT EMPIRE

ABOUT THE AUTHOR

Geonn Cannon lives in Oklahoma. He is the author of several novels, including the Riley Parra series which is currently being produced as a webseries for Tello Films, and an official Stargate SG-1 tie-in novel. Information about his other novels and an archive of free stories can be found online at geonncannon.com.

www.ingramcontent.com/pod-product-compliance
Lightning Source LLC
Chambersburg PA
CBHW060558310726
48982CB00008B/1168/J